THE EYE OF THE KALEIDO-SCOPE

A NOVEL

MARK NORBERG

The Eye of the Kaleidoscope
Copyright © 2022 by **Mark Norberg**

First edition (1.0)

Cover design by **Ryan Mulford**

CHAPTER 1

The illumination from the skylight fell in pale shafts about the old man as he eased back against his chair and sighed. Resting a paint brush still wet from recent strokes onto a nearby table, he considered the thing which had consumed and weighed upon him and which he had tended to for the last time. The sensation the small painting evoked in him, as it had done almost from the very beginning, was like being in the presence of another person – although more potent than even that: it was, he thought, like sharing the room with a parallel self. Or, like gazing into an enchanted mirror with reflections that moved and brooded independent of the viewer. As he had worked the pigments across the canvas, wresting them into their final image, this parallel companion had slowly taken parts of his own self into it, emptied him out, and then grown ever more ravishing. Now it stood, braced to its easel, and called to him in that voice, rapturously pure, with which he could no longer contend. But, he thought, he need no longer try – for the painting was finally finished.

Rising, he turned from his creation, shuffling across the wooden floorboards as he passed through the attic studio, and then, exiting, closed and locked the door forever – keeping the key gripped tight throughout the evening and deep into the night. He held onto it as one who is suspended above a bottomless chasm might cling to a fraying cord – and while it tethered him for the moment, and comforted, in its way, as an anchor to an accustomed safe reality, he nevertheless felt the slow slip towards an impending fall. It was still held fast in his palm the morning of the next day when his housekeeper, coming to rouse him, found him dead.

*   *   *

After nearly two decades directing films in Hollywood, Jeff Tanner was living proof that while you get more flies with honey than you do with vinegar, you get the most with simply a big heaping pile of shit. His latest venture, the blockbuster *Quarterback Commando* – about an NFL star recruited to lead a team of Navy Seals into the heart of the Taliban – certainly qualified as the quintessence of this axiom.

"God damn, Jeff! Another stellar week!" shouted Murch, his long-time producer and partner, loud enough to incite looks of alarm from the secretaries pretending to work just beyond the glass walls. "Get a load of these numbers – we're only down 15% from last weekend. Lewis has got to be popping his prostate!"

Jeff winced. Murch had a unique talent for turns of phrase that were often pornographic, usually misogynistic, but *always* disgusting.

"Jesus, Murch, why are you so competitive with him? He's doing his own thing now. Why do you care?"

Murch's face jolted into a frieze of disbelief at the question.

"Are you fuckin' kidding me?" he scoffed. "We totally ass-fucked that pussy-picture of his, *Finding Emily* – and who the fuck cares about 'finding Emily' anyway? NO ONE. No one wants to watch bitches in hoop skirts. They want a flick with balls! And that, buddy, is what we've got up on those screens – *big greasy, swollen, hairy balls* – and the crowds are lining up to tea-bag it!"

Murch bellowed with delight – his standard reaction whenever concocting a metaphor even *he* considered ingeniously vulgar. As Jeff watched his partner devolve into a coughing fit and down another antacid, he was stopped by a peculiar sensation. It was a feeling that had begun recurring lately. Although he had known and worked with the man for years – their partnership had been insanely profitable – Jeff had always taken for granted that the two of them existed in distinct and separate artistic spheres: Murch made the only kind of movies he could, while Jeff (bowing to the practical) made the kind of movies he knew could get made. But today, at the head of this thought, as he stopped to actually consider exactly what separated the two of them – what it was that allowed him to feel so critical of Murch and so independent of him – he found he could not name a single thing.

—ele—

"Okay, so it starts just like the real version – Pinocchio and his little grasshopper sidekick dancing around this dumpy village toy shop. Nothing but clocks and marionettes. Just put a bullet in my head, right? Hey, you listening?"

"Yeah, I'm listening," Jeff groaned in exasperation, killing the last of his second martini. Diane sat half-turned from the both of them, already fatigued.

Jeff had agreed to meet his two friends after knocking off from the studio, but was now regretting not spending the night alone. His thoughts about Murch had set something in motion – ideas he could feel moving about at the fringes of his vodka-fuzzed consciousness.

But Dirk was talking now – and both Jeff and Diane knew the general direction his story was sure to go. While Jeff's partner Murch's crassness had been a perpetual irritant to their friendship, somehow, Dirk's sense of humor – while nearly just as perverse – had an innocent, hapless quality that Jeff found endlessly entertaining. Usually.

"So they're dancing around and suddenly the Blue Fairy shows up – which is where I introduce my unique *creative* touches –" Dirk resumed with a boyish leer, restating his subject for the third time.

"Wait – is this a cartoon or what is this?" Diane suddenly interjected, having concluded that since Dirk was obviously going to finish the story she might as well get up-to-speed on what he had been babbling about the last several minutes.

"If by 'cartoon' you mean *animated film*, then yes, it's a cartoon. It's a re-edit I did of that stupid CG project they've got us working on," Dirk answered archly. "Like I said, I made a secret copy of the original files. I just explained that like three times."

"Well, I'm sorry," Diane shot back. "All I can focus on is making sure you don't break out into song."

"What are you talking about?"

"You're drunk and getting worked up. We all know what comes next."

"But I'm a fantastic singer!"

"You don't sing," Jeff countered. "You yodel."

"And at the top of your lungs. I'd like to be allowed back in here," said Diane.

"Do you mind? Do you mind? May I finish, please?" Dirk said in comically exaggerated annoyance.

"Fine. Christ. We're sorry. Continue," said Diane, always the peacemaker.

"So, in my *revised* version, they're dancing around, acting like idiots, singing about how honesty is the best policy," Dirk reiterated, building back his momentum, "when suddenly, the Blue Fairy shows up. Well, first of all, she's now topless – with *massive* areolas, nipples like plugs of bratwurst – " pausing for dramatic effect, Dirk allowed just enough time for "Oh, god, no..." – this from both Jeff and Diane, which did nothing to slow Dirk's accelerating enthusiasm: "And then we made Pinocchio go, 'Oh, Hoppy!' – that's the grasshopper's loser name – the brass were worried about copyright issues if you can believe it – 'Oh, Hoppy! What's happening?' and then Hoppy the grasshopper – looking down at his friend's crotch and to the sound of lederhosen ripping asunder – this grasshopper sez, 'looks like your nose ain't the only thing growin' Pinnoch!'"

"Uuuggg!" Diane groaned while Jeff managed a curt, "Jesus!"

"Wait, it gets worse," Dirk continued. "Without skipping a beat, the Blue Fairy lifts her skirt, and in the sleaziest Mae West voice sez, 'you want yer dream to come true? Well, first you gotta make *me* 'come true' –"

"Stop!" interrupted Diane, "I don't want to hear any more!" Both she and Jeff choked back their drinks, laughing at both the depth of Dirk's depravity and the humiliation at finding it hilarious. "And so totally wrong," Jeff added.

"I know – it's horrible. But somehow brilliant at the same time," Dirk beamed. "Except I'm probably going to get fired."

"What do you mean?" Jeff asked.

Dirk pulled out a cigarette and ignited his lighter using that fascinating, off-handed side-swipe that Jeff still could not quite figure out – "I emailed the cut to some other animators at the studio. If I could have remained anonymous, the plan was to swap it into the shareholders' private screening. But I think the CEO found out. He sent me a meeting request for Monday. I did it all on my own time – but I'm probably screwed. I know he thinks I'm a ringleader."

Jeff made a half-assed attempt at consoling his long-time pal by asserting that Family Films, Ltd. could hardly afford to let one of their top animators go – and that at worst, he'd get some kind of warning. Who knew? They'd treated him with kid gloves before. After all, this was the guy who still had naked Barbie dolls at his desk with felt triangles of pubic hair pasted to their groins. What's more, he'd yet to yodel even once that evening. All was not lost.

The text from Jeff's sister arrived just as they ordered another round: "call me. asap." Perhaps he'd spoken too soon.

~ele~

Three martinis were really not so bad, but he always forgot how tired he felt the next day. Jeff cut the ignition and popped an additional aspirin. Up and down the street, rows of oak cast a tattered flutter of shadow across lawns that stretched back to silhouettes of dark, mountainous homes. Across the street, and tight up against the crumbling sidewalk, a dense hedge ran for a good fifty yards in either direction, demarcating one of the larger properties in the neighborhood. Within its shaggy overgrowth, the ornamental grillwork of a black and rusted fence wended, leading the eye to a gate that sagged off-center at its eastern edge. The whole area was one of those strange backwaters, miles from Los Angeles, which had promised in its early days to be at the vanguard of exclusivity, where waves of elite had poured for a time, but then, when their fortunes had waned, their tide had receded – leaving behind this isolated heap of low-slung castles and mournful gardens.

The spell of the place lifted for a moment and the reason for the trip returned to the forefront of Jeff's mind. He stepped out of the car and walked toward the gate. Another surge of nostalgia overtook him and he welcomed the thousand tiny windows back into time that flew past and through him.

"Thirty years...and more surreal than ever," Jeff thought. *"Like something out of a lost Tennessee Williams play."*

Sharp movement at the edge of his vision arrested his attention and he turned in time to see his sister Ann arrive in her rental car. She hopped out and ran to him, cradling an assortment of large envelopes and fumbling with at least two oversized purses, her smile accompanied by eyes brimmed with tears.

"Well, here we are in Spain!" she said, wrapping him in a vigorous hug.

"Here we are in Spain," he returned, squeezing her back, feeling drops fall from her cheek to his, while they both laughed at the greeting they'd shared since childhood.

"Christ, that flight was awful," Ann gasped.

"You didn't have to kill yourself getting here," Jeff said, keeping his arms around her.

"No, I needed to come right away. I guess it wouldn't have been so bad to arrive in a day or two, but it turned out there was a flight out of Boston last night," she said, then adding while giving Jeff another embrace, "And I'm glad I rushed. I'm glad I'm here. With you."

He hadn't seen Ann in five years. They were both so busy now, and living on opposite coasts. Years ago, she had gone off to study English literature and creative writing and then moved to Massachusetts to teach while he went to California to make it in the movies. In those early days, when they had been off separately wrestling with their career tracks, Jeff had always felt that his sister had tried for less than she was capable. What had he wanted her to do? He couldn't say. That she had a spark of greatness had been a certainty to him. And that gift came with obligations that demanded more than teaching at an obscure liberal arts college. He, in turn, had struggled to win the respect of his industry colleagues, which had taken more years than he had expected, and even now that respect was more grudging than anything. He wondered how much this reproof of his sister had been nothing more than anger that she hadn't experienced his same frustrations.

In the end, with the advent of his immense success, this mild irritation towards Ann had eventually dissipated – although he had lived with it long enough for its presence to wear small but regrettable grooves into his consciousness. Now and again, he would brush up against them and feel shame at these tired criticisms. He needed no reminding of her true significance to him. Seeing her now, with her wonderfully harried demeanor, she gave him that unique sense of something, a kind of permanence that he had never been able to fully achieve since moving to the west coast.

"I've got the house key and the alarm codes if we need them. Jacob had it Fed-Ex-ed to the hotel," she said, holding up one of the envelopes. "But Mrs. Doss said she should be here. Let's go on in."

"Ann – you didn't get a hotel room. I mean, why aren't you staying with me?"

"Oh, no," Ann replied, and Jeff could see she had no interest in a debate, "this makes things much easier. There's no way I want you to have to worry about me while you've got a studio to run.

And it's super close to the airport for my flight to San Francisco tomorrow. Really, it's much easier this way."

They opened the main gate and walked up the path to the house, making their way through the sculptured expansiveness of the Japanese gardens that encircled the grounds. It was a bit shaggier for the wear, though retaining much of its former glory – and if an iciness had crept in among its serenity, the blanket of dead leaves seemed to encourage restoration in the mind's eye. Jeff remembered their first visit to the place, just after Uncle Aaron had really hit it big and was celebrated as a fantastic new talent, and then needed to be alone, and so had purchased the tucked-away estate. Back then, as children, they had bounded along this same path and had been struck by the sight of a slight, elderly man tending to a miniature tree. "That's Mr. Lee," their uncle had said. "He's an *artist*." The pronouncement had seared the image to the word and to this day Jeff associated it with the care of growing things.

Passing over the bridge of the koi pond, the two were stopped short by a sudden and frantic perturbation across the surface of the water.

"Poor things! They haven't been fed for days!" came a familiar voice and then the figure of Mrs. Doss, Uncle Aaron's long-time housekeeper, bustling towards them from the house. Dozens of tiny gaping mouths opened and snapped beneath them as she threw food pellets over the side of the bridge.

Her task complete, she returned to her visitors with a weary, "Oh, my dears," then reached out to wrap them both in her ample arms. For the second time that day, Jeff was home. The trio continued on into the house, holding on to each other, their voices low, speaking of the dead. They sat around the kitchen table that afternoon and talked until nightfall, the glow of the kitchen window spilling out into the quiet of the garden, its light running along the sleepy hedges, and landing in scattered flecks upon the pond whose waters had long since relaxed into a mirrored sheen.

CHAPTER 2

The fire that Mrs. Doss had started in the study before leaving had noticeably ebbed, but the leather club chair into which Jeff had burrowed and the wine which he and his sister had liberally divided – in honor of spending one last night in the home of their beloved uncle – stayed any efforts towards stoking the flames or in any way disturbing their tableau.

Uncle Aaron was dead.

It was still so strange to think. And now, Jeff and his sister had the task of wrapping up their uncle's affairs, closing down the remains of a life that had loomed so large within theirs. But Ann was talking, and he had drifted.

"You've got it all wrong," Ann continued, stretched out on the sofa and pivoting the stem of her glass between her fingers. "It all started because you were critiquing something I'd written – I was probably in fifth or sixth grade, by the way – and you told me that a true writer never states the obvious. I can't *believe* you forgot."

"Oh, yeah," Jeff drawled along with a spreading grin, "that's right..."

"And then, just to prove you wrong, I said it would be the first thing I uttered if I ever went to Spain."

"And have you?"

"Of course! And, as a point of honor, it's always directed *to* someone. Usually a flight attendant."

At this, they both cracked up.

"And so you see," Ann concluded, "you're not the only one who has lived up to their childhood ambitions."

"Oh, come on now," Jeff responded earnestly, "you're a published author. That's a fantastic accomplishment."

"Oh, god," Ann said, chuckling with a roll of her eyes, "a collection of essays is hardly the brass ring – and any time you have to put 'published' in front of the word 'author'..."

"What?" Jeff asked. "What's wrong with saying 'published'?"

"OK, yes, I *am* published. But so is a Sears catalog. No one ever puts 'published' in front of serious writers. They don't need the extra assist."

"But you've only just started. You've gotten your foot in the door. That's more than most. And you have a second book on the way, right?"

"Yes, but –"

"Well, then...?" Jeff threw his hands up as if tossing the question back to her.

"I don't know. It's all so complicated," Ann finally said, reflecting on the mess she'd left behind in Boston – her near-ly-complete first novel being only part of the problem. She looked at her older brother with an exasperated, self-mocking sigh, then relaxed her head against several pillows and allowed her gaze to travel up to the ceiling toward the gentle play of shadows to be found there.

"This next book's got me so twisted up into knots," Ann continued after a moment, "I don't know what to think of it."

She'd wanted to add more, but nothing came to her that would have been in any way coherent. There was too much that needed unpacking – but it would all have to wait. Instead, she simply added, "No, you're the one with the magic touch. You always have been."

Jeff willingly ceded to her this last word, staring into the depths of his Merlot through which the fireplace rippled with luminescent feathers – and let the silence between them answer more honestly than anything he might say. Her final thought was, he knew, Ann's way of acknowledging his past feelings towards her, while simultaneously forgiving them, and, somewhere along the way, softly questioning whether or not he had truly found what *he* had always claimed to be seeking.

"Well, yeah...I guess things are pretty great now," Jeff finally brought out – addressed more towards the fire than to her. "Every day I – well, maybe not *every* day – but *frequently* I remind myself how very lucky I've been. And really, that's what it's been – luck. I seem to have a knack for ideas that are incredibly commercial. Sure, sometimes I wish that..." The sentence was left hanging. His mind, lulled by the drink into an unaccustomed recklessness, abruptly checked itself and reared back from the sentiment – like a driver, distracted by passing scenery, suddenly taking a wrong turn onto a street with which he is not only familiar, but has been at pains to avoid. Yet the words, having been spoken, brought the thought to the fore...*sometimes I wish that*...and then to the question of why exactly he had been avoiding completing the sentence. Why *had* he? In the past several days he'd been tripping over it, stumbling around it.

What frustrated Jeff the most was the underlying sense of just how elusive any resolution was going to be. Anyone coming to the problem from the outside would most certainly suggest that Jeff suffered from "guilt" at producing films clearly aimed at the lowest possible common denominator, rather than aiming for something more socially uplifting, more artistically sophisticated. This was utter crap. Jeff had no illusions about the quality of his movies or their function as anything other than a strict commercial product – his line about conjuring "flies to shit" had entered the Hollywood lexicon for a reason – he quoted it often and earnestly. He was no artist. He was a businessman – nothing more or less than what he wanted to be. But still, something hovered. And these two opposing dialogues met and repelled each other like magnets with identical poles.

There was the feeling that in a moment these thoughts – which had been hidden for too long to quickly coalesce into a shape that could be recognized – would be finally grasped. But only, Jeff knew, were he to remain absolutely still and turn all the intensity of his concentration upon it.

A breath, a shift in his chair, and the room, his sister, the fire, all the sepia surroundings of Uncle Aaron's study returned – and in that instant, he remembered nothing except that he had been on the verge of a thing terribly important. His voice, despite his awareness of a strike and deflection, pressed forward, "Well, nothing's ever going to be perfect." He segued from this remark to the various movie sequels he was considering as his next project, careful not to betray the immense inward shift, and observed, with relief, how Ann hadn't seemed to have noticed.

"What is it?" she asked after a long pause, having turned over a quantity of competing ideas before adjusting her gaze towards Jeff's face, set in profile, still transfixed by the fire.

"What do you mean?"

"Well...you were talking about how lucky you've been and then got that weird look like you were about to dive into something really deep and then decided not to – and then just changed the subject as if I wouldn't notice."

"Okay, alright, you got me," Jeff laughed and took another gulp of wine. Ann continued to hold his face in her eyes, waiting for him to respond, but it was clear that, though he was gathering himself, he was lost in a labyrinth of tiny, disordered pieces. She looked down at the weave of her afghan, and began tracing a single thread of yarn as it moved about its looping, coiled pattern.

"Do you think he was lonely?" she asked, finally.

"Uncle Aaron? I don't know. I guess I never thought about it."

"I think he must have been."

"Why?"

"Skipping the obvious – that he lived alone," she said with a quiet smile, then more serious, "No, I think maybe because...because he cared. Maybe too much."

The comment suspended itself between them momentarily before drifting down into darkness. Ann knew her brother well enough to sense that, though silent, they were in accord on the subject, yet she was also aware that a mutual reticence had appeared, something newly present that slowed their approach to the idea. For Jeff, these thoughts of who Uncle Aaron really had been, and whether he had been happy or not, had a shape that loomed too close to his recent anxieties, as if running on tracks parallel to, or, at the very least, *towards* the same destination – a course he found he was, at the moment, unable to take. For Ann, it meant that there had been things left undone, regrets at allowing a loved one to slip away long before he had died – and the ever present knowledge that there was a Thing, a Thing that would stand sentinel, glaring and mutely demanding, that was wrapped around Uncle Aaron and this whole trip and which would need to be dealt with before returning home. Regardless, ideas had been laid bare for both of them that each recognized as leading to other, more elaborate rooms that, perhaps, should be left undisturbed.

The steam from the morning's coffee passed over Jeff's face, collecting in beaded pearls along his cheeks, and the flagstones of the kitchen floor were cool against the soles of his naked feet. It helped the hangover, somewhat. The moment seemed as good as any to try to right his ship, to level a world which had begun to feel progressively off-kilter. The appearance of Ann, showered and dressed, juggling, as usual, multiple packages, bags and purses, and heading for the door, brought a welcome distraction from the array of thoughts Jeff had no desire to contend with this early in the morning.

"Okay, I should be back from San Francisco in two or three days," she fluttered, scouting the kitchen distractedly and snatching her cell phone, car keys, notepad, and hairbrush all from disparate, implausible locations. "And, listen Jeff, if I call and leave a message, try not to take a week to get back to me. I know you're the busiest man in Hollywood, but, just this once–"

"I promise, I swear it!" Jeff vowed, with a mock Boy Scout salute.

"And about the will..."

"Stop," Jeff urged, "Uncle Aaron had a right to leave everything to whoever he wanted. I don't need *anything*."

"I know that. But I want to talk about it."

"No. You'll miss your flight."

"I don't care. When I get back, we're talking about it. I love you. Bye." And with that, she was gone.

After he'd showered and made himself some breakfast with what food still remained in the kitchen, Jeff had every intention of leaving – but the pull of the past proved too strong and he found himself drifting outside, yet again, to look at the expansive gardens where he and Ann had spent an entire summer so many years ago. He ambled along the shaggy hedges and under the trees whose trunks had thickened and whose arms had spread since last he saw them.

The old gazebo came into view, its lattices now gray with age, and with it, the sound of two children playing within, intruded on his thoughts.

"So what's this thing you need to show me?" Jeff had asked her, hanging from the rafters of the little summerhouse. Somewhere, off beyond the tall shrubberies that shaded the tiny structure from the rest of the garden, Mr. Lee's clippers could be heard grooming leaves like the quiet beat of a metronome.

"Come down from there," Ann had said, clumsily hiding the booklet behind her, "Come down and you'll see."

Jeff, dropping to the floor, accepted the carefully stapled pages, bound with a construction-paper cover. "The Butterfly Ring by Annabelle Tanner," he said, reading the front page. Then, scrunching his nose and looking up, added, "Your name's not 'Annabelle.'"

"I know that, silly. It's my pen name. Don't you think it sounds more like an author?"

"Not really."

"Well, anyway, there's a dedication page, too."

"For J.T." Jeff said – and made certain that Ann couldn't tell if he'd caught her meaning, but she seemed to think better of interrupting him. Jeff knew all her secrets. He knew she would stand and wait, and gaze at her older brother as he read her story – and it felt just like it used to when he would sit with her at the kitchen table and help her with her homework. She never needed it, but she pretended to. She had a whole catalog of ways to make him think that she was confused – and then to make him feel she was just on the brink of comprehending the assignment, if only he could help

– so that he'd patiently explain the lesson to her, ask her if now it made sense, and then she'd shine with pride when she said that yes, now it was perfectly clear. There was little else in the world, except maybe her writing, which Ann seemed to enjoy so much as watching him intently focused on guiding her towards some kind of understanding. But that summer, they had stopped doing things like that anymore and both were keenly aware that things had changed.

"Okay, see, right here on the first sentence," Jeff said, "you've lost me. You don't start by telling people exactly where you are. You need to have them GUESS."

"What do you mean?"

"Right away you have these two dumb people step out of an airplane and say 'Well, here we are in Spain!' That's just plain stupid. A real writer never states the obvious."

Had he reached out and slapped her, the offense to her feelings could hardly have been more brutal. But before he could explain any further, the tears had erupted and she had dashed off towards the house.

God, he had been such a prick.

Stepping back indoors, Jeff again had every intention of leaving. But, an empty house is, in many ways, more welcoming than an inhabited one. The enchantment of another life, laid bare and vulnerable and free from any possibility of the occupant's return, is irresistible – yet Jeff, though he had complete license to explore, still found himself not entirely immune to the transgressive awkwardness of a look-around. It seemed too soon to disturb the household, and his first inclination was to hold off at least one more day. But, finally, nostalgia for his beloved uncle overwhelmed his reluctance.

His perusal began slowly – at first, choosing to examine only those items that offered the most benign, suggested only the most chaste glimpse into the other's life: a glasses case, a paper-weight, a scarf. But the house seemed intent on drawing him from one room to another – steps led up to passageways which opened out into airy spaces portaled with verandas or balconies, always meeting the next in a variety of levels, giving a buoyancy to the setting as if each room floated independent of the last – and soon all reticence was abandoned and he surrendered to his hunger to know.

Scattered or piled upon every available surface, table, desk, couch, or chair, were the collected fragments of a life in the arts. Books and scripts, papers and pictures, curios and souvenirs from cheap to the exquisite, dusty props and studio parapher-nalia, all rested in various states of repose beneath an audience of portraits, photographs, framed vintage posters, and paintings. Each and every object whispering up a secret history to him. But rather than draw him into a contemplation of any one of its treasures, the array had the curious effect of reflecting back his gaze – so that the deeper he moved into the house, the further he seemed to descend into himself.

"Do you think he was lonely?" Ann had asked.

That had struck a nerve, certainly. But only because he had been picking at something connected – but with far deeper roots. What had it been? As he had stared into the fire, with his sister comfortably reclining on the couch opposite, his wine glass in hand, he had been going back over his conversations with Murch and the displacement he'd experienced – and she'd noticed it, evil twin that she was – and when Jeff had struggled to answer, she was right to believe there was more in his silence than they had ever covered, even in their most intimate talks. Reflecting on all this now, in the midst of Uncle Aaron's possessions, atmospheric with the expansive, unbound presence of his ghost, he approached the thought once again – and knew there was something there that must be opened. He saw himself reach for it, and then, as a diver that must head back to the surface for want of oxygen, he panicked and fled upward, back to himself, and the room. But now, the house and the articles piled about him were as if they had been his own, each thing recognizable as if he had laid it there himself. And somewhere, he knew, buried nearby, was that long lost jewel that he had come so very close to grasping.

"Everything's just as he left it," Mrs. Doss was saying, *"Just as he liked it."*

"But where are they?"

"Where are what?" said Mrs. Doss turning, stepping towards him, with a disquiet pressing in around her eyes.

"His paintings," he said. "There must be hundreds of them by now. It's all he ever talked about."

"No. No paintings."

"But what did he do with them? Twenty years holed up in this house, retired, and doing nothing but painting – he must have put them somewhere."

"I don't know," she quietly returned. "Every day, I would take food up to his studio. But I never saw anything that he did. He said that his art was just for himself."

That hardly seemed out of the usual, hardly seemed to warrant her conspiratorial manner of stepping even closer and continuing in a tone that made no effort to hide a long-buried fear.

"I would buy him new brushes, paints, thinner. All the time. But I only ever bought one canvass. One. In all the years I cared for him."

"I don't get it – what do you mean?"

"Just this: I saw everything that went in or out of this house." And then another silence.

"Mrs. Doss...are you trying to suggest that for over forty years–"

At that moment, she pressed into his hand the worn, softened paper of an envelope.

Deep within his pocket, it spurred the sudden recollection or been a response to it, and he found himself drawing out the package. The envelope opened easily. There was a key – and he knew it was to his uncle's studio, as if he was his uncle, approaching the door for the thousandth time.

The disorientation subsided for a moment, and Jeff realized he was gulping for breath. He leaned against the wall, calmed himself, and looked about him. How he had gotten this far into the house – or what the path back might be – he could barely remember. But now, he stood at the end of a narrow hallway with a small staircase leading up. The compact steps were not carpeted, but his footfalls as he ascended them were as soundless as if they had been. An arched wooden door stopped his advance.

With the key fitting perfectly into the lock, and with a reverence more befitting the unsealing of a tomb, he turned the key, felt the bolt retreat, and opened the door.

He looked up to find the room occupied – which should have brought him to a quick demand for an explanation from the intruder – yet so certain was he of that other's right to be there, so palpable was its sense of license, that he felt, strangely, that it was *he* that ought to offer an apology for the interruption – "I'm sorry, I..." he stuttered, and then, the vision just as quickly resolved itself into nothing more than a lone easel, supporting a small painting, standing in the middle of the empty room.

The air was cool and mixed easily with the soft sunlight flooding in from above. The illusion of an intruder had had a dizzying effect, and Jeff massaged his eyes as he walked haltingly into the room. He stopped and looked up once again, this time nearly face-to-face with the work of his late uncle.

Had this been the sole focus of those final decades? Mrs. Doss had intimated as much. If true, then the questions to be answered had only begun. But, that he should sit before it, that he should quietly rest upon the very chair Uncle Aaron had last used, was obvious. And so he sat.

The subject of the painting was, in itself, unremarkable. Yet the way in which it was presented to the observer was freighted with such tenderness, so carefully and thoughtfully had its imagery been arranged, that it was impossible not to be touched in an intimate way – to mourn for the thousand clumsy ways people had attempted to say what this painting said so effortlessly.

In the silence of his reflection, everything that had concerned him fell to nothing. What came, instead, was what he knew had been there all along: an overwhelming exhaustion that had finally defeated his efforts to ignore it. How long? How long had he carried it? The sense that the painting was imbued with a soul its own – was as conscious of Jeff as he was of it – was indisputable now. He wanted to put words to it, but all he could do was stare, stare deep into the work and surrender – and with that thought, the borders of the painting began rushing outward, enveloping him and, with a sudden flash, a torrent of color flung out from its center and swallowed him whole.

CHAPTER 3

"Surely, Professor, you must understand my need for absolute secrecy in this matter!" Count Von Verschlagen declared with a grand sweep of his arm, taking in the immensity of his undersea rocket base, "What I do here, I do for all humanity!"

"It's not your secrecy I object to, Count," the Professor spat back, straining against the bonds that held him and his four young associates beneath the giant nozzle of the X-15 rocket, "I am, however, strongly disinclined towards your army of radioactive zombies!"

"And the dying part! I object to the dying part!" Stuey blubbered as ignition relays began activating.

"Now, now," the Professor cautioned, turning to his comrades, "we mustn't lose our heads. Lucy, is your pet snapping turtle still in your knapsack?"

"Of course, Professor," Lucy replied, twisting her body just enough to position the buckle of the top flap towards the twins, Franny and Frankie.

"Good girl!" said the Professor.

"I think we can reach it!" said the twins in unison, swiftly releasing the clasp and dipping the tangle of their wrist bindings just inside the pack – where, with a crunch, a crack, and the flash of a small flippered foot, their hands were free.

"Quick, Franny!" urged the Professor, "Can you activate my wrist beacon?"

"Activate something!" howled Stuey. "We're about to be rocket-roasted!"

Frankie squeezed left, allowing Franny to fully extract her right arm from the rest of the restraints – and then, just as Count Von Verschlagen exclaimed one final, "You've breathed your last, Professor!" Franny's hand came down squarely on the activator button, accompanied by the burst of a pulsating bass guitar riff, trumpeting horns, and, exploding through the side of the steel hull, the monstrous – yet exquisitely polite –

"BANANA BARILLA! THE ROBOT GORILLA!!" shouted a throng of voices around her, startling Ann away from her small in-flight TV screen. Looking up at the laughter breaking out among the passengers – with heads popping up above the horizon line of seatbacks and beaming grins acknowledging the collective reaction – she sat dumbfounded at just how many of the tiny screens were simultaneously playing the episode.

Of course Ann understood that her uncle was a television icon, was aware of how much a fixture the character of Professor Puck had been in the lives of a whole generation of children, but for Ann, it had existed as a thing resting decades in the past; and it had only been now, over the last couple days, as the tributes and memorials had sprouted – whole gardens of memorial flowers appearing overnight in front of his old studio – that she had come to realize the immediacy of his legacy, and the true celebratory nature of the 24-hour marathons of the beloved, classic TV show, even making its way onto the short hop from L.A. to San Francisco.

Soon, she'd be meeting with Jacob Pressman, her uncle's attorney, and, with his guidance, hopefully make some sense of exactly what it was Uncle Aaron had left her. Ann scolded herself for not feeling a greater sense of gratitude. But thinking about an inheritance – and actually possessing one – were two very different things. There were considerations now that infringed upon her that she felt certain she would soon resent.

First and foremost was the memorial.

Jacob had introduced the topic in their brief conversation prior to her last minute flight from Boston – but she had refrained from mentioning it to Jeff. Not until she was certain she wanted to go through with it. If so, there would be no way around it: Jeff would have to help her with that whole mess. He wouldn't like it, but he'd capitulate. She had her ways. As for the money and property she was now in possession of, or how any of it might materially affect her life, she wanted it all to remain incredibly abstract. So far, so good: because it was Uncle Aaron himself that monopolized her thoughts – and the ways in which the impact of his loss had only just begun to affect her. The writer in her, accustomed to analyzing everything like a work of fiction, might have concluded that the inheritance could be seen as a metaphor for her abiding love for her Uncle Aaron: rare, opulent, esteemed – but also importunate, demanding, and exhausting.

And that was only her private, personal feelings. Now, that internal conflict contended with a celebrity status she had previously had the luxury of being all but oblivious to. That her uncle's fame was far removed from the real-life persona that existed for her and remained a living part of her was simply because, naturally, it was the last piece of him that she had comprehended. In fact, it had been years before she fully understood that her uncle was someone almost everybody knew.

To remember Uncle Aaron at the very beginning, when he wasn't anything more than just her favorite person in the whole of the world, she needed to go way back, back to a time when life was an immensity, yet circumscribed and sheltered by the intimacy of family – where everything beyond their Illinois home was a towering mystery, and the safety of the world she *did* know she did not yet want to leave. Had she been four? Yes, that must have been the summer she first flew to California to meet him. Looking out the cabin window now, it all came back, that first journey.

Then, as now, she had Uncle Aaron in her thoughts. But the memory of it in the present moment was infused and alloyed with all the events that had happened previously. She looked out through the double prism of her four-year old self – who had sat on her first plane ride, wondering just who this Uncle Aaron would turn out to be – and also down a long, long passage of having known him for decades, knowing exactly how the arc of his life and her relationship with him would bend.

And then, "Gosh, Professor, the dagger was hidden inside the candelabra all along!" intruded from the TV screen – and pulled the course of Ann's reflection through the lens of another episode, which had started playing without her even realizing it.

"Of course, young man," replied the Professor, "for as you well know: *the truth shall prevail!*"

Her uncle, as Professor Puck, was guiding his four young associates down a grand staircase. He was back in that iconic outfit that had been such a mainstay of Halloween costumes for years: the red pith helmet with the antenna and radio tubes sprouting from the top and the jacket that looked as though he might be ready to lead a marching band. They descended towards an imposing woman, dressed in violet chiffon and an explosion of feathers and diamonds about her neck, while, from behind, two British bobbies were hand-cuffing her evening-gloved wrists. Of course, Ann had seen this episode before – but there was something more, something drawing her, pulling her further into the scene.

"You see, Esmerelda," the Professor chided, "all the riches in the world can't buy a pure heart." Uncle Aaron stepped closer to the woman, and again, the sense of something acting upon Ann accelerated, something compelling her with the thought that this was far more than merely the recognition of imagery she had viewed countless times on TV reruns. "The truth shall prevail!" continued the Professor, "And certainly over a scheme to replace the Maharaja's royal emeralds with colored ice cubes!"

The woman raised her eyes to the Professor, tears glistering, and the sensation capturing the whole of Ann's consciousness resolved into two warring vistas: the scene playing out before her on the television screen, and a second, with the same players, the same dialogue, but viewed from a shifted perspective, an alternate axis – and Ann had the singular sensation of having *been there*: standing in the darkness, peering at her uncle, who stood facing the magnificent woman with her swirling fabrics and jewels, the children on the grand staircase, and the whole of them crowned by a sea of dazzling lights high overhead.

Suddenly, they all stood frozen and expectant. No one stirred. And Ann was distraught, thinking something terrible had happened. Then, a voice called out "cut!" and with that single command the entire world was re-animated. Everywhere, ranges of additional lights bloomed high overhead, her dark corner vanished and the space about her unfurled a hundredfold – out from the pitch black sprang wooden walls, angled beams, ropes, cables, rafters, crates; out into the new glaring brightness poured people in all directions, calling, moving, carrying, laughing, and then – Oh! Where had Uncle Aaron gone? Heels clicked, snapping against the cement floor, louder and louder, and, turning, there was the imperious woman in purple, towering towards her, the beams from her painted eyes swallowing Ann in their floodlights – "Now there's a little lady!" spoke the painted eyes and the red-lacquered lips, in a giant passing flurry of chiffon, feathers and diamonds. Then someone was crying, and the sound of another voice came to her, "You're all right..." it said, soothing the crying, with strong hands lifting her up, up through the passing clouds of rich perfume, up into clear air, into the face of Uncle Aaron.

There was make-up on his face and eyes too, which Ann felt compelled to point out to him, but somehow, rather than give an unnatural or heavy aspect, it seemed just right; it worked to calm the more earthbound qualities, it smoothed down the distractions, and allowed his radiating magnetism to shine undiluted. "You know who I am?" he had asked.

Yes, she had said. She knew who he was. He was her Uncle Aaron. And Ann had known they would be best friends from that moment on.

———*elk*———

"You know," Jacob told her, "your parents often mentioned you were actually on set for the last episode. Do you remember visiting California as a child?"

"Oh, yes..." Ann ruminated, recalling her experience on the plane ride, but the connections were still blurry – and, at the moment, she had no wish to delve. "But it's all a bit hazy."

The flight to San Francisco had taken its toll – she'd slept much of the way – but despite her fatigue, despite wanting to resolve Uncle Aaron's estate, her thoughts continued to be drawn back to the past, to her brother, and to the many pieces of her life that suddenly seemed on the move. Uncle Aaron's attorney, Jacob Pressman, the old family lawyer whom Ann had met many times before at her uncle's house – over his years of visiting and mingling in her uncle's affairs – leaned forward against his desk. His brow furrowed, contending with the desire to console his client – and his duty to discuss pertinent but rather cold matters.

"Ann," he said, surrendering to his professional angels, "you've been left a substantial sum."

Jacob passed a sheaf of papers to Ann, who scanned the itemized holdings.

"Not as much as I would have liked," he continued. "Aaron was never too keen on following my advice. He tended to be a bit distracted when it came to his money. We've a few debts to pay, which I'm taking care of, but the remainder is not inconsequential." Jacob paused for a moment, then added, "Of course, how you intend to proceed is up to you. You'll let me know what legal firm you'd like the files delivered to."

"Oh, god, Jacob. That's not necessary," Ann replied, "I'd be lost without you." And handing the documents back, pressed her hand against his.

"Well, that's fine," Jacob said – and again, after what he might be expected to say failed him, he merely added, "There're a few additional details to go over, but we can do that later. There's no rush."

"Honestly, just let me know what you think is best."

"Fine, fine," he nodded. "Then there's the issue of the public memorial. There are several fan organizations willing to manage the majority of the affair. But, they need your blessing, of course."

"Oh, yes, well, I suppose that's awfully nice," Ann said, nothing coming immediately to mind as to why she should object, yet feeling reticent all the same. "But do you think we really *need* to?"

"No..." Jacob offered, "but someone's going to do it. We can't stop them. And with your involvement, you'll have more of a say – be able to keep things tasteful, as it were."

"I suppose you're right," Ann said, ceding to what seemed inevitable. "But do I have to be there? In person?"

"I shouldn't think so, but...it will be in Los Angeles if
you're still around, and it would probably be sensible."

Ann smiled and nodded. She sighed and leaned back in her
chair and her eyes drifted over the walls of Jacob's office. She
felt strangely present just then, in that ordered, dark-paneled
space, a room in which she had never actually set foot, more
aware of herself, where she was, who was with her, than she'd
been in a long time – perhaps because there was nothing
among the various plaques and furniture and art to draw her
away, nothing with any personal connection to her whatsoever. It was oddly refreshing – to look out at the geography of
a room and have nothing that reflected itself back, or pushed
associations upon her. She'd grown exhausted from sifting
through the decades of memories that the death of Uncle
Aaron had unearthed. It wasn't until she'd started exploring
them that she had realized how many there were. And how
heavy. And that pulling out all that weight was going to be a
long, tiring process.

"Why did..." she quietly started to say, then stopped, the
question putting up far more resistance than she'd expected.

"Yes, Ann? Why did *what*?"

"I guess I'm just...that is...did he ever tell you *why?*" Ann
slowly drew out. "Did he ever tell you why he left everything
to me?"

"No," Jacob answered after a pause, "not directly."

Ann shifted in her chair, bringing her hand to her lips. The
Thing she had sensed last night with her brother by the fire, the
Thing that was ever near, but that now seemed bent on testing
its boundaries, that she had felt among the shadows playing atop

the ceiling and moving within the looping, coiled patterns of her afghan, was close again.

"I never ask those questions, of course," Jacob said, picking up the thread after a moment of silence, "Aaron had phoned, indicated what he wanted to do, and then stopped by to sign the paperwork."

Ann hesitated; she seemed to know that if what was hidden was to reveal any part of itself now, she must remain absolutely still and allow Jacob to bring it forward.

"That must have been thirty years ago," he mused, "The kind of transaction you do a thousand times as a lawyer. But I remember that day precisely..."

"Oh?" Ann found herself saying despite herself, transfixed by his tone.

"Yes...it was perhaps the queerest conversation I'd ever had with him. After we'd finished our business, I noticed some spots of paint on his hands. Before I could say anything, he held them up and said, '*just reaching into the void again, Jacob...*'"

It was all Ann needed. In an instant, as he relayed what Uncle Aaron had shared with him, she recalled a lost moment that brought further pieces of a growing puzzle into focus.

The tears were flowing.

Her frantic search from room to room to locate Uncle Aaron had only exacerbated what her brother had told her.

"Jeff said my story was stupid!" Ann managed to choke out between sobs and with her head buried in her uncle's shoulder. "He didn't even read it, he didn't even get to the good parts with the magician and the girl who can turn into a butterfly!"

Uncle Aaron wiped the tears from her cheeks. With his gray hair and sad eyes, he had come to look far more like a grandfather than an uncle – and Ann's feelings for him echoed that aspect. She lifted her head up and allowed him to move her to the little wooden stool next to his.

"You can not ask for more than he can give, Ann," he said, and there was more to be said, but the path was obscured – and he only added, "Let's put all that aside for now."

Ann stared down at her hands.

"You see that?" he asked, indicating a small blank canvas, braced to an easel, standing before them in the middle of the room.

"Yes," said Ann, looking up from under her brows.

"Do you know what that is?" he asked.

"What?" she replied, now giving it her full attention.

"That," said Uncle Aaron, "is the portal to everything. And you know that place as well as I do. You couldn't have written your beautiful story if you didn't."

Despite Ann's look of confusion, Uncle Aaron pressed on.

"But in there," Uncle Aaron continued, "in that expanse, into that void that reflects everything, is a place few people can go. You've gone in there – and come back. And you've come back with your arms laden with treasure. But your brother can only see the void. And it terrifies him."

And Ann finally nodded, because as he spoke, she seemed to be able to peer deeper and deeper into that immensity. Shapes began moving within the depths of the white surface. And now the shapes were no longer shapes at all, but pillars of ivory, great tree trunks of alabaster that passed her on either side, with branches miles above, fanning out among a clear crisp sky. "But why must I go in alone? Why can't Jeff come with me?" Ann asked, recognizing the landscape of this boundless forest with the crystal leaves that tinkled, and she thought of all the times – almost since she could remember – that she had been here. "I'm not sure exactly," she heard Uncle Aaron say, "but I think because more than one person makes too much noise. The things we are after can disappear at the slightest sound." And a flock of silver birds swooped overhead, then vanished, and smaller creatures scurried underfoot. "But I think that, today, if we are both very, very quiet, we might be able to, just this once, find something worth seeing, together." Ann agreed, and, for the first and only time, side by side, they moved among the trees as quiet as ghosts, following trails, listening for sounds, always searching – down into vales buttressed by snow-swept mountains, high upon cliffs that jutted out over vistas of endless frosted landscapes – and then, when they had happened upon a grove of saplings, a hush greater than the still of an arctic night descended over everything, and out from its place of hiding stepped a vision. At first, Uncle Aaron had merely motioned to stop, and Ann, holding her ground with her breath caught in her throat and eyes wide and searching, suddenly discerned a tremor of light standing before her. It was the kind of thing you would have never noticed, except if you were very old and patient, or very young and unafraid. Slowly, ever so slowly, it unfolded itself to her.

And when they had returned, Uncle Aaron began work on his painting. Ann had stayed at his side for the rest of the day, watching that first brush stroke of orchid purple slashing across the white canvas – the void surrendering its infinite spaces to that singular mind. She watched – not knowing at the time that it was an effort that would obsess her uncle for the next twenty years, nor understanding what it would all mean for her.

CHAPTER 4

F irst there had been the colors. Spiraling out from a white hot core. Then, nothingness – and the sense that he had been falling through darkness, that he had been sinking fast into a black inky night, was still fresh in Jeff's mind. That Uncle Aaron was dead, that Jeff had reunited with his sister at the old estate, was no more than a half-remembered dream. There had been a small staircase and a room. And a painting. And he had looked into it. But what happened next had become as blurred as the inky night swirling about him. There had been the panicked sense of struggling to wake up, that he might be left to die alone, high up in this far off room – but then had come his surrender to the on-rushing images, memories from the past assaulting him that would not let go – and he was pulled back under.

All he knew was that he was falling, falling, falling...

But no time for any of that. He was driving along the Los Angeles freeways to rendezvous with Murch – his new writing partner – and he cast these thoughts aside.

What consumed his attention was the absolute certitude that they both were going to make it in Hollywood. And not in any half-hearted way. No, they were going to be wildly successful. In visions that were clearer than any he'd ever experienced – almost as if they were memories rather than wishes – Jeff could see the exact sequence of events leading to the eventual formation of their own production company, then studio, and then the string of blockbusters that would make their fortune and their names. The layout of his office, the look of his desk, the lavish homes he would pay for in cash – even the people that would devote themselves to his leadership stood before him in complete clarity.

He had always been sure of himself, but today, Jeff felt invincible. He was a Titan – and Hollywood itself was nothing more than formless clay he would scoop up and remake within his clenched fists. Not even his weather-beaten Camaro rumbling along, jolting over every joint in the concrete, could shake him. This beloved jalopy would be the first to go. The faithful car that had transported him across the country from Illinois to California had more than fulfilled its purpose and would be swapped for a number of luxury supercars. He could feel and smell the interiors as if he had already taken possession of them.

He was running late, but somehow he knew he would get to the studio just in time to calm Murch down, focus on the meeting – and take a giant swing at their first big break.

ele

The pitch session felt as definite and settled as everything else – more like a formality than an exam, although he remembered being absolutely petrified at the time. Sitting there, watching

Murch lay out plans for their college-age sex-comedy to Frederick Johnstone, the head of Protocol Pictures, he could already hear the old curmudgeon shout out, "Hot damn, we got a plan!" And yet, Jeff's palms were still sweating. Not because he feared he might be mistaken, not because there was any chance they would leave this meeting empty-handed, but because as he watched Murch, he felt again how very different the two of them really were. Murch was becoming just like that cigar-chewing asshole Johnstone.

Jeff tried imagining plans, down the road of course, to branch out from his producing partner – but that only brought a cold clamminess on top of his moist palms and he cut his rumination short. He needed to be present now, there would be more than enough time to think about the future.

"And we can afford all those waterbeds?" the venerable studio chief coughed out.

"I've gone over their numbers, Fred," the VP of Finance interjected. "It all comes out to well under five million. Not a lot on the line here."

"And you're positive you've got Wanda Barton?"

"Yes, sir," Jeff answered on cue. "She's already said she'll do it."

"Christ what a rack on her," Johnstone let out through several more chews on his cigar. "And she'll show her tits?"

"She did in her last two flicks," said Murch. "You think she's gonna suddenly get bashful?"

"Well, tell you what: you get her signature and hot damn, we got a plan!"

The party that night in the Hollywood Hills, overlooking the lights of LA, was electric. Now, only sporadically conscious of time shifting beneath him, Jeff had to remind himself that the house was not yet his – and wouldn't be for several years. As the revelers danced and drank and laughed, he oversaw it all with a dual vision – how it looked now, and how it would look after his renovations. Foreseeing that the owner would need to sell it to him – and at a bargain price – did not trouble him in the least.

"I don't know how you assholes did it," Arliss was saying, "but, goddamn, four and a half million for your first picture, cheers to you!"

"And let's not forget," Murch said, wrapping his arm around their old pal from film school who had himself ascended several rungs up the Hollywood ladder, "we got total control and final cut – so long as we keep to the budget."

"Well, I still don't see how you did it. I went to those motherfuckers with a nearly identical pitch and they shot me down."

"You didn't have 'ol Jeff here with the silver tongue," Murch answered.

"Oh yeah?" Arliss asked, "And just what did you say that I didn't?"

"For that," Jeff said, excusing himself to get a refill on his drink, "you'll have to wait until you're working for us."

Murch spat out his drink and roared along with the rest of their circle and as Jeff passed on into the house, he could still hear Arliss excoriating both of them and swearing to God that he'd go down on his grandma before that ever happened.

The energy of the party was hours from cresting and while Jeff leaned against the bar, waiting for his drink, he allowed the throbbing music to replace the pulsing beat of his own internal world. This entire milieu of revelers, drink, drugs, and unrestrained sexuality was eminently calming – because it was the most honest reflection of what he carried around in tight compression from day to day. Drink was one gateway to release. Sex another. But power, this emerging power to control, guaranteed the most wanton and satisfying liberation. As he moved in his mind from room to room, he realized that there were others there who were also wondering just how *had* Jeff and his partner gotten so lucky? Someone would figure it out – and perhaps they were discussing it then – that Jeff had an uncle who was willing to pull certain strings.

The thought enraged him for a moment – as if all the other obstacles they'd overcome, all the other backbreaking work they'd put into getting where they were had been meaningless. He wanted to simultaneously cringe from the truth and throw it back in their faces with accusations that it was all just a pathetic attempt at denying their own failings. But there were more important matters to attend to that evening. Already, he could sense *her* arrival.

"You know, I liked your script," she said and offered him a plate of hors d'oeuvres she'd been picking at.

"*Waterbed Rumble*?"

"No, stupid. The one about the family in crisis."

Sally had only been dating Murch for a couple months, but she'd more than carved out a space for herself in their lives. She was dynamic, whip smart, and Jeff *wanted* her more than anything.

"I didn't know I'd given that one to you," he said with a smile, taking up a bacon-wrapped cheese curd as suggestively as possible.

"You didn't. Dennis left it on the nightstand. He won't read it, you know. He hates that kind of stuff."

It was cute that she called him "Dennis" – cuter still that he knew Murch probably hated it, but, despite his rough personality, the man was obviously putty in her hands.

"It's really not much more than a treatment with no ending. It's got me stumped."

"Well, you figure that out, and you'll really have something. So stop being afraid."

"What makes you think I'm afraid?" Jeff said, leaning in, mesmerized by her candor.

"Murch doesn't have your talent, Jeff," she said, waving away the question. "He'll never see what you do. One day, you'll have to deal with that. But not tonight."

The thing that tripped up Jeff about their conversations was wondering whether or not she really meant what she said. Sally had a kind of seductively manipulative intelligence that zeroed in on exactly what the intended target wanted to hear.

"You know, Dennis would never say this publically, but he tells me all the time you're the real brains behind the partnership."

"I wouldn't go that far. He's his own genius – when it comes to what's going to sell. The day I screw up will be the day I stop listening to him."

He saw her glance back out towards the patio where Murch and his group had moved even further away – laughing and shouting uproariously, with thoughts lightyears from what his girlfriend might be doing. She led Jeff down a hallway into the bedrooms at the rear of the house. The dim lighting coming in through the windows and the sounds of a party in full swing providing just the enveloping sense of security and jeopardy that ignited their embrace of each other. As his hands moved over her tight body and she gave herself up to him, the room began shifting, tilting, the sense of Sally blurred – and the surety of experiencing a waking reality left him. Against all his efforts to remain with her, the black inky darkness overwhelmed and pulled him under.

The sense of falling was more profound than before – as if the world itself had snapped its moorings and was plunging down an infinite shaft. How long had he been prisoner to this funneling void? His life was now alternating between moments of terrifying nothingness and violent bursts of discordant memories. Days seemed to have passed in this inexplicable torment, but the scenes and images kept coming at a relentless pace and refused to allow him to detach and move on of his own free will. Someone or some*thing* else was at the controls, but despite this, Jeff was beginning to remember a time before all this chaos – recalling a house and an attic room and a sister.

And then, just as abruptly, another meeting with Murch – one which he would forever remember as a fulcrum on which his future had balanced.

"Listen Jeff, we got to be clear-headed about all this," Murch was saying, slapping his hand against the table. "Now's not the time to go beating our meat off on something all artsy!"

Somehow, despite all Jeff's efforts and careful planning, Murch was adamant that they reject everything Jeff felt they should be moving towards.

"I understand that," Jeff said, trying to avoid sounding as offended as he was. "But do you think we can go for something a little more substantial than a road movie about three frat boys and a shipment of naked women?"

"Look," Murch said, "I get it. We got a shellacking for making it big on a low budget T and A flick. But you goddamn well know that every single one of them would trade places with us in a hot second. What they *really* want is for us to prove that it was a fluke! But we're going to show every last shit-sucking one of them. And with Johnstone willing to give us twice the budget we had for the first one, it's going to be a slam dunk."

The door to the conference room swung open and in strode Sally carrying several bags of Chinese take-out. It had been a while since their last illicit encounter, but, even so, Jeff always endeavored to appear guiltlessly indifferent in her presence.

"Are you two still fighting?" Sally sighed. "You started this conversation before I left."

"What the fuck, Sally!" Murch retorted. "We're not running a nail salon here!"

"Fuck you, Dennis," Sally said throwing her bags down on the table. "I'm going back out to get those office supplies."

Murch rose and stormed out of the room to chase her down and continue their exchange. As Jeff pulled out the boxes of food, he could hear Murch telling Sally to keep her beak out of his business – and Sally defending Jeff's position as well as his rough outline for the family drama, how it was a solid start and just needed a little fleshing out – and Jeff wished to god she'd stop. He knew how to handle Murch. Too much from her might be dangerous.

"Why are you defending him?" Murch could be heard shouting.

"As a neutral observer," Sally retorted, in that imperious tone he knew got under Murch's skin, "I think I offer a perspective you'd be wise to consider."

Jeff had once thought like Murch, that the measure of success reached no further than fame and wealth. But now, as his partner argued for those limited rewards, Jeff knew he was different. He felt things more deeply. His capacity for appreciating the richness of existence was more expansive and he was committed to opening Murch's eyes to those new, rarified horizons. But first, those tiny, disparate fragments of his grand idea must coalesce, and his script – which stood in a bare and incomplete outline – must step out from the shadows. Why not just reach in and grab it? What was he waiting for?

"That goddamn bitch," growled Murch on his return to the conference room.

"Let's just relax and enjoy our lunch and pick up our discussion later," Jeff said, sliding Murch's order towards him.

Murch folded his hands and with a great sigh rested his forehead against his interlocked fingers.

"Sorry I've been on the edge today, Jeff," he said, suddenly seizing Jeff with his eyes, and a chill cut through the room as he followed with: "We gotta talk something out."

"What do you mean?" Jeff asked, feeling that every word from that moment forward must be weighed with the utmost care. If this was leading where it potentially could, never had things been more precarious.

"I was really hoping to avoid this discussion, Jeff. But I need to clear the air. Last night, I found out Sally's been cheating on me. And you know who with."

Jeff set down his fork and leaned back from the table. His read on Murch revealed nothing. His partner seemed far more calm than he would have guessed in this moment which gave Jeff the sudden hope that things might be salvageable, if navigated delicately.

"Okay. Fine. Let's lay our cards out on the table," Jeff answered coolly. "We can be adults about this. There's no reason why this has to change our business relationship."

"Agreed. But Sally's going to have to go. I can't have her here. That's too much stress. I know you like her a hell of a lot but I won't be able to concentrate on anything."

"Alright. Okay. If you think that's best."

"And that asshole Kurt. He's gotta go too."

"The sound guy?"

"Yeah."

"But why Kurt?"

"I don't want to have to be wondering if they just fucked."

"Wait. You're saying *Kurt* and Sally? Really?"

"Who'd you think I was talking about? You know of someone else?"

"No – of course not," Jeff countered, careful to contain his explosive sense of relief. "I just didn't know who it was for sure. But Kurt. Wow."

"Well, I just wanted to clear the air and let you know where things stood."

The conversation continued with Murch never once noticing Jeff dabbing the perspiration from his upper lip. And as for Sally, well, Jeff silently promised to figure out a way to extricate himself from that mess immediately.

But Murch was right.

Now was not the time for risks. Now was the time for carrying on, steady as she goes. But Jeff knew he must never allow himself to become distracted or to forget his quest for something higher. And it was so very easy to get distracted, so very easy for twenty years to roll on by and see those first, pure ideas plowed under by money and fame and the attendant routines of both. So very easy to forget that those thoughts had ever existed at all. And then, once forgotten, when those long lost dreams stirred themselves from the farthest recesses, to register them only as the natural, middle-aged discontentment with life and then with a general resolve to dismiss them.

As he struggled with this tension, this need to stabilize the center, he was carried forward and brought back to his place on the floor of a dim attic studio in the house of his deceased uncle.

Raising his head from the dusty floorboards, there it stood, once again, staring down at him – that small, seemingly unremarkable painting.

Despite his disorientation, despite the slowly dawning panic at how long he had been there, sprawled out – the sound of someone knocking at the door to the studio only now reaching his consciousness – his eyes stayed fixed: he had forgotten the way in which that work had been freighted with such tenderness, so carefully and thoughtfully had its imagery been arranged, that it was impossible not to be touched in an intimate way – and all those obscured things that he had buried and forgotten, the things he knew he must confront – the box deep in his mind that contained them, finally opened.

CHAPTER 5

The flight attendants were coming down the aisle with the drink cart and Ann hoped that a stiff one would get her to stop endlessly reviewing her compounding problems. Jacob had been a saint – walking her through all the confounding minutia of the estate – and giving her wonderful guidance on exactly how to proceed with the public memorial, which she now accepted as a necessity. But goddamn it! There had been several points on which she needed Jeff's advice and despite multiple calls she had been unable to reach him for the last several days. Where the hell *was* he?

Ann settled into the seat, exasperated. She'd be back in Los Angeles within the hour and would be able to drive to his house if need be. No sense in getting all worked up. Jeff was who he was and that was that. He'd get back to her as soon as he could. Furthermore, she had to be honest: a large part of her annoyance was no longer having the overwhelming problems of Uncle Aaron's estate to divert her from all the unresolved issues she had tried to leave in Boston. That buffer of distraction, unfortunately, was now greatly reduced.

She thought back to that first evening with Jeff at Uncle Aaron's house. He'd tried to inquire about her new book and "how things were going," but she'd kept the conversation focused on her brother's problems – deftly avoiding talking about "The Thing" that was, in actuality, beginning to overwhelm her.

Here it was then: her sudden departure and arrival in L.A. had been made possible by a fortuitous late night booking. Yes. True. But the real reason had been the desire to get away from everything and spend a good week or so in California being able to breathe. No such luck. What had seemed immediate and importunate and frantic 72 hours ago, back home, was all returning, and with a vengeance.

"Now what the hell is that supposed to mean?" her agent's voice groused over the phone.

"Just something my uncle once said," Ann tried not to laugh, but Jill – a veteran of decades in the publishing biz – flew off the handle so easily it was hard to resist the temptation to provoke her. "I'm not ready to go back into the void. Not just yet. Too many moving shapes...whatever..." At this point, Ann was desperate for any distraction – even if she wasn't making any sense.

"Honestly, I have no idea what you are talking about. What does any of that have to do with the book? Or the contract I need you to sign?" Jill contested.

Nothing. And everything. And she'd just had another quarrel with Michael over money which had gone unresolved and still sizzled. This fight with Jill was unfair. Jill had no idea that Ann was jacked up on adrenalin from that impending, ticking time bomb.

"*Nothing, I guess,*" *Ann said, pacing in her kitchen, trying to stall as long as she could.* "*I'm just not in a good head space right now.*"

"*You're getting us off track, Ann. Barker's wants to publish.*"

"*Yeah – if I change everything.*"

"*Ann, think carefully about this. Please let's not have an argument about artistic integrity when I'm trying to get you a deal here. A deal that can open all kinds of doors. All they want is the central character warmed up a bit. Throw in a relationship subplot – it won't change a thing.*"

"*No. No. That's the whole point of the book,*" *Ann replied, getting heated once more.* "*The whole point of the book is a narrative as cold and analytical as any male writer.*"

"*Nothing would fundamentally change – you've captured that brilliantly. Adding a touch of humanity is a small price for a first novel.*"

Nothing would fundamentally change...

Christ, how that was true. Somehow, her agent had a knack for instigating these kinds of conversations – needing to discuss artistic issues that invariably yanked at highly sensitive personal complications – at the worst possible moment. Last time, it had been an eleventh hour plea to accept a smaller speaking stipend in exchange for a write-up in a college journal. This was not long after Ann had discovered she was being paid a thousand a month less than a male colleague – and would have to confront her dean. Now, she was being asked to water down the lead character in her first real novel which jabbed at raw and numerous insecurities.

So humiliating: Michael had needed to borrow money again and then, after she'd given him this new "loan," he had gone be-

hind her back and charged her credit card for additional expenses – and it was not the first time. Things would be coming to a head soon. But Ann was too honest with herself, at least in this regard, to believe that she would do anything about him just yet. No, she had convinced herself that with everything going on, now was not the right time. And, she would continue dragging this – and her torment – out for who knows how long. Everyone around her, Jill for the moment, would pay the price.

"And the ending. It's all wrong," Ann hurled at Jill. "It really needs to be completely rewritten."

"Now you're just fabricating problems that don't exist. It's bull-shit."

"I'd rather self-publish."

"I just don't understand you. You made all kinds of revisions to The Glass Corset. You deleted whole essays! You completely reversed your perspective in your chapter on performative feminism!"

"Exactly. A book of essays. Who gives a shit?" Ann paused for a moment. This was getting them nowhere. She restarted, shifting to a tone she knew Jill would not contest – at least for now. "Honestly, Jill, I can't have this conversation right now. I've got to fly to Los Angeles, meet my brother who I haven't seen in ages, and handle all kinds of family crap. I'm just not in the proper frame of mind to make any decisions that I know will have long-term ramifications."

"Alright, alright, you're right. I'll let Barker's know we'll get back to them," Jill said, her voice falling into resignation. "And I'm really very sorry about your uncle. What do you need me to do?"

"Nothing for now. I'll call you when I get back."

I'll call you when I get back.

That was more bullshit.

The flight attendant handed Ann a Bloody Mary and moved off with a smile. Ann took a sip and wondered how it was that she was, yet again, engaging in more self-deceit. She and her agent both knew it would be Jill that would call back – and call back steamed after giving Ann more than enough time to keep her word. And, no doubt, just when Ann would be at the peak crisis with that asshole in her life. But was Jill right? Was she really being totally unreasonable? The one thing that was certain was that this novel was rapidly becoming an obsession, and she'd become more radically territorial than ever before.

It was also bullshit that *no one* cared. A few had. A marginal few. That first book of essays had been a minor hit on the college circuit and the talk of numerous literature departments. She'd connected issues of body image dysmorphia, Neo-Liberalism, the infamous San Francisco lesbian band *The Lickety Splits*, and the poetry of Gertrude Stein in a way that excited fiery debates on topics that the collegiate literary establishment had long ago decreed had gone stale. But mainstream success had eluded her. The people that had bothered to read it had recognized her talent – but getting a reviewer even on the fringes of the popular mainstream to take up the work had proved impossible. It was a conundrum she'd completely failed to anticipate. For her, the entire battle had been the creation of a work that could justify its existence, authoring a work that was *substantial*. What had never occurred to her during the three year writing process – fraught with unyielding torments about her talent or ability to complete the work – was that she might achieve her goal, was that she might find herself the creator of a showpiece of scholarly writing and then discover *no one cared.*

There was that "no one" again which galled her and made her feel disgustingly petty. Why was she so dismissive of her admirers? And, furthermore, why wasn't the work itself enough? Why did the lack of establishment acclaim embitter the whole undertaking? She could not escape the thought that her personal life had become so unfulfilling that she had come to expect her professional life to compensate. Maybe she was overthinking the whole thing. It must be said that those enthusiastic responses that she so quickly dismissed had not been inconsequential: they had temporarily pushed Ann's insecurities about her talent into the far corners of her mind. Prior to committing to that three year effort, whether or not she had enough skill as a writer had seemed her number one problem. Now, she no longer questioned if she was any good – but whether or not she could get the world to agree.

Which brought it all back to the question of why she was so adamant about not wanting to make any changes to her first novel. Acquiescing to the publisher's request pretty much guaranteed she'd be in every mainstream bookstore in the country. Barker's was no joke. If any other writer had come to her with the same problem, she'd have immediately diagnosed the issue as an artist pulling away from having to confront their doubts. She'd tell the poor soul that, obviously, if you accept the publisher's advance and the work goes to print, and yet *again* you find a lack of critical interest, you'll have nowhere to run – that while the life of the perpetually undiscovered poet may be a discomfiting existence, it does, however, have the advantage of providing un-limited opportunities to talk about "might-have-beens." But this explanation – like all the others – was immediately swallowed up at the slightest approach, which prevented any kind of percep-tion into the heart of the matter.

Side-stepping this mess brought her back to an early child-hood memory, to the first time she and her brother had spent the summer alone with Uncle Aaron. They'd been eating in the formal dining room, French doors open to the summer air, and Uncle Aaron had asked, as he always did, his question for the night. The one he chose this particular evening was the first one Ann remembered not being able to answer immediately.

"Would you rather be rich and famous but know that your endeavors were worthless – or brilliant and unloved?"

"Would I know that I'm brilliant?" Ann had asked after a moment.

"You're in sixth grade – what difference would it make?" Jeff interjected.

"Yes, Ann, if you want," Uncle Aaron had replied, ignoring Jeff's outburst. "But I'd advise against that part."

Jeff had, of course, immediately announced he'd rather be rich and famous – and maybe because of the terrible fight she'd had with him earlier, maybe because of the tears that she could feel were still threatening to spill, she announced her opposite opin-ion. To this day, she felt as if she had been trapped by that pledge, as if the universe had happened to select that one moment, for the first and only time, to actually bother listening to her. It certainly had listened to her brother. She had watched as Jeff had glided from success to success, landing a first film within two years of being in LA and then buying his third home before he'd been there for five. Meanwhile, she'd clawed her way to a second-rate professorship. Oh, it was true that within her tight circle of English snobs, her name carried some cachet – but it was nothing that would provoke anything more outside that circle than a polite smile.

And with her brother, it was best to avoid the subject all together. Things were much better now, as adults, but without saying anything, there remained that sense that, despite his professed admiration, internally, he was at a loss to understand why she had not been far more successful. In a way, to be totally fair, Ann had always felt a perverse satisfaction in his expectations. It was flattering to have the person that knew you best be so sure of where your talents could – or better yet *should* – take you.

But the expectations had been hard to bear. Despite the massive effort that had gone into completing *The Glass Corset* and now the novel *Dancing about Architecture* – a fictional story loosely based on the life of designer Aileen Grey – Ann's life bore a shape contorted by the pressures of wanting approval, most of all, her brother's. Even simple conversations were checked short by remembering his first words of disdain at something she had poured her soul into – and then the horror that she might, despite herself, do the same to another. "I'd really like your honest opinion," was about the worst thing a student could ask her.

"Well, of course, but you understand, it's just one opinion – and you've got to be able to move past even the harshest criticism or you'll never survive," was her stock response. A particular exchange that frequently resurfaced was from a conversation that had occurred during one her worst bouts of writer's block.

"It's about a genius goldfish," the grad student had said, leaning forward in the office chair, "who realizes he's just a goldfish. Can't talk, but can understand everything that's being said around him. I mean, geniuses happen in humans all the time. Surely they must happen in the animal kingdom – so I think it's entirely possible that an Einstein goldfish could be that smart."

"Yes," Ann had wanted to say, "but where does it go?"

But she'd lied, as usual, and said he was on the right track, and then he had gone off, written the novella, and it had, indeed, been a minor miracle – and a publishing hit. And she'd hated it: a work that had every cliché in the book – as well as a few new ones.

But what really galled her was that the ending so closely mirrored that of her new novel – at least thematically. As things stood, *Dancing about Architecture* concluded with an archangel and a demon debating how best to torment the protagonist, Alice, a mortal that had spurned them both in the pursuit of her career designing cathedrals.

"The application of physical pain is so very easy," the demon said, "and encourages so much creativity. There are endless avenues to explore. Why do you resist my suggestion?"

"On the contrary, it's more tempting than you can know," said the archangel, "as much as I hate to admit it." Looking down at the

body of Alice, lying in the hospital bed, he reflected on all the crimes against God and heaven she in her willfulness had committed, and then added, "But suffering leads to expiation. And that I cannot allow."

In the end, the two celestials decide on death, and the eternal damnation of Alice's soul. Her student's story, similarly, climaxed with the sentient goldfish finally managing to communicate by spelling out words using food flakes and then conveying the rudiments of the meaning of life to his young owner before being eaten by the family cat – both works arguing that the loss of a great talent, of an unfinished masterpiece, was the greatest tragedy of all. Right now, she wasn't so sure. Right now, total oblivion was sounding pretty goddamn restful.

"You can still keep the angel and demon arguing at the end," Jill had said, "You can still keep Alice dying. You can still keep everything else. Just give her a boyfriend. Give her a boyfriend that cheats on her. Some bullshit thing like that. What's the big deal?"

Ann had wanted to say it was about artistic integrity. Had wanted to say it was about not compromising with commercial pressures. Which of course it was. At least somewhat. But she pulled up short. Worse, the suggested revisions actually made a lot of sense. Yet, despite being able to intellectually accept that, she found herself resentful towards them. It gave her a headache knowing that Jill would see right through her and figure out Ann was prevaricating around something deeper.

Suddenly, somebody else was talking – and it took Ann a second to realize it was coming over the intercom, *"Ladies and gentlemen, we'll be arriving in Los Angeles in twenty minutes."* Christ, thought Ann, my mind is spinning. As she was informed that the flight attendants would be making a final pass through the cabin, she considered attempting a deep dive into her purse in search of a lost bounty of ibuprofen, but, realizing that would entail bending over, she surrendered the idea and leaned her head back against the window.

It doesn't have to be so complicated, Ann thought to herself. I'll be back in LA shortly, I'll have a lovely time with my brother, we'll hold Uncle Aaron's memorial, I'll fly back to Boston, I'll sort out my personal problems, I'll tell Jill that I'll accommodate the changes Barker's wants but I'm re-writing the last chapter, and that will be that. See? Simplicity itself. Why is that so difficult?

But any clarity from trying to see things from a dispassionate viewpoint was fleeting. Everything in her life had seemed to contract into a giant interconnected ball of knotted, tangled yarn.

It was "The Thing" – the only word she had for it – a Thing standing sentinel, glaring and mutely demanding, a mass born of the death of Uncle Aaron which had ensnared parts of herself into it, parts which had, previously, operated as distinct and independent spheres: her contentious relationship with her boyfriend and her connection with her brother, these were now both enmeshed with her book and her agent and that summer with her uncle – and pulling on one disrupted the others, or brought them into even tighter collusion. Worse, her comprehension of these distinct events was starting to blur, yet, she could feel her thoughts working in unison to draw her back to those earlier memories, as if to say the thread starts here – and from here it must be unraveled.

Ann returned to her view through the cabin window, to the flight back to Los Angeles – and to thoughts of her brother, and to the billows of the cloud tops, like bleached exhalations from the void, gliding by.

CHAPTER 6

"Jesus Christ! Where the hell have *you* been?" Diane shouted across the bar. Making her way towards Jeff through
the early evening crowd, she grabbed him by the shoulders and
continued on with only slightly less pique, "I've been trying to
get ahold of you for three days!"

"I know, I know, I'm sorry," said Jeff, passively falling into
Diane's quick hug and allowing her to lead him to their table.
Patrons sat in clustered groups and the establishment had the
relaxed feel of professionals gathered for well-earned cocktails.
Then Diane was speaking again, but Jeff could tell by the tone
of her voice she hadn't asked him anything important yet or
anything he needed to respond to – and bought himself a few
more moments of unfocused consciousness by joining in with
her husky laugh over something she'd just found amusing. He
had told no one the reason for his nearly three day absence – and
had definitely decided this was not the time.

He would have preferred extending his seclusion even longer,
but Jeff had retained enough sense to recognize he needed this
dry run before returning any of the numerous messages now
clogging his machine – including his sister Ann's. She would be
returning from San Francisco tomorrow: he might be able to

evade Diane's scrutiny, but his sister was in an entirely different
league.

"And Murch is losing his mind," Diane was saying, wrapping
her jacket around the back of her usual seat and taking up the
drink she'd started before Jeff's arrival. "He was ready to call the
cops. Thought you'd been abducted."

Now it was obvious he needed to speak, and Jeff resigned
himself to the fact that it was simply going to be an effort to
sound coherent and engaged. "No, I know, I called him this afternoon and smoothed things over," answered Jeff, immediately
perceiving that Murch was another universe of conversation he
needed to avoid. "I reminded him that I had to take time off for
the funeral, but of course he forgot. He'll be fine."

"And you?" Diane added, "How are you doing?"

"Fine. Everything's fine," he said, horrified at how mechanical
he was sounding – and how oblivious Diane was to it.

"Well, I'm just glad I'm in Marketing and two floors down. I
can't imagine what his assistants are going through," Diane said.

"You don't have to take his shit," Jeff said, rubbing his eyes
with his palms. "I'll talk to him."

"You're the boss," she said, and again fell to laughing over
a story that Jeff was certain was truly hysterical. But now, she
might as well have been sitting on the other end of the bar. As
he watched her continue on, animatedly describing the various
characters they both worked with, every so often throwing off
one of her signature gestures, Jeff could gauge just how lost he
really was – Diane was the last person he'd ever thought he'd be
unable to connect with. She'd been like a second sister to him.
And, except for Ann, there was no one that could more easily

read him, read his thoughts, know exactly what he needed to hear – or what he was going to say. And she was the first person he thought of when there was a problem, when he had to admit he needed advice. But things were different now. Now, everyone, even Diane, was beyond arm's reach, was being swallowed up by the fissure torn open by his recent revelations.

The full collapse had not happened yet, and might not happen for some time, but he could see that everything was larger, more imposing, or, maybe, people had gotten smaller, and would continue to get smaller, and, eventually, be swept away. Even the air was thicker now and drew his attention. It seemed to be hiding things. As deeper and deeper into his surroundings he tried to peer, shapes had begun moving within those depths. Objects were swooping overhead too, just beyond the periphery, then vanishing, and in the nooks and crannies, tiny creatures darted.

It had all started with the pounding.

He had been reaching for something...something which must be opened...

And then the pounding, and Mrs. Doss was calling to him, and he realized he was on a floor, and then that he was at Uncle Aaron's. Mrs. Doss must have had a key or forced the door, but he had drifted away again, and only knew that Mrs. Doss had knelt next to him, shaking him roughly and asking if he was alright. He had answered her but she had not seemed to understand. Then she had said something about a horrible painting – taking up a dirty sheet and throwing it over something near him. Why did he remember that so clearly? Why did he remember her talking

*about a painting? There had been no painting in the room.
Had there?*

"Alright," Diane's voice said, and though carrying no un-
usual emphasis, in fact quite subtle now, it managed to bring
Jeff back, lift much of the fog, and allow him to freely breathe
for a moment as the world seemed to deflate, almost returning
to its normal size. "I really need to know what's going on."

"What do you mean?" Jeff asked, laughing at Diane's expression of disbelief – which he seemed to see perfectly
though his eyes were closed and his head was now resting in
his hands. In the days since his experience, since his blackout,
since he had refused Mrs. Doss's plea that he go to the hospital – and somehow made his way back home – the shock of
being back among the living was staggering.

"I'm not going to dignify that with a response," she scolded. "Even Murch would be able to see you're a man on the
edge."

Jeff sighed again, brought his face up to hers and knew he
was caught. "I had an experience. Very intense and very hard
to explain."

"Like what?" Diane asked, leaning in and suddenly understanding that things were worse than they appeared. "What
kind of experience?"

"I saw something that...that I'm having difficulty understanding."

"Like what? Like a UFO? Like that kind of something?"

"No," Jeff chided, more at himself for saying anything to
begin with. "Nothing like that."

"Well, then like what?" Diane said gently, but with eyes creased at the edges with worry.

"I don't know what exactly. Maybe I was just light-headed for a moment. But I was at my uncle's, and I saw something. Like a bright flash of something – and then, it was like I could see myself, everything that brought me here, I saw it all rushing past, you know? But, at the end of it – for a second, I could understand it, and saw what I wanted, really wanted – and, for the first time, I wasn't afraid of it, but then I just...I couldn't breathe anymore. And...oh, I know it doesn't make any sense..."

"No, no..." Diane said and reached out to take Jeff's hand in hers. "It doesn't have to make sense. It's really okay. You're okay."

Jeff wanted to tell Diane that he wasn't. That everything had shifted, and he really was starting to believe he might not make it out again. But he only managed a small sound in the back of his throat before putting his face down onto the table, into his crossed arms, and exhaling.

"Listen to me Jeff, you're exhausted. I'm taking you home. You can get your car from the garage tomorrow."

The ride back with Diane and the fresh night air with the car windows down seemed to revive him. As the cool wind whipped about them, he could still sense giant shapes moving about, gliding like Chinese dragons, but the city lights and traffic kept them in the distance and at bay. And as Diane spoke, he could follow precisely what she was saying – even respond cogently – though the experience still seemed once removed from reality, like watching everything reflected through a mirror. One of the few things that took no effort was the memory of Mrs. Doss. Something she had said kept needling Jeff. What was it again? He almost had it, but no, it was gone again.

"I didn't realize you had family here," Diane was saying as she drove. Then, spurred by Jeff's look of confusion, added, "When I heard you had a relative in town that passed away I was shocked. I guess it was your uncle? You said you were at your uncle's? Is that right?"

Jeff looked over at Diane, thinking how thoughtful she was and feeling bad that he was only now considering her kindness in taking him home. He wondered if he was like that – normally, that is. He wondered if he would have done the same for her – or called a cab. Or even done that. He saw that she was hoping for a response and that providing one would make her feel better. He groped around for something appropriate but banal.

"Yes, well, that's all true. But I guess I don't have an uncle anymore. He passed away, as you know. My sister and I are having to take care of the estate."

"I'm so sorry to hear that, Jeff," Diane said, and he could hear in her voice she seemed to think this cleared up a lot. "How's that going?"

"Fine, I guess. Ann's dealing with everything," he said. "It's what Uncle Aaron wanted."

"Must be something in the air," Diane said after a pause and with a short laugh. "Something about 'Aarons' this month. The great ones are leaving us left and right."

"What do you mean?"

Diane looked over at Jeff as though now he really *was* losing his mind. "You telling me you didn't hear Aaron Arbuckle died?"

At this, Jeff was thrown – especially since he was certain he'd been exceptionally focused the last several minutes. Why was she asking him about what they'd just been discussing? Then, the pieces came together for a moment and he understood. "Actually, I did know," Jeff said, meeting her gaze. "That's my uncle: Aaron Arbuckle."

"What?" Diane said and Jeff was sure the car swerved. "You're joking."

"No," Jeff whispered, shaking his head.

"Your uncle is *The Professor and the Groovy Gang*?!"

"Yes," he replied, "Didn't I ever mention that?"

"No, you asshole! I never knew Professor Puck was your fucking uncle!"

Jeff mumbled an apology but Diane was now far too distracted to notice. "You know I *worship* that show!" she declared and again the car seemed to be destabilizing. In a passion, she continued: "God! Are you saying you never noticed the Banana Barilla doll in my office? Jesus, and you know, back in college, I had the whole Professor Puck getup – the 1949 Radio Hat, the coatee jacket, the jodhpurs, boots, the whole getup. Christ, I loved that show!"

Now it was Jeff's turn to really laugh – the thought of Dianne swaggering around like Uncle Aaron in that red pith helmet, radio tubes standing out like bug ears, and the rest of her looking like a cross between a British soldier off to fight Napoleon and Fritz Lang was more than enough to bring him closer to his old self, to give him a beachhead, however temporary. For the second time that night, he was almost revived.

"Well, I'm glad you think that's funny," Diane snipped. "I think I looked really cool."

"I'll have to tell you all about him sometime," Jeff said, and relaxed back into the seat. Yes, perhaps talking to Diane about Uncle Aaron would help. Perhaps verbalizing everything that seemed to be massing in a siege about him would calm him down. And as the street lights streaked past he felt himself submerging again, back into the past, waves of memories rolling over and pushing him under. Would he tell her about that first funeral long ago? Would he tell her about the car accident? And being called to the principal's office, the long walk down the waxed brown and white checkered floors thinking he'd been found out for sprinkling bent staples on the auditorium seats, then waiting as Mr. Diller kept him terrified and alone sitting in front of his big empty desk, then, that imposing man finally entering, lowering himself slowly into his creaky leather chair, tenting his fingers before him, staring down at Jeff from behind black-rimmed glasses, and regretfully informing him that both his parents were dead.

He had started crying. Great streams of tears. And then an arm had comforted him. And still the sobs erupted from his chest while hands continued to soothe and voices worked to calm. Wiping his eyes and nose with his sleeve, he wondered what Diane was doing at the funeral – No, no, that was the arm of Mrs. Doss, come from California with Uncle Aaron to be with him and Ann. And thinking that he'd never noticed how much like Diane the voice of Mrs. Doss sounded. It's okay, it's okay, she had said. Your uncle and I are here. You're going to stay with us for a while.

All that following summer, not once did they discuss why they were there, why they were spending those beautiful summer months at Uncle Aaron's. Neither he nor his sister gave even a hint that the two children gallivanting and cavorting around the Arbuckle estate, playing around the gazebo, were not having the time of their lives – were not spending those glowing sun-swept days in carefree bliss. It was their secret pact, and would not be broken for many years to come. Not that they would have had a chance. Jeff wouldn't have allowed it, even if Ann had wanted to. Yet, he had known she was in pain – far more than he – that she was yearning to move closer to him, to go back to the earlier times, before the loss of their parents, when they could read each other's minds, when they seemed almost to circle a mesmerizing secret. But that was over. And even though they spent most of their days at the estate in each other's company, it was an illusion, an elaborate theater show that concealed a new and impassable gulf. Let her suffer, he remembered thinking to himself – angry and ashamed that she could be so needy, that Ann would ask of him something she should be able to handle on her own.

"I'll tell you all about it, sometime," the words tumbled out of Jeff, and he felt again the wind on his face and watched as the road ahead began to take gentle twists and turns and resolved itself into the route to his Bel Air home.

"That's okay, sweetie," Diane said softly, patting him on his arm. "Everything's going to be just fine."

———*ee*———

As the sound of Diane's car faded, Jeff had intended to go right to bed. Laying down on the sectional sofa, he closed his eyes, promising to call her (and his sister!) back in the morning. She'd let herself out and, perhaps for a while, he had dozed off, because he seemed to recall those scenes of the funeral – the quiet lines of people, most of whom he barely knew, the big, cavernous sanctuary with its sparse white walls, the priest in his vestments, the soloists standing off to the side and at the center of it all, drawing everything to them: two caskets set end to end, two caskets like two closed eyes standing vigil over the mourners. He wondered what mom and dad would have thought of it all – and could come up with nothing. Even their memories were now locked away and silent. Then, of course, his mind had turned to Ann and Uncle Aaron. With Ann, he had his anger to keep himself safe from her. But with Uncle Aaron, there had been nothing but guilt from the beginning. Even at 14, he had known enough to be appalled at himself for sitting in that pew, dark coat and tie, and failing to resist contemplating all the new advantages that being taken under his uncle's wing had suddenly opened up to him. But he had kept his secret safe, even from Ann, and they had flown to California to spend the next six months of their lives with Uncle Aaron.

As they had begun their new reality on Uncle Aaron's estate, Jeff had come to regret every careful chess move that had boxed him into his tight, distant corner – but once he had achieved some measure of calm, isolated though he was, he was terrified of coming down from his battlements; and so watched from a distance as Ann and Uncle Aaron grew closer. Maybe it would have happened anyway. Maybe Ann and Uncle Aaron were just more simpatico. But, whatever the reason, he was the outsider, though no one could be accused of treating him with any less affection.

In the end, Uncle Aaron must have known how Jeff had felt, must have sensed and then regretted not working harder to reach out to a young boy obviously in deep pain over the loss of his parents – because, years later, after Jeff had returned to Los Angeles, having been remitted to Illinois with Ann and picking up what remained of their lives with relatives closer to home, then graduating from Chicago University Film Studies – his uncle had all but rolled out the red carpet for him, and worked to open several key doors into the Hollywood industry. Jeff's natural gift for the work was irrefutable and that he probably would have, eventually, made it on his own was clear. But to say that Uncle Aaron hadn't played a significant role in his early career would be wildly unfair.

These were the thoughts he would have carried off into slumber, remaining faithful to his promise to Diane – but then he remembered, or, to be more precise, was intruded upon – quite violently.

He remembered! Yes! There HAD been a painting! But it was uncanny: what it depicted hardly mattered to him now. No, it was the *way* in which it was presented to the observer – the *way* in which it had been rendered with such tenderness – that it cut

Jeff so deeply. He wanted to mourn for the thousand clumsy ways people had attempted to say what this painting said so effortlessly.

As if it were before him, he saw again the glint of light just to the side, and turning, the blinding flash, and then the colors: the sense of a rent and rip of atoms, the day itself cracking in two – massive voids exploding outward – merging, twisting, screaming – planets tumbling into the abyss, red giants falling in flames among a hail of comets and stars – the cosmic maelstrom collapsing to the point of a needle inside his own mind. There! That tension between a soul standing before the galactic eminence – and the audacity of its spirit!

For the first time in a long time, he knew, really *knew*, exactly what he wanted. And, he was not afraid.

Stumbling into his home office he pulled a packet of legal pads out from his desk and began furiously writing down everything that he could remember. His great unfinished script – the one that had plagued him for years – suddenly came into crystalline focus. Over the last 72 hours he had been wrestling with his original moment of insight in the attic studio – where, without warning, he gazed directly into that blinding sun. But the vision had been too staggering. And his mind had gone dark. Then, recovering, for three days he had thrashed about without sleep, futilely punishing himself with curses and ramblings and drink to remember the vision exactly as it had appeared to him. Now, here it was again! And this time, he was prepared. This time, he would not yield to its terror or its sickening entropy. Now, he would fight through that veil of awful mystery to capture it. On into the night and through to the first sharp beams of dawn, pricking at him from beyond the tops of his orange trees, Jeff worked until the script was finished.

He awoke to the phone ringing. He had fallen asleep at his desk and his first reaction was panic at the thought that he had merely dreamed of completing the script. His second thought was that it might be Ann, standing furious, at the front gate. A swift glance at the security cameras confirmed there was no one there: it was just the phone, just Diane.

She could wait. Things needed to be put in order. Had his meeting with her and their ride home together – and then his revelation – been a dream? Impossible. For there was his new script, in a pile of seven legal pads, spread out across the desk top. A hasty survey of the pages confirmed that the five acts were indeed all there and, spot checking random scenes, he breathed no small sigh of relief that the lines of dialogue were not only as clear and cogent as he'd remembered them – but, in many cases, even better. However, a more thorough review would have to wait.

Diane was calling again.

"Have you returned to the land of the living?" she asked with a forced jocularity.

"Yeah," laughed Jeff. "I think my fever broke." Which was true. He was wiped out and exhausted, and he felt as if he had just come out the other side of an intense bout of the stomach flu – but, he was feeling much more like himself again. And the intensity of the last three days was like the experience of another person.

"Well, you need to get down here as soon as you can. Murch has the whole place in an uproar."

"What's happening this time?" Jeff said, making his way to the kitchen and a pot of cold coffee from two days ago.

"I have no idea. But the message I got from him this morning was that the production logo needs to be redone. Our two notes were, 'Make it last longer – and more sparkles.' And he wants it by the end of the week. Jeff, you know that's not how I work."

"Alright, yes," Jeff said, "I'll get there by this afternoon."

"Okay, well, hurry."

"I just gotta take a shower and clean up a bit. I won't be too–"

"Holy crap!" Diane suddenly interjected, "I buried the lead!"

"What? What's going on?"

"All I can say is, be prepared for more yodeling than you can handle."

"Oh boy, what's happened to Dirk this time?"

"You didn't hear about it, did you?"

"No – what happened?"

"I probably shouldn't bring this up now, but I think you should know. In case he calls you or something. Or shows up stumbling around your front yard and singing. Dirk and his cartoon, the one with the pornographic Pinocchio – they fired him."

CHAPTER 7

*H*is face was a gun. Alice could no more escape the brutality of its beauty than she could outrun a bullet. Despite knowing that he was annihilating her, was pulling her down piece by piece, she had continued to sacrifice herself to him for the last five years. This was the mortifying secret of a woman whose fame was built on her image as a powerful feminist trailblazer – one of only a handful to ever make it in the male-dominated world of architecture.

Alice stepped among the hulking blocks of granite and marble. Piled beneath the cranes and scaffolds, they awaited their placement within the main tower of the basilica – giant puzzle-pieces that would fuse into a holy mountain. Here, at the construction site, surrounded by the great stones that would soon become her crowning achievement, she was fully herself – confident and unafraid – yet as he came towards her, she prayed to those silent rocks for deliverance.

"Thank you for meeting me here, Michael," Alice said and felt the first pangs of what leaving him for good was going to mean. Those sorcerer's eyes of his, and that face and perfect chin were pressing into her and already working their toxic alchemy. Only by concentrating on the presence of her surrounding work could she *continue: "You've wanted to visit the site for a while. I thought you might like to finally check out the progress we've been making."*

"But that's not why you've asked me to come, is it?" he answered.

"No," she said flatly, then continued with what she'd very carefully practiced over the past week. "I can't see you anymore. I appreciate everything you've done for me and our time together, but you don't love me, Michael. Yes, you love things about me. You love my career, and you love my lifestyle, and you certainly love my money. But so long as none of that changed, you could just as easily swap me out for any number of women. I honestly wish you all the best. But what we have isn't good enough for me anymore."

Although she hadn't been expecting any serious rebuttal from him, any overly heroic effort to change her mind – she had been expecting <u>something</u>. Instead, he merely nodded, gave her a look of complete acceptance, and walked off. As little as she had suspected he cared for her, it was less even than that. Yet, she had done it; she and her incomplete blocks of stone were finally free.

Ann sat back in the booth and let her hands slide from the keys of her laptop. She took a deep breath and realized she could feel her pulse behind her eyes. Goddamn coffee. Goddamn book revisions. She felt herself in that purgatory between neither liking nor disliking what she had written – and then the memory of some far-off pledge made by a novice writer, a writer that she no longer knew, to only put down what was *brilliant*. Well, *that* had been discarded since page one. Time for a break.

At least she'd finally connected with her brother. Or, rather, she'd finally gotten him on the phone and listened to a cockamamy excuse about taking three days to call her back. But why he insisted on these elaborate fabrications to cover up what had clearly been some kind of three-day binge was beyond her. He sounded awful.

Nevermind.

She'd gotten his answers to her questions regarding the funeral and the estate. More importantly, he'd concurred with her plans for a public memorial – and had agreed, miraculously, to speaking at the event for the family. She suspected that he hadn't really been paying attention to everything he was agreeing to – but she would deal with all that later. For now, she had a few days to relax. And to try her hand at slapping into some kind of acceptable shape these stupid revisions that Jill had insisted on.

Looking back at her laptop, she tried her best to be objective.

The prose was somewhat tortured, but *so what?* She thought. *Let the reader suffer.* Grabbing a wadded-up napkin, she passed it between her hands, squeezing it into her damp palms. The new scene with Alice and Michael did not yet have a specific place in the novel – probably towards the end, if not the end itself – but, as of now, it floated on its own little island in space. She decided to let it marinate for a while, and if it still felt solid by the time she wrapped everything up in LA and returned to Boston, she'd whip out an additional five or six scenes that could be sprinkled throughout the book, not cause too much harm, and be satisfactory to the publishers. And, better still, get Jill off her back.

At first, she assumed the young woman who had moved to stand next to her was the waitress and Ann was on the point of ordering another cup of coffee (and asking whether or not brunch could be charged to her room) before looking up and realizing her mistake. The curious young woman staring down at Ann, as well as the equally curious young man at her side, were not more than 25 – nor, obviously, part of the wait staff.

"Excuse me – are you Ann Tanner?" the girl asked, clutching a book which Ann could immediately see was a hardcover copy of *The Glass Corset*.

"Yes," replied Ann, though perplexed – not by being recognized, so much as by the girl's expression which seemed to indicate that Ann should know who she was.

"Is this a good time?" the girl said, reading Ann's confusion as possible irritation. "We can reschedule if you like."

"Reschedule?" asked Ann, still unsure as to why they didn't simply ask for the autograph since they'd already said hello.

"Yes," the young man adduced. "We're from the Professor Puck Society. We're the ones who were sent your email from your lawyer, Mr. Pressman?"

"We're here about the memorial," the girl broke in. "You said you spend your mornings here and that we should stop by today."

"Oh, my goodness, yes!" laughed Ann. "I'm so sorry! The book you're carrying completely threw me. I thought you were oh well, never mind! Please, have a seat."

"I'm Brenda and this is my boyfriend, Paul," the girl said excitedly as the two flopped down in the seat across from Ann and extended enthusiastic handshakes – all of them breathing sighs of relief that the mutual awkwardness had passed. "This is so amazing to meet you. I mean, we're obviously huge fans of your uncle, but when I found out that Aaron Arbuckle's niece was the author of my new favorite book, I about hit the ceiling!"

"The way the book's been selling, I really didn't think I had any – fans of my own, that is," Ann said.

"Well, you've got a big one right here!"

"She's an English major, Chico State," Paul added. "It's where we met."

"I've read this cover-to-cover three times. I think it's one of the most important works of feminist writing in the last 50 years. Would you mind signing it?"

"Of course," Ann said, "I think I have a pen here." Ann reached down to open her purse and immediately panicked at finding a writing implement among its bulging contents. Then, taking the plunge, managed to pull out a laser-pointer. "What do you know? I thought I'd lost that," she said, dropping it back into the bag.

"Here – use mine," Brenda offered, and Ann took both the book and fine point marker into her lap. She finished the dedication with a flourish, and passed the book and the pen back to the girl.

"*To Brenda,*" the girl read out loud, "*I finally found one! Sincerely, Ann,*" then, hugging the book to her chest, said, "You won't be able to say that for much longer, Ms. Tanner – I think it's the sleeper hit of the year. Anyway, I don't mean to take up so much extra time. I know this is supposed to be about the memorial."

"Not at all," said Ann. "I'm in no rush. And, honestly, I'd much rather talk about literature. Did you read the book for a class or on your own?"

"Oh, it was assigned – but I would have read it anyway. A good friend had been raving about it before I saw it on the syllabus.

I hope you don't mind me saying, but I think you've pushed feminist thought into the next century! I *so* connected with your assertion that true feminism is fighting for a set of principles that nurture the feminine side of *all* genders."

"Oh, well, thank you," Ann said, "I very much appreciate that."

"But what really strikes me," Paul interjected, "is the way Brenda says you insist that we use the very strictures we've been struggling with for centuries to craft our own ends, to remake our world."

"It was certainly one of the harder points to convey," Ann said, warming to the conversation by the earnestness of her admirers, "I've often thought that, yes, corsets – my central metaphor – confine and restrict, but they also give shape, form, and protection."

"Well, it made the biggest impact on me," Brenda said. "In fact, it gave me the courage to finally recognize the relationship I'd been in for the last three years was a crutch."

"Oh, really?"

"Yes. Your final plea to cast off those cycles of stasis we're constantly falling into really hit home. It made me see all the ways I was accommodating a person in my life who was never going to change. And if I hadn't moved on, I'd never have been open to meeting Paul."

"You are a real inspiration to her," Paul said, then added, "And to me. We're getting married in September."

Brenda gave her fiancé a quick kiss on the cheek and Ann had to laugh at herself – couples showing each other genuine affection still managed to prick her – a too harsh reminder of what she'd never gotten from Michael. She congratulated them on their engagement and conveyed an air of sincere delight in their upcoming union and asked with interest about their future plans without either of them knowing any better.

"Well," Ann interjected after a moment and before they could get too off-topic, "why don't you tell me about your thoughts for the memorial, and let me see what I can do? But I'll warn you, I've never worked with a fan club before."

Although Brenda had seemed ready to respond, it was Paul that now took the lead. "That's alright, we're old pros at this," he said, leaning in, "We're the president and co-president. Oh, there's lots of Professor Puck fan clubs out there, but we're the biggest one by far. Anyway, of course we'd want to start the event with the traditional career overview, a slide show, clips from *The Professor and the Groovy Gang,* and testimonials from those that knew him. But, afterwards, we think we have a really great idea to end things with a bang – and attract as many people as possible–"

" – Not that it wouldn't be packed anyway," Brenda said, obviously overcome by the desire to inject honest flattery. "But we thought that if we could tie the event to your uncle's favorite charity, the Children's Convalescent Center, we could really do some good."

"I think that sounds wonderful. What did you have in mind?" Ann asked, again noticing Brenda's obvious desire to continue interceding by clamping her hand down on Paul's forearm and by assuring Ann, "We want to do something very respectful. To honor the dignity of his legacy."

Ann nodded her agreement, but couldn't resist adding with a laugh, "Or, at least as much dignity as possible when we're talking about a man who co-starred with robot gorillas..."

"Yes, to show our respect," Paul agreed, but clearly not finding any humor in Ann's comment.

"Paul's a composer, you see," said Brenda.

"Oh?" said Ann, suddenly sensing that things might get strange.

"Yes – he's really amazing."

"Oh, I see," said Ann – and then, more cautiously, "And, I take it, ah, you've written something for the memorial?"

"Yes. An atonal opera based on the adventures of Professor Puck."

"An opera? About my uncle?" Ann asked, though it came out sounding far more baffled than she had intended.

"Yes. About the TV show. But it's not what you think," assured Brenda. "Not stuffy at all. And it's only an hour."

At this, Ann, at least her expression, lost the ability to filter any amount of bafflement, though it was now clear that her two guests did not possess the ability to accurately read her. Were they completely crazy – or just off-beat? Ann seriously hoped it was the latter. In the last 24 hours, she'd gone from resigning herself to a public memorial to firmly believing it was exactly the thing she needed. And right now, the *last* thing she needed was having to start the planning from scratch.

"There are a number of exciting innovations I'm utilizing," Paul continued, hitting his stride. "Unlike conventional bourgeois musicals, all the duets are a half-pitch apart with the accompaniment in a totally different key. It's all about giving the finger to convention. Just like Professor Puck."

"It's surprisingly difficult," Brenda said in an air of great confidentiality, "but there's never been anything like it."

Now, it was Ann's turn to lean forward and, with the greatest care to affect an attitude of respectful calm, said, "Well, it all sounds wonderful, but, I'm – "

"I'm not explaining it very well," Paul blurted out. "Really, if you see it, you'll see that it's, well, what it's *really* trying to do is capture what Professor Puck was really all about: all the, you know, heartache in the world, the kind that – that – " and he trailed off, stumbling over an impassioned plea he hadn't had any idea he'd be called on to make.

Once more, it was Brenda who came to his rescue. "Those deeper things – the kind of things that, you know, spoken words are just too clumsy to say," she said. "The kind of things no one can *ever* say. What you really should do is come to one of our rehearsals and – "

Brenda would have continued on with her explanation, but Ann gently held up her hand as if to ask Brenda to slow it all down, creased her brow as if in sympathy with them both, and nodded. She'd used it on many a grad student who'd burst into her office to fling themselves at her mercy for a better grade. From anyone else, it might have come off as belittling or offensively arrogant – but Ann was a master at situations like this and was able to bring the discussion to a gentle but definite close.

"I'm really very sorry, but I'm just not confident that that's our best route."

An uncomfortable silence was all that the couple could offer in response and Ann could see that the two of them saw, finally, that they'd failed to make their case – that the amazing meeting they'd probably spent the last week enthusing over was a bust. Brenda looked down at her lap and said, quietly, "Well, we like it, anyway."

Under normal circumstances, Ann would have stopped the interview then and there, performed a marvelous bit of deflection, bucked up their spirits with some noncommittal ambiguities, sent them on their way, and made a mental note to never see them again – having a strict policy to avoid drama at all costs. And there was, certainly, drama here – and it certainly could cost her. But maybe it was the fact that she could still see the dust jacket of her book tucked in the crook of Brenda's arm, maybe it was Ann's lingering irritation at Jeff – or maybe it was the sheepish way Paul had received that quick peck on the cheek from his girlfriend that filled Ann with some kind of faith in a couple that in all likelihood would see their dreams ultimately beaten down. Maybe it was a combination of all of it together – but, for whatever reason, Ann threw all manner of caution to the wind and decided to do something for these two odd ducks that had somehow found each other. And found her.

"Listen," she said to them, "I tell you what: I have to get rid of literally thousands of pieces of memorabilia of my uncle's. I don't want them, I have no room for them. Now, I have a company that's going to be managing the estate sale next month, but, in the meantime, I'll have the housekeeper put together a crate of items directly related to Professor Puck and the TV show. They're yours, if you like, to auction off at the memorial for the Children's Convalescent Center. What do you think of that?"

The blank stares she received from both of them convinced her she had totally taken the wrong tack. They were obviously more attached to that opera of theirs than she'd surmised – and, so it appeared, were unwilling to accept any kind of substitution. But, having committed to her present course of action, she felt duty bound to see it through. "Of course, you'd be welcome to anything you like," she flung out, "as a thank you, for all the hard work you're putting into this."

Brenda's hand clamped down again onto Paul's arm and Ann was sure it was a prelude to the two of them storming out. Instead, they turned to each other with wide-eyed stares, then turned back to face her and cried out with the enthusiasm of game show contestants on a hot streak.

Laughing, Ann added, just as a precaution, "So, is that a 'yes'?"

"Are you kidding?!" asked Brenda. "That's the most incredible offer in the world!"

"No one is going to believe this!" cried Paul – and Ann, watching the couple cling to each other amidst their shared euphoria, was certain that was no exaggeration. After taking a bit longer than she would have expected for both of them to calm down, they discussed some of the more mundane details of the memorial and it was agreed they would speak over the weekend to iron out the rest.

"And listen," said Paul, as the couple collected themselves and ambled out of the booth, "if you change your mind about the opera, even at the last minute, we'll be happy to perform it. The whole cast will be there anyway – they're all in the fan club, of course."

"My schedule is going to make that pretty difficult, but I deeply appreciate the offer," Ann said, shaking their hands one last time. As she watched them leave, and then stop for a final wave on their way out of the restaurant, her universe felt empty of something, as if Paul and Brenda had filled it with material it had sorely needed. For a while, and she wasn't even sure how long, she sat and stared at the exit, unwilling to sever the train of thought which was following them out into the world and wondering how it was that they spent their time and days together. And, just as she always did, she wondered not about their peak moments of joy, but about those average evenings spent at home, the kind that a relationship like theirs accumulates mountains of, the days of living in each other's company, not speaking for hours at a stretch, nor desiring it, because just the presence of the other person is more than enough.

She thought of her brother and realized they never discussed each other's relationships. Why was that? In fact, she didn't even know if he was currently seeing anyone. She took it as an accepted fact that he had no idea about her. Then, as though she had touched an exposed wire, she quickly sat up in her seat, flipped open her laptop and began writing again.

The seraph and the gargoyle laughed. Some prankster – or maybe just random chance – had contrived to turn their marble faces towards each other. But now, as Alice approached, the pair seemed not so much in conversation as ignoring her. She'd left the foreman's trailer to clear her head and found herself wandering among the statuary. Although they awaited placement in the, as yet, unfinished exterior niches and tympanum, they seemed ten times more powerful grouped en masse, and Alice suddenly had the wild idea to leave them as they were. Again, her mind was wandering just when she needed all her powers of concentration.

Michael would arrive in an hour. And she had just realized that asking him to meet her at the construction site was another humiliating defeat. Even in the midst of severing herself from him, in the midst of reclaiming her self-respect, she was capable of unconsciously undermining every one of her specific intentions. She'd told herself that having him meet her on her turf would put him in his place – a powerful visual reminder of exactly who she was. And, when she broke things off, decisively, against this backdrop, he'd leave a shattered man.

But now she could see what she had really been up to. It was bait. It was an inventory of all the money and prestige she brought to the table, and everything he'd be losing. It was an ante meant to bend him back to her, to convince him to beg forgiveness. Yet all she had really done was give him an opportunity to demonstrate even more clearly how little it all meant to him – to wildly inflate the heroism of any refusal – which she was now certain would be his reaction. But, it was too late to think about all that. She'd set this in motion and would carry it through. She would stand here and wait for him. And then, she would hold her own, as implacable as this seraph and gargoyle, whose private joke now seemed obvious. As she stared further and further into their faces, the remnants of their conspiratorial chat echoed from their stone mouths: "You want to torment her?" the angel had asked the gargoyle, then continued

without waiting for his answer: "No, no. Don't give her failure –
give her a dream!"

Once again, Ann sat back and looked at what she had written. Was it what Jill was asking for? Like so much in her life, she had no idea.

CHAPTER 8

"I just can't understand it," Diane spouted again, watching the blur of the interstate from inside the cab of Jeff's Testarossa – "He won't return my calls, and as far as I can tell, he's not responding to *anybody*. I even tried calling his mother – and even *she* doesn't know what's going on."

"Did she say what he *is* doing?" Jeff asked, trying to keep his eyes on the road, knowing that Diane's facial expressions when she was this upset were almost worth risking an accident. *Ha!* he thought to himself, *at least I'm getting my sense of humor back.*

"She says he sits in his room all day staring at a *wall*," Diane recounted, "Seriously, Jeff, I'm really worried about him."

It did seem out of character for Dirk. But, gripping the wheel tighter than usual, Jeff's thoughts could not stay faithful to Diane's concerns and he found himself, again, reflecting on his three-day bout of *whatever* it was he had experienced. He had thought it was finally behind him. That had turned out to be comically optimistic. Even now, nearly a week later, he had to concentrate to keep Diane from suspecting anything. The experience was still goading him on, pushing him towards some kind of singular vision.

"Look," Jeff said, trying to calibrate his tone to as off-hand a manner as possible, "I know things are not going great for Dirk right now. But come on, people get fired, he's an adult, he'll figure this out."

"I know, I know. But this time, I really sense he's on the edge..."

Jeff floored the engine – ostensibly, to pass several slow-moving cars ahead of them; in truth, to push Diane off the subject of Dirk. He knew she put up a good show of nonchalance whenever he offered her rides, but her muf-fled squeals when he really let things rip (which he never failed to find opportunities for) unmasked the touch of the thrill-seeking bad girl she normally kept rigorously buried. The gambit paid off. The exploding engine pressed both of them down into their seats – Diane's hands clenched at her seatbelt, she stifled a small gasp, and Jeff knew he could move the subject of their conversation on to *real* problems. Problems that needed the dedication of her full attention.

"So, anyway, did you read the script?" he said as Diane brought her hand to her heart and worked to slow her breath-ing.

"Of course," she said. "And next time you want to do that, give me a half-second warning, would you?"

"*And?*"

"And nothing. You know I've always said that you should try to stretch yourself. You know I think you've got a lot more to give as a writer-director than you've shown the world so far."

"Yeah, but is *this* the script to make that stretch?"

"Well...look," Diane said, and suddenly Jeff felt a sinking nervousness, "any script, no matter how good, can turn out any number of ways. But that's not the point."

She shifted in her seat to turn to him as best she could. "Here's the thing," she continued in that matter-of-fact attitude he prized so much, "you're looking for guarantees where there are none. This could easily be the worst thing you've ever done – or something quite special. But there's no way to know until it's all over. You just have to stick to your guns and see your idea through."

"Is that all it is?" he said in mock surprise.

"Yes, asshole," Diane laughed. Then, giving his arm a squeeze, "For what it's worth, you can count me in."

Alright. He had Diane. The project was halfway home. And that strange burning energy he'd become infected with warmed anew with her endorsement. But they both knew the rest of the way would be a far steeper climb, and with a far less tractable person: Murch. Just how were they going to get *his* approval?

"You're going about it all wrong," Diane offered after they'd deliberated without landing on anything concrete. "If you want Murch, you don't come at him head-on. You need an end run."

"What are you talking about?" Jeff interrupted, "That's exactly what I'm saying I want to do. You've seen the financial estimates I pulled. All based on a very conservative boutique rollout, and low-balling averages for very similar films. Murch is a numbers guy. He'll see the dollar signs –"

"OK, that's where *you're* wrong," Diane said triumphantly, "He's *not* a numbers guy. Everybody thinks he is. *HE* thinks he is. But at heart, Murch is all about instinct. Gut instinct. And if it doesn't grab him by the balls, he won't go for it. You've got to paint a picture for him. You've got to give him the biggest hardon for this picture. You do that, he'll say yes to anything."

At this, Jeff had to concede the point. Diane had stripped the issue down to its core and laid things bare. But how to do it? Just how does one entice the mind of a man whose spectrum of intellectual interests falls somewhere between monster trucks and porn? As usual, Diane had ideas.

As he listened, Jeff's mind, to his dismay, kept leaping about – wanting to fully consider the game plan Diane was carefully illustrating but, ironically, now that Diane was totally focused on his movie, Jeff could not stop jumping back to their discussion about Dirk. Winning over Murch was essential. Yes. But after that? Dirk's recent catastrophe was a stark warning – a flashing red barricade against looming dangers. He saw that the biggest mistake he could make would be to dismiss Dirk's fate as being Dirk's and Dirk's alone. And it was clear that Diane was not fully aware of the immense risk. No: Dirk's defrocking was far more the norm than the exception. Even if Murch signed on to everything, Jeff would need to be supremely cautious.

Now that he was about to step out from the protection of his nearly infallible sense of what makes a corporate blockbuster, he'd have to thread a very fine needle indeed. The vision he had committed to pursuing had cheated his grasp several times before, but *this* time, he'd outfoxed it and, at present, with Diane at his side, he stood holding its slippery form tight, with fingers buried deep. He was not letting go.

Yet, Jeff still had the presence of mind to acknowledge that it would place him at the mercy of innumerable foes. For a project like this, everything would be harder – the money, the casting, the distribution – all the normal challenges would be doubled just for the lack of nudity alone (and how he would get Murch past *that* one, Diane had, so far, noticeably avoided). Worse, for those that would recognize the project's full potential, how many would rather undermine a producer with Jeff's stellar box office record – than see him lavished with the additional rewards of critical acclaim?

But if he could realize a tenth of what he saw, victory would be assured – and Diane was right: if things did happen to go south, it would still be worth it a thousand times over.

As they continued driving and plotting – Jeff having put together enough of Diane's discourse, snatched in staggered bits, to sound coherent – he recalled a lunch he had had with Uncle Aaron. Actually, it had been the last one they ever had – and it had been almost a decade ago. Funny that he didn't immediately remember it that way but as just one of a string of visits to catch up with each other.

"Sorry for taking so long to see you again," Jeff had said. "My schedule's been crazy." He hated lying. But when the truth would have taken an hour to unpack, and much of it painful to the recipient, a lie might not be the moral choice – but it certainly was the compassionate one. "But anyway," he continued, "how are you doing? How's Mrs. Doss?"

"She remains willing to put up with me," his uncle laughed, "And, you know, being a recluse suits me. I'm happy with my books and my painting."

"You ever going to let us see these masterworks? Any gallery would jump at the chance to show your work. You know that, right?"

"Well, I'm content to keep my art for myself. How's your latest project?"

His third film with Murch, Gloves of Iron *– about an assembly-line worker in a steel mill who overcomes adversity to make it as a champion boxer – had been green-lit and was on track to start pre-production in a month. As he described the project, Jeff kept thinking how different Uncle Aaron looked. For Jeff's first two films, he'd needed so much help – and Uncle Aaron had been a wellspring of advice, connections, and, when the circumstances arose, a reliable string-puller. He'd seemed a giant.*

But now, as Jeff's success had propelled him to the upper echelons of Hollywood, Jeff saw that he hadn't really needed his uncle at all. And he'd learned several valuable lessons along the way. Especially about being rich: One, you are always aware that you are rich. Two, you are always aware that your money exists quite apart from you – and, what's more, although it does your bidding, it has absolutely no loyalty. And three, always there is that small needling sense, ever present in the back of your mind, that it is forever looking to betray you.

And although Uncle Aaron had greased wheels to a certain extent, it was not really anything that Jeff, himself, could not have done. Furthermore, perhaps, he had asked for his uncle's help more out of charity than anything else – a way to allow a retired actor to once again feel a part of the game. Had he done his uncle a disservice by creating a false sense of purpose and importance? Looking at him now, Jeff tried his best not to see the real truth –

that his uncle was a has-been, and a part of Hollywood history that had long ago been put to pasture. And, if he was truly honest with himself, it was the reason he'd put off seeing Uncle Aaron for so long.

"Jeff," his uncle said, resetting their conversation, "your mother and I were never exceptionally close – not like you and Ann – but when she died, there were some regrets. I don't mean to say that I wouldn't have done the same had she lived, but I promised to make sure you and your sister got what you needed. I only want to know that you are okay."

"I know, uncle."

"What I'm asking is, do you have what you need?"

"Yes. I mean, look at me – things could not be better."

"You're sure?"

"Of course – and you know, every day I'm amazed to find how really easy it is to be successful. Murch and I have made every film we set out to. Its was all so scary at first. But not any more. Now that I have learned my lesson."

"And what lesson is that?"

"The most important one," Jeff answered, and now it was his turn to laugh: "It's infinitely better being rich than being poor."

Uncle Aaron shut his eyes meditatively. "Yes, well, I don't think too many will argue with that," he conceded. It was then that the check arrived and the conversation was dropped. But the matter persisted for Jeff. He knew Uncle Aaron well enough to see that he had been prepared to say something further, that his initial expression of support was the prelude to a pointed question – more than likely about Jeff's relationship with Murch. Jeff could guess how a man as independent as Aaron Arbuckle ultimately viewed partnerships.

"You're in your head again," Diane laughed, "and you missed our turnoff."

Jeff let out a groan of annoyance and headed for the next exit.

"Listen to me," she said, and Jeff could hear a new tone of tough love, "I can see you're scared – and maybe for the first time in your life. Just don't stop listening to those voices you're hearing. And for god's sake, when you make your pitch to Murch, *prepare* what you're going to say. You're a goddamned, deadlining, last-minute tap-dancer. And one day that's going to catch up to you. Don't let this time be that day."

Again, Diane was right. He *was* a goddamned tap-dancer.

And never more so than with his uncle. In the end, he had come to the preposterous, pompous conclusion that, with his own star still on the ascent, trifling with overly sentimental relationships could distract and threaten his continued advancement – justifying it with the promise that once he had plateaued, once he had secured his status inside the Hollywood machine, he could afford to reconnect without being false to either himself or his uncle. If only that had happened. By the time of Uncle Aaron's death, the two of them had not spoken in years.

Unconsciously, at least at first, his grip tightened once more against the steering wheel.

———ele———

The glass shattered against the dresser. Had it slipped or had she thrown it? Ann was not falling down drunk, but she was sauced enough not to give a shit how it had happened and ordered up another from room service. Goddamn Jill and her revisions. The whole thing stunk. The whole idea of crow-barring in a plot that betrayed everything the rest of the book – everything her career – stood for was repulsive. She was *not* signing off on a character that not only couldn't pass the Bechdel Test – it hadn't even studied for it. She was *not* saddling Alice with man problems! And where the hell was her wallet?

She and Jeff had finally met for lunch and spent the afternoon catching up. But he'd been distracted, as usual, and distant. Maybe things would never again be the same. Maybe this was the best that could be achieved this late in the game.

Tossing up piles of clothes and shoes and towels lying around everywhere – how many goddamn towels had they given her? – and bedsheets twisted and sprawling over half the room, tripping her as she scavenged through her splayed open luggage, make-up bags, charger cables twined with necklaces, and earrings, and now she couldn't even find her fucking purse. And wait – why, exactly, was she looking for her wallet?

God, if Jeff could see her now he'd go catatonic doing one of his internal inventories of all the ways her life was not precision-crafted to rocket her to world-wide acclaim like his was.

Well, that's *another* reason she had not wanted to stay at his place.

I like my mess! I work better in chaos! Except when I need to find my GODDAMNED WALLET!

The sudden awareness of her foot was confusing at first, as she grappled with why she should be feeling her foot at all – and, also, what exactly she was feeling – then yelled out "Fuck me!" as she looked down to discover a mess of blood and broken glass. Hobbling over to the bed, she pulled out a piece much smaller than the shard she was sure she'd just stepped on.

A nearby and still damp towel cleaned the wound and she chastised herself that she had been the one to throw her cocktail – inadvertently or not – across the room in the first place. The adrenaline rush from the instant vision of bleeding out on the hotel floor had done the trick. She was sobering up. Lifting the towel up from the sole of her foot and seeing that the cut had already sealed, she took a breath – then looked about her and knew she had to stop running.

Ever since she'd arrived in LA, since that first night with her brother, she'd known she was in high avoidance mode. That Thing she needed to do needed to be done *now*. And then she realized it was not her stupid wallet she'd been looking for – it was her cell phone. Which still didn't help because that, too, would be in her purse. Which her exhaustive reconnoitering had failed to turn up.

No, no, if I don't pick up all this glass, I'll just step on it again.

Getting down on all fours, she began carefully collecting the triangular fragments scattered over the beige carpet. *I'm so glad we don't have to mow carpet*, she thought as her hand carefully spread out over the fibers. *That'd be <u>another</u> thing I'd let get out of control. Certainly couldn't keep it like this – all uniform and crisp.* And the individual strands of the pile marched on and on, dissolving into the distant corners of the room, and they were like people, just millions of us, all the same, she thought, woven into our tight little spot and crowded around by a million others no different than we are, when you really look at it.

"Everyone has their time," Mrs. O'Connor had told her as they sat together in the office, waiting for some relative of hers to come and pick her up. The office secretary seemed intent on convincing Ann that people die and there was never any very good reason for it.

I think I get that, Mrs. O'Connor – Ann had wanted to say, but she was too distracted by the scene taking place in Mr. Diller's office. Jeff was seated in front of the principal and seemed to be crying. Jeff was the one who needed help right now. Her brother was in pain and she should be in there, she should be the one telling him things would be alright.

You see, Mrs. O'Connor, Ann would have told her, I'm okay because I have Jeff to look out for me, but he has no one. At least, that's what he's thinking right now – that he has no one. And I just need to tell him that he's wrong. He doesn't need to look out for me. This time, I'll look out for him. If I just let him know that, because he doesn't know that, then he'll stop crying.

But, Mrs. O'Connor had not let her see Jeff. In fact, no one did – for several days. She didn't know where he had gone to but before she knew it, Uncle Aaron and Mrs. Doss had arrived and things had begun to calm down. And, things had also changed. When he returned from his short absence, Jeff was different.

When he returned, from wherever it was he had been, they weren't secret friends anymore; they were barely brother and sister. The problem was, Ann was the only one that seemed to see it – because although secret friends might end their friendship, they can't end their secrets. She knew all his tricks; she didn't watch her brother from the audience, she watched from the wings. Yes, Jeff was a brilliant performer, but Ann could see he was deep, deep inside himself, hiding away from everyone and manipulating his outward persona like a marionette. At first, she tried a frontal assault, hoping that the direct approach would crack the shell. Then, after seeing that fail miserably, she thought playing the distressed little sister, the helpless waif shivering in the blizzard of tragedy might arouse some latent feelings of protectiveness. That too backfired. Jeff grew even more remote and Ann knew she needed to summon her most profound witchcraft to save him.

The problem was, as intimately as she knew her brother, his powers of perception were ever greater. She saw that he'd be able to decipher any scheme she might consciously employ against him. It was not until years later, looking back on that summer with Uncle Aaron, that Ann realized exactly what she had done. Without understanding it at the time, she had labored for weeks to craft a story for him – a story with elements specifically embedded in it to sabotage his defense mechanisms and draw him out and back to her. She had written "The Butterfly Ring" not realizing any of this, only knowing that he had to read it. It was even dedicated to him, which might have been her fatal mistake.

His first rejection of the story had sent her into a panic, but, a few days later, after leaving the manuscript out on the kitchen table inadvertently, she returned to find that it had been moved to the coffee table next to Jeff's favorite chair in the drawing room – and she was certain his curiosity had gotten the better of him. However, her efforts at uncovering his reaction – and at restoring their bond – had been to no avail. Jeff had continued on with his detached existence and she had had to resign herself to accepting that it might be years before their relationship was mended.

But even now, decades later, Ann was still at a loss as to how her dark arts had failed her. Magic had been on her mind often that long ago summer. And how art was not really so much the act of creation as of conjuring up an idea from a hidden dimension, siphoning it away from some pre-existing, cosmic source. Uncle Aaron's house was infused with this sensation. As she had wandered through its halls and rooms, she often felt as if she were not actually moving at all, but drifting through corridors in her own mind.

Eventually, of course, the magic had waned, reality had returned, and Ann and Jeff had been sent back to Illinois. In the days and months that followed, she thought often of her Uncle Aaron, sitting alone in that house, and wondered whether or not he was lonely. She began writing him and, in many ways, he became her new secret conspirator. They understood each other in ways that only she and Jeff had previously. More importantly, it was at this time she began to really write in earnest. Uncle Aaron insisted she send him everything – poems, plays, essays, and, especially, her stories. Always, he wrote back with glowing praise. Always, he responded with detailed encouragements. From anyone else, she would have said they were being disingenuous or ignorant. But with Uncle Aaron, because of their deep understanding of each other, she knew without question that he was being sincere – and that he believed she had real talent. Their relationship flourished through the years, and when the time came for college and decisions about careers, he paid for the best schools for both Ann and her brother.

Then, things transpired to once again change everything. After graduation and landing an adjunct professorship, Ann worked assiduously at becoming a professional writer, crafting hundreds of short stories and poems which she was certain were good enough for reputable publications. But, after countless submissions, no such offer was forthcoming. Sure, there were regional quarterlies who would print anything she sent them, but the major publishing houses were totally uninterested.

To Ann's credit, she never flat-out asked her uncle for anything. But as the years dragged on and she grew more discouraged, she would hint that a connection with a literary agent or an introduction to a high-profile magazine publisher would be extremely helpful. Yet, never once did he respond to these intimations. Never once did he acknowledge what was repeatedly implied, however obscurely. To be sure: his letters were overflowing with absolutely sincere praise, with an enthusiasm that grew by the month and with an unbounded generosity of affection towards her and her gifts. But each succeeding letter would be devoid of even the slightest hint or acknowledgement that he could be of any service to her career at all. He could not be ignorant of her plight or have missed the messages clearly embedded in her letters. She knew he had the same powers of perception as she did – maybe greater. And as her bitterness grew at the world's refusal to open its doors, those feelings leached into her bond with her uncle. No, she did not stop writing to him – though perhaps not quite so often – and anyone intercepting her letters would have observed no change in either the length or tone – but to a fellow magician, to a co-conspirator, Ann's slow withdrawal from the relationship would have been as a sea-change.

Ann sat up on the hotel room floor and sighed.

A leaden exhaustion descended and Ann recognized it as the now familiar hangover from digging about the past. One of her professors had once told her that the greatest crime is a person unaware of who they really were – and that, furthermore, it was a condition of which we are all guilty. If true, Ann had thought, we are forever condemned to be nothing but a planet of criminals.

She had sought self-awareness anyway. What else was there to do? There were too many unpacked moments from her past that felt like the massive blocks of stone amongst which her character of Alice walked. The question was whether or not, when the excavation work was complete, her pieces could be reassembled into something new and useful, into anything like a soaring cathedral.

The knocking broke her train of thought and she became aware that she was still sitting on the floor. "Room service," a voice called out. Scrambling to her feet and navigating the obstacle course of items strewn about the room, she managed a meek "yes?" The boy at the door held out her requested cocktail, which she simultaneously realized she'd forgotten – and was also delighted to remember – and noticed the bellhop was also, oddly, carrying a purse that looked very much like her own.

"You left it in the restaurant, ma'am," he said, passing it to her, and then, as a loud buzzing noise erupted from deep inside its contents, "Someone's been trying to reach you." She thanked him – and managed to tip him a twenty.

After sliding the chain back into its slot, she leaned against the closed door and swiped her phone, which had started buzzing again.

"Hi, Michael," she said, realizing she had run out of rope. "How are you?"

CHAPTER 9

The opening to the film was perfect.

The bright, unbounded sky blazed down upon the golden wheat. This was America's heartland – where the soil itself was infused with freedom, and those born and bred to its fertile cradle worked the land, not for profit, not for fame, but for that dignity which can only be earned by the honest toil of the hand and the heart. Here, amidst these sprawling fields, in this quiet little town, our story begins...

At least, that was the perfect opening to the film Jeff would have *liked* to communicate to Murch – accompanied, as he had *tried* to rehearse, with a description of a bird's-eye camera shot soaring over Midwestern farmlands – and, he would have had plenty of time to practice it all if he hadn't been totally broadsided by the chaos breaking out around him.

Diane had met him that morning in the parking lot looking frantic.

"Thank god you're here!" she had said, grabbing his wrist and pulling him along with her into the building. "It's Dirk. He's here. He's in your office. And he's on a total bender!"

"I can't deal with this now," Jeff said, suddenly gripped by desperation and confounded by what was happening. "I've got to face Murch in thirty minutes!"

"And it will all work out just *fine* – but not if Dirk goes ballistic!"

It had been two days since Diane had last raised the alarm about Dirk – and Jeff had thought they were in the clear. No such luck. By all accounts, Dirk had truly gone off the deep end and had broken into their office building sometime around dawn. Looking for Jeff, he had made his way to the breakroom where he had attempted to kill himself by sticking his head in the microwave. Diane had arrived just in time to prevent him from seeing that it wasn't plugged in – and had convinced him to talk things over with her first. She had sequestered him in Jeff's executive suite before anyone else had shown up.

"It's over! My life is completely over!" Dirk wailed as Diane pulled Jeff into his office and secured the door. No sooner had they caught their breath than Dirk, swaying on his feet near Jeff's desk, bent over to vomit in a small trash bin – and missed by a good three feet.

"I'll get it. I'll get it," Diane said, rushing back out again to grab a roll of paper towels. Jeff eased his friend to the ground and begged him to calm down.

"No, no, you don't unnerstand," Dirk drawled through his slobber. "They're gonna put me in jail!"

"Listen to me, Dirk," Jeff said. "You can't go to prison for making a video."

Dirk's eyes lolled about in confusion, trying to focus, "What're you fucking talkin' about?" he said and began dry heaving directly at Jeff. It was then that Diane sped back into the room with a mass of paper towels in each fist and began mopping up Dirk's mess.

"I don't know if he's tried to explain it to you," she said, dropping puke-soaked wads into the waste basket, "but as far as I can make out, this has nothing to do with that movie of his at all."

"What?"

"No – they don't know anything about that," Diane went on excitedly, "But, apparently, his boss at Family Films was embezzling money – and, before he could get caught, figured out a way to pin it all on Dirk."

"Holy shit," said Jeff, his mind spinning.

"They're gonna put me in jail!' Dirk cried out again, finally succeeding in disgorging more of his stomach contents onto his shirt.

"Diane, seriously," Jeff demanded, "I don't have time for this – Murch is expecting me. I have to go *now*."

Leaving Dirk to Diane's ministrations, the stench still in Jeff's nostrils, he raced to his business partner's office and to the most important meeting of his life.

"You tell that cunt-lipped asshole that his offer is dry-fucking us with a burlap dildo!" – Jeff heard Murch scream from the other room – "And use those exact fucking words!!"

Jeff's partner had – completely without warning and just as Jeff had begun describing the opening to his film – leapt from his desk and bounded out the door to his office. The fracas had obliterated Jeff's narrative flow, but the break provided a tiny reprieve to collect his thoughts and keep his stomach from churning. The insanity with Dirk, who at this moment was being guarded by Diane just down the hall, had left him totally discombobulated. As the room seemed to sway, he sat dumb-founded as to how the entire day had gone from pandemonium to worse.

"Sorry, buddy!" Murch shouted, coming back and throwing his hands in the air as he flopped back down into his seat. "You know how those shit-suckers need to be bitch-slapped. Now – take it from the top again, I already forgot where we were!"

"Yes, well, um, as I was saying," Jeff began to stutter, and was furious with himself for feeling so distressed. Yesterday, it had all been crystal clear. He had come back to the office with the whole project making absolute, perfect sense – the entire story worked out from beginning to end and with an unquestioned certainty that it would be a breeze to articulate.

Diane is going to have a field day with this. Jeff sighed to himself. She had told him he wasn't sufficiently prepared. *Why didn't I memorize this spiel word-for-word??*

The few short quips he'd thrown at Murch to get the meeting set up were a masterclass compared to this floundering. "So, yeah, just to give you the big picture, it starts with, like, corn-fields, you know, and shots of silos, and stuff," he finally got out.

"Got it. It takes place in a shit-hole," Murch said to hammer Jeff's point down.

"Well, not exactly, we'll capture the, you know, blue-collar, the American, you know, romanticize it more than that," Jeff countered and began to really be thrown by just how lost he was finding himself, how nervous, how changed from before – and saw that those times before, when he'd felt so revived and energized, those times articulating it all to Diane, he had actually still been in the throes of his inspired fugue. Still been resonating from his encounter in his uncle's attic. Now that his head was truly clearing, the whole thing was morphing into an unwieldy concept that was making him sound like a crazy man. No! No! He could still remember, could still see the vision of how his story would rivet audiences and express ideas that –

"God-damn granny's ass crack!!" Murch suddenly screamed, staring at his computer and jumping up from his desk again, stopping Jeff mid sentence.

"Jesus Christ, Murch! I'm trying to explain something here!" Jeff shot back, still reeling from the interruption.

"Yeah, but did you see this?! Did you see this!?" Murch shouted, stabbing his finger at his computer screen, "Seven fucking nominations! Seven! That ass rag!" Then, stomping back out of the room, started howling, "Get me the fucking trades! *Where's the fucking trades*?!?"

Alone again, Jeff sunk his face into his hands to calm himself down. He was not going to succumb to this. He was not going to allow himself to mentally snap in front of anyone, let alone Murch. He'd fought battles and held his own with some of the most powerful people in Hollywood. What was wrong with him? And why did this project seem so goddamned important? All he knew was that for the first time, he was afraid Murch would tell him no. They'd done eleven pictures together and never once had he ever wondered if his partner would come on board. But this was different. This movie would be unlike anything they had ever done before – and that confidence with which he had envisioned laying everything out to Murch had evaporated, had now been replaced with the clarity that, of course, there was no way in *hell* Murch was going to agree to this.

As the sound of Murch continuing his rant echoed from the outer office, it was then that Diane came rushing in. "Where's the first-aid kit on this floor?!"

"I've got a bunch of Band-Aids in my desk," Jeff murmured, still holding his head in his hands. "What happened now?"

"Dirk fell over and cut his face on your air purifier."

"What? Is he okay?"

"Yes, it's all under control – Ted from Finance is sitting on him, but we'll have to get the blood out of the carpet later," she said exiting in a rush and nearly colliding with Murch on his way back in – who yelled at her about still not having the promo done, to which her retort of, "Not going to fucking happen, Murch!" could be heard trailing off and away down the office.

"Here!" stormed Murch, slapping the front page of Variety down onto his desktop and in front of Jeff – where *Finding Emily* was the banner headline. "Seven fucking nominations!" Murch raged, "Seven golden butt plugs for that piece of cunt rot!!"

"Jesus, Murch!" Jeff said, overcome with exasperation. "Calm the fuck down! *Why* do you give a shit?"

"You want to know why? You want to know WHY?" Murch said, and, cutting himself off, charged back to the door and shouted out, "Bonnie! I want every fucking copy of today's trades out of this office and fucking burned in the parking lot!"

"Right away, Mr. Murch!"

"And why am I hearing yodeling?!?" Murch demanded as he barreled back into the office and threw himself once again into his desk chair, turning to Jeff and fuming, "Is the whole goddamned office losing its mind?!?"

Jeff's head reeled in his effort to get control of this meeting while the insanity of this decades-long conversation erupted yet again, and he found himself shouting, "Stop being so competitive with Lewis! The guy's a nothing! You're worth ten times what he is!"

"You didn't know that butt cyst in film school!" Murch said with the venom of a betrayed mafia don. "He threw his fucking weight around, let me tell you! He threw it around!" This outburst was accompanied by Murch's eyes speeding about his office as if seeking a collection of poison-tipped daggers – then he flung his hands up in the air and exclaimed "Well, I'm an asshole! What can I say?" From this, he folded his hands, leaned in and said, "Now! Take it from the top again, I already forgot where we were!"

Taking a deep breath, Jeff, aiming his last ounce of concentration at Murch's Cro-Magnon brow, launched his attack.

"It's called *Summer of the Rainbows*," Jeff said with a slow and deliberate intensity, savoring the title he'd finally landed on, the one he had concluded gave the film the exact dignity and flair it deserved – and then, just as Murch started to respond, Jeff pounded the desk with his fist and jumped back in with even greater fervor: "Forget what I said about cornfields and that small town crap!" The vision was swelling – along with Diane's words about grabbing Murch by the balls – and the feverish high it brought with it was urging him on, goading him to expel any shred of caution; and he did, becoming the human conduit of his exultant muse and proclaiming, "This is a film about something REAL – about how shitty the world is, how it's too much so you try to move on! About the struggle and the fight! About LIFE!" Then, rising from his seat, Jeff took the entire room as his stage, "Because it's about a woman – and she's DYING, Murch! Yes, DYING of LUPUS! And you know what else she has?!?" Murch stared back wide-eyed and stunned, managing only to shake his head in the negative as Jeff continued, "A DAUGH-TER, Murch! A daughter who DOESN'T want her to DIE!!"

Now it was time for the coup de gras – he threw his body forward onto Murch's desk, bracing himself with his arms out-stretched, and seethed, "And you know what else it's about?!?" Jeff's voice soared into ever higher registers – "It's about telling Lewis to go FUCK himself up the ASS!! It's about making a movie that's going to shut that cocksucker up ONCE AND FOR ALL!"

Jeff fell back into his chair, needing to catch his breath. The thought that came to him now, as beads of sweat broke out across his forehead, was that he was back to his normal self again, that lavishing Murch with his vision had broken his brain fever. But what he was starting to understand was that although he was feeling more and more himself – and that his feet were closer and closer to the ground – the experience had been like the aftermath of a flood, where the receding waters reveal a new, altered landscape delivered from the cataclysm. And, he was also accosted by something else: two totally competing impressions of what had just happened. On the one hand, part of him felt that he'd been quite profound, that he'd managed to convey the outlines of a truly epic picture. But, on the other hand, it might have been the stupidest thing he'd ever said in his entire life.

Murch leaned back in his chair and began tapping the tips of his fingers against each other. His eyes narrowed to slits. "I just have one question for you," he said quietly.

"What?" Jeff asked in a near whisper.

"Does it have balls?" came Murch's words, "Does it have big greasy, swollen, hairy balls?"

"Yes, Murch," Jeff said, realizing that, somehow, miraculously, he'd done it. Somehow, he'd actually gotten Murch to sign off on this. "Yes. Yes it does," he repeated. He also knew he had no clue how he was going to make any of it happen.

CHAPTER 10

*R*ow upon row of their young faces looked up at her in silent ardor. The lecture hall of *The Marie de Gournay Lyceum for Women* was packed and overflowing with students, faculty, and their guests – all sitting in that kind of hushed active silence that kindled with anticipation. Ann stared at the faces of those young women, determined that she would somehow not betray them – although she knew she was a fraud.

She looked down at her notes, then brought her eyes back up to her audience – and her voice, amplified by the PA system, filled the space with an assertiveness that belied her true feelings of shame and doubt: "Every morning, most of us step into our bathrooms and confront the glass corset." There was a rustle of murmurs of assent, and Ann continued authoritatively, "We stand before the judgment of that constricting frame which does nothing but reflect back the most pernicious societal edicts about who we are supposed to be as women, and worse, our own traitorous acquiescence to them." The outbreak of applause hit just in time to cover the tremor in Ann's voice and make her extended pause seem like an intentional courtesy towards her listeners. The truth was, she had been on the brink of drowning.

This memory of her one and only speaking engagement of note – following the publication of her book of essays – kept recurring to Ann as she wandered along the blocks of hotels surrounding LAX. Although her foot was still a bit sore, there was no discernable limp; and, she'd needed a walk after her conversation with Michael. It also wouldn't hurt to finish sobering up. Her purse with her ringing cell phone and Michael on the other end of the line had arrived at the moment of her determination to finally make a clean break with him. Something she should have done years ago.

At its worst, her relationship with him had been intensely degrading. At its best, she had experienced a constant, low-grade ennui, a state of perpetual dissatisfaction and irritability with the world. This she was able to mask with dazzling aplomb, deceiving even her most intimate friends – and her brother – with a perpetually sunny persona. Indeed, she was able to go weeks believing it herself, and was able to compartmentalize those emotions so well that she was often quite shocked to rediscover them when they erupted to the surface – as they invariably, eventually did – and then, just as invariably, plunged her back into depths of self-loathing.

Her rambling excursion down the boulevard with the night traffic rushing along took her past a convenience store and to the purchase of a pack of cigarettes. The nicotine rush was intense, as it had been months since her last smoke. As the sidewalk glided beneath her feet, the cigarette and the hammering of her heels on the cement seemed the perfect accompaniment to her fury towards Michael.

The catalog of emotions assaulting her now so perfectly mirrored the night of her speech at the Gournay Lyceum that it was *that* particular event she found herself fixating on, and not this evening's trauma. That night, two years ago, she had reached a level of wrath so acute that she had nearly become unhinged in front of three hundred bystanders – an episode that ever since had hovered as an omen. Every particle of her rational, conscious mind and shred of self-respect had stood in horror of her submission to him. Why had she not broken things off the night of the speech? Why had she let this relationship drag on for so long?

As she looked back at the woman she had been, it was all so perplexing – because the woman looking out over all those young listeners themselves searching for answers from a champion of feminine independence, *that* woman had known everything Ann knew *now*. She had been just as aware of his games and manipulations. That woman had known that her relationship with Michael could not have been a more clichéd example of melodramatic dreck – the kind that the worst literary hack would have laughed off the page. Surely, there must be an explanation – a conk on the head from a falling flower pot? – to explain how a woman of her intellect and education could, after a one-night stand with a bartender, allow him to move in with her after less than a month. And then continue putting up with it for years.

Had the audience known the details, she could only imagine what the Q & A would have been like.

"So this man that you met one night in a bar: a month later was living with you and, if my notes are accurate, you began paying for his car insurance?"

"Yes, that's correct."

"Why?"

"I didn't want him using my car. It was an imperfect solution."

"And, you also knew that he was sleeping with other women?"

"I didn't know that for sure."

"But you suspected it–"

"Yes, yes," Ann would have said, *"I've been through all this before. I have nothing to say in my defense – except that I knew every second how stupid I was being. How much I was putting myself at risk. And how I was making a mockery of my book, my own moral compass, and that I'm standing before you now as the world's biggest hypocrite."*

"Then why? Why do it?"

These were the voices Ann had heard in her head, the voices she knew had every reason to ask, that weighed on her then as now and provoked at that podium the tremble in her voice and the tremor in her hand, and with which she had had to grapple every second of her speech to keep from falling apart. And, she also knew that these voices were behind her drive to reach out and reconnect with her brother, to stay and unravel the complicated riddle of her Uncle Aaron, and that maybe, all of it together when peeled back, when sifted down to its essence, would help her understand this thing about herself.

"To answer that, to answer why," she would have told the audience, *"I'd have to be more honest with you now than I've ever been, even with myself. I'd have to tell you things that will only come to me in their truest clarity years later. But, as you are a memory, as you are a moment that seems to have attached itself to me in a way that seems important, maybe I have a responsibility to answer you,*

though none of you will ever know it. I only know that if I had to do it all over, I'd do it again. And, I know that every single one of you is capable of the same."

Had she dropped her guard that evening at the theater, had she stepped off of that stage and sat among them and poured out her heart, she would have told them that it was all to experience something she had never in her life dreamed would ever be possible. She would have had to confess that from her earliest age she had experienced lusts for the male form that, even now, as an adult, she found breathtakingly, prodigiously carnal. But, not just any male form. She seemed to have been cursed with an obsession for the Adonis.

"But, yes!" they would have said. "We *all* like guys who are hot. How does that explain anything?"

In fact, it explained *everything*, because Ann would have said that it was to this type of man that she was attracted *exclusively*. Only the face and body of an exquisitely formed god fit the bill – the kind that was impossible to land. It was a curse; it was a calamity. And she had endeavored for years to rid herself of it. How she pined to find average men enticing – but even above-average men, men that she intellectually could see most women would describe as "handsome," left her cold. But what was to be done? These were not things one merely turned on or off with a switch. These were biological hard-wirings, embedded far below the level of conscious thought, the roots of which descended even deeper, and which forever remain out of touch. There had been no shortage of gentlemen whose conversation and wit she had adored, but as stimulating as their intellectual intercourse had been, none of them had been able to translate

those feelings into physical attraction. No, for Ann, it was all
or nothing. You either matched her extraordinarily constrained
parameters for exceptional male beauty – in which case she was
ready to bed you right there and then – or you did not, in which
case, as far as Ann was concerned, you might as well have been a
stamp-collecting eunuch.

The second major component to this situation was Ann herself – and she was far too intelligent and self-aware not to know
how much her own appearance, how much her *judgment* of
her own appearance, fueled her difficulties: Ann, in all honesty,
was plain in face and form. Not ugly, but missing the rigor of
bone structure and alignment of muscle tissue that lifts a face,
at minimum, into the "interesting" category. For Ann knew her
appearance lacked any of the subtle hooks or tiny barbs that
allow a woman's aspect to adhere afterwards in the memory.
When it came to men, in true democratic fashion, they typically
responded to her as she to them: with total disinterest. But just as
she was too self-aware to ignore the problem with her looks, she
was also too self-aware to deny what she was sexually capable of
– that is, what she would be willing to do were there nothing to
restrain her. In a way, her physical blandness had been a godsend.
This was the true glass corset for Ann. This was her bondage
and her salvation – and she had long resigned herself to a life
of singlehood, and had concluded it was probably for the best.
Then, however, it happened. She met Michael.

She had dropped into a local tavern on a whim for a quick
cocktail before heading home, and the man who met her across
the bar had stepped straight out of her most potent fantasy. To
her eternal embarrassment, the only way for Ann to describe

him was in the lurid argot of literary trash. The sole descriptors that came to her mind could only come by scraping the barrel for worn-out chestnuts and tawdry symbolism: *this was no man. This was a bull in heat – with caramel skin, coal black eyes – a brooding stallion with a ravenous grin that marked him instantly as a master in the art of female pleasuring. Worse, he had made it immediately clear that he was ready and willing to prove it to her.*

Now here's where things got tricky. Ann's first instinct was to pay her bill and leave. But then, those same intellectual pistons which ordinarily powered her rational thought process, with which she scrutinized the world and analyzed its problems, came to bear. Yes, in the midst of doing exactly what any sane woman would have done under similar circumstances – *no good can EVER come from sleeping with a bartender* – her superego asserted itself and in the most professorial bearing told her to STOP. RIGHT. THERE.

Paradoxically, it had been her rational, feminist side which had betrayed her in the end. "By leaving," it had insinuated, "you admit you are no match for a man. *Stay*, and you demonstrate how he can be used. Remain unscathed to the last – and you win." This argument had been her real moment of weakness.

But Ann had seriously underestimated both her own abilities and Michael's – and the next day, after he had taken her into realms she had never dreamed of, it was too late. It was over. He had awakened lusts in her and then, demon that he was, *delivered* on them with acts of physical intensity that acted on her like a drug – and with such power that heroin would have been easier to kick.

The sound of a low-flying jet distracted her for a moment. Ann looked up to watch the mammoth craft pass by overhead. She followed it as its landing gear retracted and it ascended out of sight and she thought about the tremendous weight that can be kept aloft, if only there is enough thrust. Jesus, what a metaphor for her life! And just how much lift did *she* require? Her audience may have been surprised to learn how little she really needed from Michael. Other women, if there had been any in his life, really didn't matter to her at all. Why should they? She had no tender feelings for him. She didn't need flowers, she didn't need chocolates. And, she didn't need conversation.

A good thing, that, because – despite his prodigious talents – he was a dullard. Once his stud services had been rendered, she was able to return for stretches at a time to a state of relative calm and to enjoy her solitude. But all the garbage that Michael did put her through, or rather, that she *allowed* him to put her through – the financial assistance, the free room and board, the gym membership – had to be met with an equal and opposite force. On that point, she had made her terms quite clear. She wanted sex – lots of it – and she wanted to show him off from time to time.

The other big problem was that Michael managed to give her exactly enough to fulfill their bargain but nothing more – a precision-calculated quid pro quo talent at being worth just *slightly* more than what it cost her in her pride. That he could so carefully balance on this edge, that he could so easily refrain from being generous with her needled her endlessly. She longed for him to violate her in some way, to hurt her with enough intensity to overwhelm this barrier. But he never did. He always kept his antics just inside her threshold of tolerance. For if Ann's brilliance was deception – towards both others and herself – Michael's was gauging just how far he could push a lover and still remain within her graces.

But that night years past, standing before a hall full of admirers, among whom were many of her friends and colleagues come to hear her speech and applaud her winning the Lyceum's annual literary award – that was the moment that Michael chose to subtract from his surplus by failing to show up, texting her curtly, just before she went on, "Sorry can't make it." Walking out to the applause, shuffling her notes carefully on the lectern, it was not the betrayal of her principles that overwhelmed her with anguish, it was the humiliation of being jilted in front of friends who would see right through any excuse to explain his absence – and knowing that her evening of triumph, her speech and accolades, would be forever tainted by this blow.

Ann's cigarette had almost burned down to the filter and she quickly scanned the sidewalk and store fronts around her for a place to extinguish it. If she was going to be irresponsible and smoke, she could at least be tidy about it. An ash can next to a darkened laundromat caught her eye and, approaching it, she found herself arrested by her reflection in the window and flinched. She'd aged in the two years since she'd met Michael. She was older. Heavier. She studied her plain face and her plain body. *Never ponder your problems when you've been drinking*, she tried to remind herself, but she was seized again by Michael's affront two years ago at the Lyceum. *I should have ended it then*, she thought. But, instead, she had listened to her pride – "So long as you leave because you're hurt, you've lost. So long as he can get to you, he's won."

I should have told my pride to fuck off and saved myself two years of torment.

If she'd explained herself, if she'd thrown herself on the compassion of her audience, would her sisters have risen up and absolved her of her hypocrisy? Or would they have scorned her on the spot? How often had Ann wished for the mercy of the latter – a quick end to her pretense and her suffering. *But I didn't,* she thought, *I didn't because I was a coward and a fool. Which is why I decided to finally end it tonight. Why I decided to make a clean break. And when he called, I had every intention of following through on that vow.*

Except that I didn't.

I didn't say a goddamn thing I had wanted to.

All because his face is a gun.

A fucking gun.

CHAPTER 11

From the deck of his Hollywood Hills bungalow, Jeff gazed over the sprawling city. He'd bought the pad partly as a getaway and partly as a solution to hosting soirees without having the riffraff tramping through his Bel Air home. Now it served as a bunker. Although Murch had signed off on *Summer of the Rainbows*, Jeff needed all the space he could manage to plan for the coming battle. It would be a fight to the finish. It would be a fight to the death. And knowing all this, he should have been terrified – but he wasn't. Things had changed. Somewhere, deep inside, Jeff was growing increasingly confident that he was on the verge of something extraordinary.

Then there was Dirk. There was no way he or Diane would have been willing to leave him alone. They'd only been half kidding when they discussed putting him on a 24-hour suicide watch. Somehow, they'd calmed him down enough to get him out of the studio, into a car, and delivered here. He'd clearly had much more to drink than either of them had suspected because he'd passed out immediately in the guest room – and had been that way for the last eight hours. But let him sleep. Tomorrow, Jeff would walk through Dirk's story with him one more time, try to get more answers, and maybe get his lawyers to stop by and offer some counsel.

He looked out again over the city. Its pattern of far flung lights continued on with shimmering indifference and Jeff considered how even the most powerful man in the world would not be able to hold its attention for more than a moment. Jesus, everything had been swimming since Uncle Aaron's death. Everything had been thrown into upheaval. He let the cool night air and the glowing vista take his thoughts where they would. The moving sparkles worked their magic and charmed his attention and, spectral sirens that they were, beguiled him away from his troubles – up he floated and felt the tug of familiar currents, pulling him back towards familiar depths, and to his uncle's garden where he drifted along, watching his sister run among the carefully manicured shrubbery. At first it seemed as though he were chasing her and she was laughing – but then she stopped, looked about and he saw that her eyes were red and her face was wet. And he knew she was looking for him, that he was hiding from her, and that he'd been hiding from her for a long time. And then, he wasn't near her at all, but watching her, secretly, from a window. She called out to him one last time, ripped a fist-full of leaves from the nearest bush, threw them disdainfully behind her, and fled off to the secluded gazebo – where he knew she'd sulk until dinner time.

A spider crawling along the sill of the window and up along the wall drew his attention back towards the small space where he crouched. It was a hiding place he'd discovered inside the broom closet of the kitchen. It seemed as though the cabinetry had been added at a later date and that, rather than remove a window that served to balance its particular part of the exterior, it had been left in its place and relegated to a merely ornamental function. But, for Jeff, it provided the perfect portal from which to spy, unobserved, on the bulk of Uncle Aaron's vast garden. His eyes kept moving upwards towards the ceiling, where, for the first time, he noticed several compact shelves containing various glass vials, like a spice rack.

Without having to inspect them, he knew they were not spices. The location of the little shelves, high up in a broom closet, was exactly where one stored dangerous chemicals, things to be kept out of the reach of children. Jeff was certain he would not have known exactly what was in the bottle he took and placed in his pocket – only that he knew enough about poisons to see that the markings on the label clearly indicated it as such. Ann would not be back for some time and Uncle Aaron was off in his study and would stay there until called by Mrs. Doss – who had left to buy fresh salmon for the evening meal.

Sitting at the long, imposing kitchen table that seemed to have been carved from a single block of wood, Jeff thought how all of them finding him there, slumped across the table top, would have the precise impact he desired.

He'd tried before, although it had been hushed up and dismissed as a momentary lapse of reason following the shock of his parents' death – but they'd kept him in the hospital for a few days, and then, when he appeared not to remember anything about the incident, brought him back home to his sister, his relatives, and his uncle. They'd thought the whole thing was behind him and had been assured by the doctors that there was no chance of a relapse. But he'd kept the boy who had done it hidden away, deep, deep, inside the fortress where the real Jeff had come to live – so as to watch the world from a place of safety. And that other little boy, deeply hidden away, never made a sound and Jeff knew that, unless he went looking for him, he would remain buried forever.

But something had changed that summer day for both himself and for his sister, out there in that garden. A phone call had come, and, for whatever reason, Jeff had gone looking for that little boy, had run away from Ann, had holed up next to his secret spying window, and had found his phantom friend once again. And then, sitting at that long imposing kitchen table, with the bottle in his pocket, he had started thinking again about that little boy he kept hidden away, and how that little boy would want him to open the bottle and see what was inside. That's when he saw the story.

How he had missed it was only part of the mystery. The carefully stapled papers had to have been there the whole time, but, however it happened, Jeff had only noticed it then. Sliding the stapled papers from across the table he flipped open the cover and recognized it as the story Ann had tried to get him to read earlier in the summer.

Her stupid ideas...

More out of a sense of fun – cruel curiosity to see exactly how bad her writing could be – Jeff strolled out of the kitchen and into the drawing room where he plopped down into his favorite chair, and read on. And this was the other part of the mystery: by the time he was finished and had experienced the adventures of the magician and the girl with the butterfly ring, he no longer sensed the presence of the little boy that had been hiding deep inside. In fact, he had the distinct impression the little boy was now inside Ann's story, that he had traversed the conduit from Jeff's mind to the printed narrative and was off having all manner of adventures on his own. In the boy's absence, Jeff forgot the existence of the bottle in his pocket.

That evening, sitting down to dinner with Uncle Aaron, his sister, and Mrs. Doss, it was as though a hard, constricting carapace had finally split and fallen away from his body. He felt freer than ever before and when Uncle Aaron, in one of his rare, whimsically bombastic moods began serenading Mrs. Doss – and she, more shocking still, broke into song with *him* – Jeff howled with delight, erupting in unrestrained glee for the first time since the tragedy.

"Listen to those pipes!" Uncle Aaron had exclaimed at the conclusion of their duet, "Mark my words, Aggie, you could have starred on Broadway!"

Mrs. Doss blushed in embarrassment – and countered by asking how anything could be worth giving up her life of luxury cooking meals and cleaning up after such a fine gentleman as Mr. Arbuckle. The two continued their back and forth teasing and even Ann joined in the fray – taking Mrs. Doss's side of the argument, and Jeff, feeling spent, finally noticed the make-shift family that he'd fallen into, really saw who his uncle, Mrs. Doss, and his sister really were. And what, perhaps, he'd been missing. And then he remembered, suddenly, the bottle in his pocket, and was ashamed. He fled from the table and rushed outside to dispose of the hateful item in the trash bins behind the garage.

Jeff felt the terrible guilt of that moment pierce him in the present. He had been an asshole then and was still one now. Maybe he was too confused as a child to fully comprehend the on-rush of all those emotions – too overwhelmed to let any of them know all that they had done for him. But, Jesus Christ, by the time he'd moved out here, by the time he was in his twenties and had accepted his uncle's generous help, you'd think he would have been more grateful. But, he'd cut things off to "prove" something to himself – and the renewal of their friendship which he carelessly assumed would eventually happen, never did. And that was a shame that could not be extinguished. There wasn't a dumpster big enough to toss it in. Jeff cringed at the thought of how much the old slurs about his lack of talent had perturbed him and how much they were really responsible for his withdrawal from Uncle Aaron. He'd been made aware of pronouncements that his fantastic rise had all been courtesy of his family connections. "Yes, but you know he's the nephew of Aaron Arbuckle," they'd said, "Of course he was escorted right to the top." He looked back at that thin-skinned careerist through the eyes of a man that now was actually quite proud of his heritage – and wished he'd talked about it more. Why hadn't he stood unabashedly with a man who had conquered twice as much of Hollywood as Jeff ever would? Maybe that would have stopped him from push-ing so hard for this film project. The question disturbed his fresh confidence, and brought within range, once again, that uneasy feeling that this might just be the one movie beyond his reach. It held him fixed, staring out at the stars for answers.

Into this state of deep self-reflection, Ann dropped with her late-night call.

"Well, thank you for picking up!"

"I know, I know," Jeff laughed with sincere remorse, "I'm a terrible brother."

"No, just rude," said Ann. "I love having to wait three days on average to get a call back."

"Oh, god, I deserve it. But rest assured my life sucks right now, so the universe is on your side."

"You want to talk about it?"

"Not really. It's all crap that I'll eventually figure out somehow."

Now Ann laughed. Her personal life might be in tatters, her integrity shot by her continual capitulations to Michael, but she still had her brother. Yes, Jeff was still the distant soul that she longed would come a bit closer – but he'd changed in the last few years. And days. And it was nice. Yes, there was still a lost, far-away quality about him, there was still the sense that she'd disappointed him in some vague way – she'd disappointed herself, after all – but there was also an honesty now and a grounded acceptance about who he was and an openness in allowing Ann to see it. And this gave her hope because only a secret ally could tell her all that without saying a word. Ann would have liked nothing more than to relax into their reawakening bond – just as they had done last week on her first night in LA. But, sensing the hour, she had to forego that pleasure for the moment and get down to business.

"Okay, I'm really calling to give you an update on things," she said, shifting into her faculty chair mode, "It looks like we have a buyer for the estate. They're offering the asking price and I'm not really interested in waiting around for a better offer. You good with that?"

Even at his most contentious, Jeff would not have offered a hint of resistance to anything Ann wanted to do in any family affair – and she knew it – but this was all pure Ann: needing to spell out everything. He happily conceded to her view of things.

"Terrific. Now, more importantly – have you been to the house and gotten everything you want?"

"Yes. I did that yesterday."

"Great. The estate sale is next week so if you have any last minute desire for a second look, you still have time. Now, how's your speech coming? Are you ready?"

Secret, reawakened bonds are indeed a beautiful thing. But, they also come with a heavy toll. One of which is being able to compute, down to the nanosecond, the exact length of time at which a pause becomes an indication of either not being able to answer a question or the formulation of a BS smokescreen.

"Jeff!" Ann scolded – almost instantly – and with some actual bite, "The memorial is *this Friday*. You are speaking for the family. You are representing our entire line of ancestors – in front of potentially 800 plus people – so don't screw around with this."

"It'll be ready! Geez!" he said, laughing again, and starting to get a bit light-headed as he realized he had no idea what he could, should, or would say.

"Well, just remember, you can't blow this off because I'll have my hands full running interference and coordinating with the fan club that's put the whole thing together."

There were a few additional incidentals, mostly about the program for the memorial and where to park. But Ann, not wanting to impose more than necessary this late at night, indicated she was wrapping up. But before she could actually end the call, her brother paused, and then, in the most direct way, said, "I'm glad you called, Ann. It's nice to hear your voice."

There are, it should be noted, also very nice things about secret, reawakened bonds. Most notably, that it can suffuse the simplest of sentences with whole passages of meaning. Ann knew instantly that Jeff had much more on his mind, that he wished for her to stay, to keep him company, that he was apologetic for not having been a better host during her Los Angeles visit, and that this incipient change she had detected had not yet run its course. Also, that no response was necessary – that he would pick up the remnants of his thoughts momentarily. And so, she waited.

"I was actually just thinking about Uncle Aaron when you called," Jeff said, as if to a confessor. "Do remember that night he sang to Mrs. Doss?"

"Of course I do! Our farewell meal."

"What?" Jeff asked, startled.

"Yes! Don't you remember? We were leaving the next day to go back home."

"Oh, god...that's right..." Jeff said, then fell to silence again as a deluge of memories rushed in, filling in gaps that he had not recognized were there. The process was disorientating for a moment – "I had completely forgotten...Aunt Lynn had called that day...and wanted us to come back to Illinois to start school and be with the rest of the family."

"I was miserable," recalled Ann, the memories flooding back for her as well, "but *you* couldn't have been happier. I never saw you laugh so hard. I knew you had been having a hard go of it that summer, but I was crushed. I *desperately* wanted to stay."

"No, no. I think I was sad too…you know, if I'm honest about it," said Jeff, stopping himself from being totally candid, and proving there were some things that must be kept even from a secret bond.

Ann then seemed to lean into the conversation herself, finding aspects that she, too, needed to assuage. "That was the last time I saw him at his house. Did you know that? Oh, I wrote to him constantly, we were furious pen-pals. And he visited me now and again, but it was never really the same. With school and the jobs, I never had a chance to fly back to see him in his own element. I'll forever regret that."

"He adored you, you know."

Yes, Ann said, she knew. Then, hoping he would be able to recall a point which suddenly urged itself on her, she asked: "Do you remember that last time you saw him? Here in LA?"

"Oh, probably we went out to dinner or something," Jeff replied, too late to stop Ann from understanding all the extra baggage that he was clearly still struggling with as well. "We'd do that…periodically," Jeff continued, "But no, I don't really recall the last time. I got busy too, and, well, things happen and…"

Ann was ready with the assist, faithful pal that she was: "Well, we're going to make it up to him," she announced, and then, "We're going to show him a terrifically good time. Not to worry. The kids I'm working with are going all out."

Then, it really was time to go, and to fall asleep with all their plans, and questions, and regrets, and resolutions floating about, with none of those dreams promising to stay or any of those worries guaranteed to fade off into forgetfulness. "And as for the speech – just say something true, Jeff," Ann finally said, "Say something real."

After Ann had gone, Jeff spent another hour or so watching the night sky and trying to come up with the truest thing to be said about Uncle Aaron – or *anything*, for that matter – but words would not come, only images, and as exhaustion settled over him, he began drifting off on the deck chair, and moving, as on a river, back to his childhood, back to that summer with his uncle. First, it was to glide among the fulgent blossoms of Mr. Lee's garden, pass slowly above the koi pond, fly around the old wooden swing and through the gazebo – and from there, he drifted into the house, around its many rooms, through the kitchen, past his secret hiding place, then up a small staircase, and into the attic studio. Here he was held, for just a moment, waiting. And the attic returned to its present, dusty state, and Jeff was no longer a child, but himself again, entering that upper room exactly as he had less than two weeks ago. And it came to him that he had seen something, something standing before him. Something Mrs. Doss had thrown a sheet over. He was certain it was something he had recently remembered, too – something he had felt was the key to much of what he had been experiencing. He felt as if he had forgotten something else, a question or perhaps that he'd left something important there. Whatever it was, he could feel it, sitting quietly just outside the periphery of his consciousness. The last thing on his mind before the dark of sleep came to him was the echoing question,

What was it?...What was it?...What was it?

CHAPTER 12

Out of the giant darkness, demon thrummings of bass violins shook the theater – the cheers nearly as booming – and suddenly, up on the screen, a crack and flash of lighting, and an iron cauldron appeared; and from its luminescent, turbulent green brew, purple ghosts shrieked skyward; and as the song started, 900 applauding fans joined in –

Look out, folks! It's a ga-ga-ga-ghost!
Look out, gang! It's a Dracula's fang!

It was the opening to the show's third season, the season that had introduced the iconic animated credit sequence and, by this point, the crowd was on their feet and dancing –

Everybody's runnin' from those thrilling chilling creepers!
Everybody's flyin' from those fearsome frightful creatures!

Several fans cos-playing the lead characters rushed out on stage and took up positions directly in front of the foot lights, frolicking in sync to the footage playing behind them –

But with Lucy and Stuey
There's sure to be grins – Ha! Ha!
And let's not forget
Those super-smart twins – Ta-Dah!
With Banana Barilla

Right by their side
They're here to thrill ya!
A spook-tacular ride!

Swelling to the bombastic finale, the chorus of voices rang out–

Yeah! We're glad you came!
Yeah! You'll have a bang!
With that kooky Professor and –
The GROOOOOVY Gang!

A massive trumpet splat concluded the anthem and the image faded to black. Ann thought the raucous ovation that followed could not be topped – but then, a classic sepia publicity photo of Aaron Arbuckle, from his early career in motion pictures, suddenly filled the screen and the response surpassed deafening. From her vantage point in the wings, hidden in the shadows and looking up at the giant picture of Uncle Aaron, Ann held tight to the velvet scrim as waves of nostalgia broke over her to the clapping and cheering of the packed house. She felt as if, in some way, through her, he could hear it too. And, even though he shunned publicity, she was certain he would have been humbled and grateful for all the people who had come tonight and who were now on their feet.

Then, the image of him alone in his studio, alone in that house, reappeared to her for an instant – and, also, those regrets that she had not been there for him. But there in that moment, hearing the roar and shout of those fans, she knew that if he had ever felt abandoned by the world, he had been terribly mistaken. Or at least ignorant of the possibilities for connection that had stood ready for him. But did that absolve her? What exactly was the price for pulling away from someone? The answer was just another reason to have worked so hard to spare herself too close a look. But now, she needed to look hard and to look close. And still the applause went on. She turned again to his picture spread out above her, canted by her perspective, and wondered.

Was there an emptiness, Uncle Aaron?

She wondered if she would ever know. The distortions that occur the nearer we draw to a person made that difficult. She had continuously misunderstood him – and in many ways still did. Who had the clearer picture of her uncle? Herself, having stood close-up to him her whole life, craning her neck to take in all that he was, or those who looked and cheered from afar, but could see him head-on and in his totality? No, she thought, maybe the closer we get to a person the more we see the truth of them, because those critical distortions become foregrounded and enhanced. And the trick, if there is one, must be to compensate for those distortions – and only hope that those we love do the same for us.

Ann looked over at Brenda just then, standing by her side, and smiled. In their scant time together, she had found that she was recognizing much of her early, tentative self in this young woman. Brenda and her fiancé Paul had been phenomenal, working at break-neck speed to pull everything together and Brenda had thankfully, finally, found a moment's peace to take it all in and ready herself for the program. Ann reached out and squeezed Brenda's arm, compelled to express her feelings; and Brenda nodded and smiled back – and after Ann had whispered some additional encouragement and straightened her dress, Brenda silently walked out onto the stage where a single spot illuminated a podium set to the side of Uncle Aaron's picture. The audience took their seats and a respectful hush filled the old movie palace.

"Tonight," Brenda began, speaking with tender reverence, "we celebrate the life of a man who brought joy to millions."

It was a beautiful and heart-felt opening tribute – and Ann felt a slight surge of pride in listening to a fellow English major strut her stuff. And, again, she thought of how much this entire event would have meant to him.

This is for you, Uncle Aaron, what I should have done long ago.

To think that it nearly didn't happen, or that it hadn't been her idea at all, only served to make Ann even more grateful to Brenda and Paul.

They had met her that morning in front of the movie house, and though they still had their quirks, she'd grown quite fond of them in the few days that she'd known them. One could say that the canted front-row view of their personas no longer seemed distorted at all. It was not only in their unwearied response to life, their enthusiasm, not only the endearingly respectful attitude towards Ann herself, but, it was also that knowing them a bit better now, she saw they had, at the bottom of it all, a profusion of real goodness. Her first impression of them in the restaurant had not been incorrect. Yes, they were a couple of odd balls – how else to describe two people who could argue the meaning of life or, just as easily, how to avoid condensation on a fudgesicle? Regardless of their absurdities, the truth remained that they cared deeply for each other and it bled out into every aspect of their lives. And being around them, observing them, she became aware of a certain influence upon her, of being able to peek, now and again, at life through their uncommon, lovely perspective.

She'd needed it; the morning had not started well. Having dreamt about Michael, she'd awakened in a foul mood and spent the start of the day still unable to get that phone call out of her mind. Christ, how many days ago had it been? Three? Four? Her failure to stand up to him, to end things with Michael then and there, pecked incessantly. When he had called, she had intended to use the credit card charges as a way to springboard up into enough anger to tell him it was over. But, shrewd Lothario that he was, he preempted that whole line of attack by apologizing, unprompted, for what he had done and promising to pay her back. Then came that warm whispering baritone syrup, seeping into every secret chamber of her mind, and she'd folded. Somehow, he always managed to simultaneously fire every humiliating desire – assuring her of his eagerness to satiate them – while at the same time, and without directly addressing them, activate her deepest fears.

Without exposing himself to any direct criticism, without saying anything that could implicate him, he somehow managed to send snakes inside that intoxicating syrup – snakes that found their way around anxieties she was appalled to realize she had. And after every encounter with Michael, she was left with little forked tongues of panic over leaving him, little hissing voices that told her she'd never really be able to find the one thing she desired more than a man like Michael, more than the perfection of male beauty – and that was a soul mate. They told her that such a thing didn't exist, and that her only real chance at happiness would be in the intense sexual compatibility she felt with

Michael. Yes, she'd folded – and gone out to walk the streets of LA at night and then dedicated the last several days to hating herself. Her one escape had been to commit to working furiously on the memorial with Brenda and Paul.

Ordinarily, during those previous occasions of going back over and evaluating her troubles, she would reluctantly conclude that the voices were right. The years had rolled on and failed to provide her with any direct evidence that she was mistaken. She certainly had not had the opportunity to see first-hand what any kind of idealized love might be like. And so, most days, it remained buried. But now and again, such as today, when given a chance to have some real time away from him, small windows of an alternative world would open. The physical distance of 3,000 miles between herself and Michael was immensely fertile ground for fostering her romantic imagination. More than that, was the presence of Brenda and Paul. And, that afternoon, when she had met them – and a host of volunteers from the fan club at the Aztec Orpheum Theatre to help set things up – she kept finding herself slipping behind that lens of their perspective, glimpsing the refreshing contentment of a deeper love. But, they were just that – glimpses. And glimpses were not enough. Ann resolved, after an hour or two of this vacillating, to live with her decision to stay with Michael and, like an adult, to stop entertaining these fantasies of a permanent separation.

It was Brenda who had been the first to arrive at the theater, and Ann had almost not recognized her: dressed as Lucy – the Professor's niece – but in her disguise as The Martian Mistress (from the famed episode of the same name), Brenda was stunning in her flounces of burnt orange crinoline, chrome chest plate, tiara, and laser rifle. Then Paul had come bounding from around the corner, outfitted as Stuey – replete with his trademark green and purple turtleneck – and leading a motley gang of assorted characters from the show including a very impressive Count Von Vershlagen, and an extremely large somebody in a robot gorilla costume – and all of them laden with boxes, bags, cartons, and backpacks.

"Here she is everybody!" Paul had exclaimed, "Our patron saint, Ann Tanner!" Surrounding her with ecstatic faces, they lavished on Ann appreciation and warmth, and, if they now and again seemed a little too eager to please, she had only to recall her own failings and immediately forgave them. Like Brenda and Paul, these were people bound together by nothing other than a common passion for a man that had meant something to them, which was just *that much more sentiment* she could funnel upward to Uncle Aaron.

The sound of keys in a lock had brought everyone's attention to the main entrance where Sherwood Jones, the ancient manager who seemed to have been built right along with the rest of the Aztec, appeared, showered them all with sprightly salutations, and escorted them inside. Now it was Ann's turn to be gobsmacked. The interior of the Aztec Orpheum had been recently restored to its full 1930's golden-age grandeur. Three mammoth cut-glass chandeliers, sculpted to resemble dahlia blossoms, hung suspended from the platinum-deco ceiling – a canopy held aloft by eight limestone pylons, embossed in gold leaf and entwined by replicas of the great stone snakes at Tenayuca. A grand staircase leading to the second floor balcony arced around a ring of fountains plashing at the base of a 20-foot turquoise statue of Tezcatlipoca – the Aztec god of night and memory. And that was just the lobby.

"How did we ever get this place?" Ann was finally able to whisper as the group crossed the plush carpeting, her eyes and mouth gaping.

"Easy – the new owner is a member in good standing! Isn't that right, Sherwood?" Paul said without any attempt to hide the boast.

"Quite so. Mr. Volks has been a fan of your uncle's forever," the old man replied, "Couldn't wait to offer his hospitality for the memorial. This is an honor, miss."

Paul tipped his head towards Ann to say in confidence, "And wait until you see what comes next..."

They entered the theater proper; and if the architects and designers had been aiming to cast the observer into a state rivaling religious awe, or to drive her to the precipice of artistic rapture – they had achieved their wildest aspirations. No empress, no tsar, no sultan had ever walked within a palace like this. The essence of luxury oozed from every surface, cocooning the visitor in almost suffocating decadence. *Jeff is going to absolutely lose his mind over this*, Ann thought, and couldn't help but feel a little thrill of hubris knowing that, since the place had only recently reopened, he'd almost certainly never been there – which would give her the opportunity of finally presenting her brother with a maneuver he couldn't possibly top. She looked out at the over-flowing flourishes, the architectural showmanship, and thought of the hundred, if not thousands, of craftsmen whose talents had been pooled to realize such a masterpiece – and the idea arrested her. Because despite everything, despite the collective impact of all that magnificence, somehow the whole experience miraculously trembled just shy of overkill – and that was its real achievement. Cutting through it all was the clear perception that this was not some forbidden temple – this was not ground that only the exalted few could transgress. This was a monument built *by* and *for* the common man, as a respite from the cares of the work-a-day life. And for that, all its excesses were readily forgiven. And, as she had said to herself, as an added bonus, Jeff would never be able to top it. So there was that, too.

Best of all, tonight, Uncle Aaron, you sit with kings.

"Yeah, it's alright," Paul shrugged at Ann with exaggerated indifference as they finished their tour, "if stunning opulence is your thing."

Brenda pulled up close, taking Ann by the arm and, guiding her to a set of double doors off to the side, whispered, "But what's in *here* I'd take over this ol' dump any day." They entered into a spacious conference hall, far more modestly fashioned than the rest of the facility – functionality being its primary pur-pose – with rows of chairs facing a low stage positioned against the far wall. Streamers and balloons had been wreathed about the platform with a small podium standing front and center. And all around the room, the comrades of Brenda and Paul, who had cut out from the full tour early, were just putting the finishing touches on the rest of the decorations they had brought with them. Covering the walls were posters and photos of Uncle Aaron in his various movie and TV roles, but mostly, of course, from his eleven-season run as Professor Puck.

"Here's where we'll hold the charity auction, after the main program," said Paul.

"It's lovely," Ann said sincerely and then, proceeding to the next logical question asked, "Have the auction items been dropped off?"

"Not that I'm aware of," said Brenda, and a momentary look of concern shot among them, until she added, calming them, "I'll check with Sherwood and find out what's going on."

"Well, let me know right away," Ann offered. "That crate should've been here by now."

"I'll take care of that as soon as I check on the Green Room," Brenda said, scurrying off, "The special guests will be arriving any minute. And you know how they are!"

"Should we be helping her?" Ann asked, casting a worried glance as the double doors closed behind Brenda.

"Heck no! We've got bigger fish to fry – front of house duties wait for no man!" Paul said, throwing several empty bags and boxes into a closet.

Ann deferred to his judgment with a quick nod, but then felt compelled to address another matter that had been on her mind. She pulled him aside, and sincerely and plainly, leaving out all the stupid English professor flourishes, expressed her gratitude for everything he and Brenda had done. "Seriously, this is absolutely overwhelming," she concluded, "and I don't know how I can thank you enough."

Paul was caught tongue-tied, and flushed, "Aw, you know, we're – we're thrilled to do it."

"And I'm really very sorry we're not going to be able to hear your work tonight."

"Well," smiled Paul, and waved the thought away, "it's probably for the best."

"Oh?" Ann asked, and this time her concern about Paul's opera was genuine.

"My lead is out with laryngitis. He claims his vocal cords were shredded by the libretto. I say he wasn't using his diaphragm properly. But that's how it goes with these divas."

He laughed and then suggested they proceed to the main stage for the final meeting with his team of organizers and the theater staff assigned to help them out. He had decided, in that instant, to scrap his usual message demanding that everyone work to top themselves and, instead, to go with simply thanking them for all their hard work. After speaking with Ann, he too was feeling grateful.

Moments later, they stood with his crew who had gathered in a circle on the stage of the main theater. Ann listened as Paul went through a rundown of the evening's program: footage of the TV show's classic animated opening credit sequence to start things off, then, welcoming remarks by Brenda who would introduce clips of Aaron's early films paired with remembrances by fellow co-stars, followed by a special screening of the fan-favorite episode, "Murder, a La Mode" – after which the proceedings would wrap up with Jeff's eulogy (*assuming he remembers to show up*, Ann nervously thought to herself), and then it was over to the community room for the late night auction. And, sprinkled throughout the night, special vignette reenactments of famous scenes from *The Professor and the Groovy Gang* performed by Paul and his fellow members.

Ann smiled as she watched Paul's liveliness orchestrating those around him. It was clear that he was now in his element. That deferential shyness which he typically exhibited around Brenda had disappeared and he'd become possessed of a whole new sense of confidence and self. Also, Ann could not fail to notice that Brenda, whenever possible as she rushed to and fro, stole glances up at him and beamed with pride.

With a hearty cheer, Paul and Brenda's assortment of *Groovy Gang* celebrants – along with members of the theater staff in livery teleported right out of the 1930's – leapt off the stage, marched up the aisles, and burst through the theater doors to take up their positions in the front lobby.

Almost immediately someone shouted, "Oh my god! Look at that crowd!"

In the past two hours, the block in front of the Aztec Orpheum had gone from empty sidewalks to throngs packed up against the glass windows and spilling out into the street. The clamor of their revelry reverberated throughout. The uninitiated observer, those unfamiliar with the passing of Aaron Arbuckle, might well be forgiven for concluding that the event was some kind of celebration – and for their shock at learning it was, in actuality, to honor the recently deceased. But something there was in the life of the man, something in those rare appearances that he gave, but, mostly that something to be found in the exuberance of his performances, the vitality of his presence, that made those whom he had touched feel that the only possible way to remember him authentically was in the spirit of joy. And not, as might be assumed, under a pall of sorrow or regrets. The Society had been exceptionally deferential to Ann – who had heartily agreed with the tone of the event and that their initial instinct was spot on. In fact, she insisted on it.

A commotion at the center doors stopped everyone in their tracks as theater security opened and quickly closed the entrance to allow two scrambling members of the fan club – two actual twins dressed as Frannie and Frankie – to enter the building. "You should see the line!" they gasped in unison, "It just keeps going! Must be at least three blocks long!"

"We're gonna have to turn people away," said a close replica of the Professor's assistant Lucy.

"No – this place has got closed circuit monitors," said Paul. "We'll televise the show to them – and have overflow seating out under the stars. Tell Sherwood we'll need to get that set up pronto! Now let's move, people! Move!"

And with that, the members of the first official Professor Puck Society – passionately abetted by the staff of the Aztec Orpheum – flew into action. The white-gloved hands of Sherwood Jones flicked a series of switches, and if the lobby had been impressively dramatic before, it was all magnified exponentially as array after array of additional lights flared up and cast everything in a dazzling radiance: uniforms shined, balustrades glowed, and murals turned luminous; the military precision of the organizers entranced those lucky enough to have an unobstructed view from the outside; shoulder to shoulder, the eager ticket-holders watched enraptured as the concession stand sprang to life, velvet ropes swung into place, ticket takers moved to the ready, and old Sherwood, surveying it all with a sharply critical eye, made one final pass to ensure that all of it was up to the standards expected of the venerable landmark, and, seeing his small army having conducted themselves above and beyond the call of duty, shouted out his famed cry of, "Incoming!"

The great brass doors parted and in poured the excited, expectant crowds. First came the special guests from the Children's Convalescent Center, Aaron Arbuckle's cherished cause. Escorted by a platoon of Groovy Gang cos players, their young faces radiant, they glided along in their wheelchairs or rode on the shoulders of robot gorillas. Next came the hardcore fans, those for whom arriving early and waiting in line with other enthusiasts was half the fun – and dressing the part was de rigueur. Of course there was the healthy assortment of Professor Pucks wearing his trademark red pith-helmet radio hat (and, also, a number sporting his various alternative outfits) as well as meticulously crafted imitations of his faithful companions – but that was just for starters. Seen throughout were those steadfast friends and allies of the Professor: Miss Sharp, Mentar the Great, Pollyanna Pipsqueak, and the Wave Wizard – and all of these heroes could be seen mixing fearlessly with some of their most dastardly foes: Green Gecko, The Crystal Witch, Freaky Face, Dr. Monocle, Esmerelda Diablo, and of course, Count Von Vershlagen.

There were, safe to say, no shortage of the more regular "civilian" type of fan, those with no less enthusiasm than the others, who counted the eternally re-running TV show as a staple of their childhood, but who didn't quite have the wherewithal to come in costume – yet who gaped and awed and celebrated the industriousness of those that did. Nevertheless, the numbers of extravagantly costumed guests was so great that it required a disciplined attention to spot any of the actual celebrities in attendance: was that Buddy Coleman (Arbuckle's co-star in two westerns) speaking to a Glitter Girl? Was that Joan Fisher (a rumored ex-flame) standing at the bar? And there, laughing it up with sportscaster Bronson R. Wallace was certainly Cecily Gray!

Moving like morays through the sea of excitement were members of the press corps with camera lights coruscating and mics and booms outstretched, capturing the magic of the evening for various newspapers, magazines and TV stations, interviewing celebrities and fans alike. For the most part, their questions were only of the most superficial variety, and they seemed content with merely exploiting the crowd for their uninhibited affection for a genre show.

A bright flash off to the side hijacked Ann's attention, and she was drawn to the words of a tall, self-conscious fellow standing next to Paul and being interviewed by Channel 5.

"The Children's Convalescent Center has grown beyond its original name," the man was saying. "Now, we primarily care for disabled children in need of adoption."

Ann stepped closer and found herself mesmerized by his intensity. He had an incredibly animated face, the kind where the brow is constantly on the move and with eyes that looked out into the world with a penetrating search for understanding. He would not, most likely, be described as traditionally handsome – but his lean physique created any number of fascinating deep angles to his cheeks and chin that set off his mouth in an extremely sensual way. But all this was merely a gateway beckoning her in – it was his words which kept her captivated. She watched as he detailed the work of his non-profit and how the lives of thousands of children had been uplifted, and how many more children there were in Los Angeles alone that needed the services of his organization.

"Typically, there are only thirty to forty residents that we can support at a time," he explained. "We're currently housed in a wing of the Freemason General Hospital, but that building is no longer up to code and is being demolished. As of yet, we don't have a new home." It was here that Paul stepped in to add: "We're hoping tonight's auction will raise awareness for the plight of the Center."

At the conclusion of the interview, Ann found herself following Paul and the tall man from a distance, and was glad for her anonymity – that she could move among the crowd unmolested, free to pursue her thoughts. The man she was following represented the rarest of the rare: a type only once in a great while that she'd meet – a man who could hypnotize her not through his features, but his mere *presence*. If she'd been asked what exact elements combined to create such an effect, she'd readily admit the formula was a bit mysterious, but definitely contained a large measure of the quality of "selflessness" which, although she could not hear his words, she could see him embody simply by the way he listened so carefully to Paul and allowed him to dominate their conversation. How different from Michael, she thought. But before she could permit herself to be swept away fantasizing about what life might be like with a man like that, an announcement was made indicating 15 minutes to the start of the program and she was seized by the sudden panic that her brother had not yet arrived.

CHAPTER 13

The mad chaos of the Green Room, crammed with a constant influx of guests and crew confabulating over the food and refreshment table, was keeping Brenda in an emotional state equally turbulent. At the moment, a new crisis was breaking out between two exhaustingly dramatic members – both scheduled to perform in several of the evening's skits – over an alleged spot on a costume, allegedly the fault of the other, allegedly done on purpose.

"That's not paint from his sword, Howard," Brenda was insisting while insinuating herself between the two combatants who had been known to come to blows. "That's condensation from your fudgesicle."

"Impossible!" the man dressed as Phantom Fireman asserted, wielding his frozen dessert like a conductor's baton.

"Trust me – I know fudgesicles," demanded Brenda, and, marching him to the other side of the Green Room added, "Now stay away from each other or you're both out on your ass!" Before the other could speak, Brenda's phone let out an importunate ring.

"Save it, Howard! This is an emergency," she said, holding her ground. "Yes, I was calling about the delivery truck!" Brenda yelled into her phone – partly to compensate for the noise (along with a finger in her opposite ear), partly to shut up Howard, and partly because she was justifiably pissed off. "A crate was supposed to be picked up and then delivered here to the Aztec Orpheum! What? What?...Yes, okay, I'll hold!"

It was bad enough that there had already been a mix-up as to what time everything was supposed to begin – an email had erroneously gone out to half the membership indicating 7:30pm instead of 8pm – but now, the star attraction, at least from the club's viewpoint (an entire *crate* of Professor Puck collectibles!), had been lost in transit, and here was Brenda awaiting a THIRD manager to explain exactly where their delivery truck had disappeared to.

"Brenda! What the hell is going on?" came the perturbed voice of their eternally cranky Secretary-Treasurer, with a screech undaunted by any finger in any ear, or the fact that the person she was addressing might be on the phone: "I thought you said we'd be performing the opera tonight!"

"No, Charlene, we can't," Brenda said, not trying too hard to hide her exasperation. "We sent out an email about that a week ago. Plus, Gilbert has laryngitis."

"But why can't Paul do it? I mean, the rest of the cast is all here!"

"Charlene," Brenda said, locking eyes with her comrade, "we - don't - have - approval. End of story."

"But we're ready to go!" Charlene pleaded, unconcerned with anyone's authorization. "At the very least we can tell everyone to go back to the playhouse and we'll do it there – once we're through here, that is."

"Look, if you can get people to agree to that, maybe. But I don't know who's going to take on the lead. And don't even think about asking Paul. He says the part shreds his vocal cords," Brenda concluded, and then quickly added: "I know: why don't you talk to Howard about it?"

Pushing her two problems onto each other was a stroke of genius – and just as the manager came back on the line: "Hello? Hello?" Brenda shouted into the phone while stepping away from Charlene and Howard – who had immediately fallen into an excited comparison of personal affronts perpetrated over the last hour alone. The result of all this maneuvering was that she was barely able to make out the voice at the other end explaining that the truck had somehow been sent to the wrong theater, but was now on its way.

"You sent it to the wrong theater?!" Brenda responded, "How many Aztec Orpheums are there?!" The propitiating tones offered by the delivery representative were not enough to stop Brenda from cutting him off with, "Just make sure it gets here in the next 20 minutes or we're not paying a dime!"

"Ten minutes, everyone! Ten minutes to curtain!" a voice cried out, provoking an extra flurry of people shoving past each other to get to their destinations or desperately grabbing one last mouthful from the buffet.

Back in the main lobby, Ann was about to try phoning her brother (for a second time) when in through the front doors he burst along with a woman Ann recognized as a colleague – and a fellow, looking pretty woozy, whom she had never seen before.

"Where in God's name have you been?!" she called out. "I was about ready to send out the cavalry!"

"Sorry, there's traffic backed up for blocks," he said, propping Dirk up in order to gesture towards Diane. "Ann, you know my Marketing Manager, Diane Hernandez, and this is a good friend of ours, Dirk Jarvis."

"So pleased to meet you!" Diane declared. "I'm a diehard fan of your uncle. Wouldn't have missed this for the world!" The two exchanged a quick handshake as Dirk hazarded a vague wave in Ann's general direction and mumbled some kind of greeting while staring off at no one in particular.

"He's going through a rough patch," whispered Diane.

"Does he need anything?" asked Ann, wondering why he'd been brought in the first place.

"No, he'll be fine!" countered Jeff as Diane slipped her arm around Dirk to stop him from slumping against a couple chatting just behind them – an action that did not go unnoticed by Ann, but who turned to her brother to address far more serious matters.

"And you have your speech ready to go?" she asked, looking him dead in the eyes and activating those resurgent connections.

"Of course," said Jeff, tapping his breast pocket. "It's right here."

"Uh-huh," said Ann, unconvinced. "Just be sure that it is."

Before his sister had enough time to fully engage her black magic mind-reading skills – and realize he had absolutely *nothing* prepared – Jeff's eye was caught by a young woman, trying her best not to look too agitated, running up to their group in a rather impressive Martian Mistress costume.

"Ms. Tanner, I'm so sorry to interrupt, but we need you backstage. The show's starting in five."

Allowing herself to be led away, Ann called back to her brother, "You're on in almost exactly an hour. *Please*, Jeff..." she urged, letting the sentence hang incomplete, not needing to say anything further.

Jeff smiled past a lump in his throat as his sister disappeared off into the crowd and he felt, once more, the ground falling out from underneath him – exacerbated by the escalating anticipation in the lobby – as announcements continued over the intercom urging people to take their seats and ushers pressured them towards the theater doors. Dirk let out a small moan and began leaning more heavily into Diane. "Jeff," she said, "I don't think he's going to be able to handle going in there."

Nodding his understanding and agreement, Jeff pulled over a theater attendant. "Excuse me," he said, at his most charming, "is there some place our friend can sit down? He's not feeling his best."

"Of course," said the eager young man and immediately proceeded to escort the three of them to a conference hall, right off of the main lobby. The room, obviously set up for some kind of presentation but vacated for the moment, contained a small stage at the far end, rows of chairs, and decorations and posters celebrating his uncle's TV show. Diane eased Dirk down onto one of the chairs where he closed his eyes, screwed up his face, and began whispering something unintelligible.

"You'll be able to hear what's going on over the intercom," the attendant explained, flicking a switch by the door, which brought into the room the echoing hubbub of the theater audience finding their seats – and then, nodding, he politely left Jeff and Diane alone with the ailing Dirk.

The two stood looking down at the train wreck they'd brought with them. Obviously, this was far from an ideal set of circumstances, and while Jeff and Diane could be guaranteed to disagree on any number of issues, they had both immediately concurred that Dirk could not be left home alone – and Diane had been particularly insistent on not missing out on the memorial. Taking him along had been the only real option.

"Well, *I've* definitely hit the jackpot," said Diane after a moment, scanning the Professor Puck images plastered around the room. "And don't think you're getting out of this without hooking me up with something from the show. Dealing with this character, you *owe* me."

"Not to worry. There's a whole crate of props and costumes that'll be here tonight. I'll snag you something," said Jeff, and then, looking down at Dirk added, "But, you're right. What are we going to do with this poor fool?"

"I'll worry about him," said Diane. "You worry about that speech."

Jeff sighed a quiet "thank you" and while Diane sat next to Dirk comforting him, Jeff began a slow walk around the room to collect his thoughts. Yet again, his life had the feel of an impending collision. This entire predicament had happened with the relentlessness of a runaway semi-truck – and no matter how he'd bobbed and weaved, the barreling inertia of Dirk's unspooling calamity had plowed a mile-wide swath right down the center of it.

Of course he'd not been able to write anything! Of course he was totally unprepared to give a speech tonight! Because: the fact was that Dirk had somehow become entangled in a bigger mess than either he or Diane had dreamed possible. As the story now went – and it was highly probable it would continue to evolve – Dirk, who had made no secret of his distaste for the recently appointed head of Family Films, Ltd, was being accused by the company of embezzling over $200,000 in miscellaneous funds. According to Dirk, it was all a set-up. Yes, the money transfers had been executed from his computer and using all of his passwords which, ordinarily, would still not be enough to convict – except that a witness had come forward claiming to have seen Dirk in the act. What no one knew – but which Dirk claimed as the truth – was that the witness (an assistant producer in his office) was having a secret affair with the company president and was, quite possibly, a party to the whole scheme. If true, the perpetrators had been quite clever. According to Dirk, they had been using his company ID codes to manage their digital heist in order to provide cover should a surprise audit require them to hide their tracks. Which was why those *exact* circumstances – a surprise audit initiated by the new parent company in New York – had nailed Dirk and not them. However they had done it, their plan had come off brilliantly.

Now, there were several universes of things Jeff was fully prepared to believe about Dirk – especially in the realm of immature, sexual pranks – but there was one thing his friend was not, and that was a thief. Or a liar. Both he and Diane had known Dirk for years and were convinced this whole mess was nothing but a big heaping pile of shit that had been dumped on Dirk for no other reason than that he was a convenient fall guy, already disliked by the malefactors, and one with just enough documented, marginally-unacceptable incidents at work to make the story stick.

Jeff, true to his word, had held council with his own legal team, but his lawyers had regrettably concluded that, barring any new exonerating evidence – and considering the evidence against him, and the powerful corporate urge of Family Films to keep their chief executive unsullied and especially considering the witness – there was little Dirk would be able to do to stop the wheels that had been set in motion. The poor guy had watched helplessly as lifeline after lifeline had disappeared one by one. What he *did* have was a trial date, a pending legal suit for the stolen money, and a brand-spanking new drinking problem.

Jeff and Diane's 24-hour suicide watch had turned into a week-long affair and had created a number of cascading catastrophes for Jeff. First and foremost, with an alcoholic, suicidal depressive under his wing, was his inability to get the kind of substantial pre-production work done on *Summer of the Rainbows* necessary to make him feel at ease. Diane had been a real trooper and done her best to stop by for baby-sitting duties to allow Jeff a modicum of time by himself – but it had not been nearly enough.

Everything about his pet project seemed to be collapsing in on itself. He'd passed his rough draft on to a writer he trusted for a final polish, but the pages coming back were moving the script in the wrong direction and rather than smoothing over its rough edges, at least in his estimation, they were making certain flaws appear even more ungainly. His meetings with his production team were not going much better. First, no one seemed to fully share his enthusiasm – not overtly, of course, but in that even worse, faked-interest way which meant everything they communicated was suspect. And second, Murch had only agreed so long as filming could be completed in the short five-month window between now and the start of their "next epic blockbuster": *Car Crash Kings 3* – and securing the right cast was proving expensively difficult. Boutique films like *Rainbows* rose and fell on the names above the title and the salaries for the people he wanted were pushing the budget into very uncomfortable territory.

But none of this was a match for the war of extremes breaking out in his mind. On one side, a growing sense of impending, cataclysmic defeat – apocalyptic scenarios of the whole project disintegrating around him should that delicate, effervescent faith in his script evaporate. And on the other, glimpses of a new potential horror: that *failure* was his true lineage. And that failure now would unleash unending failures tomorrow – that his commercial self confidence, the one that he'd relied on for decades to identify sure-fire hits, would also reveal itself to be fraudulent. Hard to believe, but for the first time, Jeff saw with perfect clarity just how lucky he'd actually been – and he gasped at what lay on the other side of his reality, saw that thing which snuffs out Hollywood hopefuls by the fistful: a bottomless pit of paralysis and despair, which he'd never really confronted, and from which, were he to fall, he doubted he could ever recover.

But no! Something *had* appeared to him! Something had happened to him that night in his uncle's attic, something that had long laid buried, had sprung to life: a white-hot core that, now and then, would send out the slenderest of beacons, radiating spears which, despite their delicacy, had the concentrated power to obliterate all his monstrous fears – leaving only himself and his vision. The experience had not yet vanished. He could still remember: he had been Superman.

But that moment of confidence – was it real, or only an illusion? That was the torment. Because *in* that moment there was nothing about which he had been more certain – but *now*, all he had was the memory of that courage. He knew there was one and only one way to discover the truth: complete the film. He also knew there was still time to save everything. There was still time to pull the plug before any damage had been done. No one would think anything of a producer with a track record like his suddenly sending a project back into development.

Christ, who was he kidding? There'd be massive relief if he quit. He could probably even give most of the staff a month or two off before coming back hard and heavy for *Car Crash Kings*. He'd be a hero – and the whole crazy thing would be completely forgotten in a matter of weeks. The prospect of chucking it all and returning to that familiar terrain was alluring. All that lunacy would go out in a wink. Could he do it? Could he live with himself never seeing where those flashing, penetrating beams were leading? The question hurt almost as much as the struggle itself. And, as Ann might say, "Well, here we are in Spain…"

"You got this, buddy!" Dirk suddenly called out before drooping back against Diane and stammering something about wanting everyone to be happy. The interruption was enough for Jeff to look up and find he'd already lapped the room several times without realizing it. *Judas Priest,* thought Jeff, *I really have to concentrate. I've got less than an hour.*

CHAPTER 14

"We had less than an hour!" bellowed Caroline Morris from the main stage of the theater – apparently not realizing that the podium *with the microphone* was miked – a point observed by Ann and which was confirmed when the woman leaned in even closer to shout: "Only fifty-five minutes for each episode! But that didn't stop us from changing the world!"

The audience roared its approval. But Ann, watching from the wings and despite the memorial proceeding flawlessly (at least so far), could find nothing that did not irritate her – including Caroline Morris and her inability to understand the basic principles of sound equipment. Jeff's antics had guaranteed Ann's nerves would be laid raw. And right now, the only part of Ms. Morris' speech that connected was her lament over the pressures of a TV production schedule. Time might be a power as unstoppable as it is stingy, but this tenet was never more distressingly real for Ann than when having to deal with her brother. Forty-five minutes before he needed to get out on that stage – and it was all Ann could do not to feel his panic.

He'd better be pulling something brilliant out of his ass right now, she thought just as her acrimony was further stoked by

Caroline Morris re-telling for the umpteenth time her completely fabricated story about declining an invitation to the White
House in favor of attending a fan convention.

Oh, lord, she's laying it on thick, she thought, wanting nothing
more than for that woman to put a big giant sock in it, but also
knowing that the longer she droned on, the longer Jeff would
have to prepare.

The venerable actress who had brought the character of Esmerelda Diablo to life – and parlayed the part into a recurring
role as a major villainess – had certainly carved out a place for
herself in the world of pop culture. But the role had not led
to much else and it had been clear in the decades following the
cancellation of the show that Ms. Morris thoroughly intended
to squeeze every last drop of its residual acclaim right to the very
lip of her grave.

"But," Caroline Morris continued, in her seemingly endless
quest to find yet another tired phrase to over-dramatize, "none
of that could have happened without YOU, the FANS!"

More jubilant applause burst from the audience and Ann
knew all too well what was coming next. Not because she had
stayed connected in any real sense with the show over the years
– she hadn't at all – but because Caroline Morris was one of
the few colleagues that Uncle Aaron had ever permitted himself
to bring up – on account of him not being able to abide her.
"When I chose to leave the show..." *Here it comes...* "When I
said, 'I must move on'..." *bullshit detectors on high alert...* "It was
YOU, the FANS, that DEMANDED my return!" *Oh, god, why
are they encouraging this?* "And THAT was a call I could NOT
refuse!" As the room exploded in thunderous cheers, Ann had

to concede that the woman had her shtick down to a science – but was completely immune to any admiration for it: Ann knew Caroline's full story, and if the truth of her full story was *'I wanted more money, they called my bluff, and I came crawling back'* – who wouldn't want to shellac over that with a generous trowel of BS?

Ann paused.

Her elevated level of snark had caught her unawares and she found herself chagrined. The stress of worrying about her brother was getting out of hand. She walked away from the wings and further backstage to clear her head. *Now I'm just being vicious,* she said to herself, *what did that woman ever do to me except fight for a little bit of attention?* To Ann's credit, that same woman had scared the piss out of her as a little girl – and to this day, Ann's visit to the set had fused both Caroline Morris and Esmerelda Diablo into a corner of her childhood. But that had never fomented disdain like she'd just experienced. Ann knew she was projecting her own frustrations on an easy target.

Obviously, the reason she was being so petty, why she was screwed so tight, was that careless brother of hers. Without any consideration, once again, he'd waltzed in and completely up-ended her carefully laid plans. She'd *begged* him to have something prepared for the evening. She'd even used her super powers to communicate it – and he'd shown up, totally unprepared. He'd left her more apoplectic than at any time since the news of Uncle Aaron's death. And who was that drunk basket case they'd dragged along with them?

But then, strange to consider, after letting things settle further, she saw that no, even that was not entirely the truth. Jeff could be an asshole, yes, but he was only being himself. And who knows what else he was grappling with? This wasn't about him. She was stewing over something else. Something evasive. And this new insight – that there was something just beyond, pressing itself against her thoughts – created a curious stillness about her.

Without exactly knowing why, and feeling that she must be careful to remain in the shadows, Ann suddenly decided to make her way back to the edge of the proscenium – rather than check on Jeff or return to the Green Room to verify the delivery of the delayed auction items, which was precisely what she knew she should be doing. Instead, she stepped cautiously to a small gap between the stage wall and the grand drape which allowed a partial view of the audience.

At first, she assumed that her interest was in seeing if she would be able to catch Jeff somewhere in the audience – which would be exactly where he *shouldn't* be if he was out practicing his speech. But the suspense she was experiencing was wildly disproportionate with that alleged goal.

In a moment, she realized her true aim: it was *not* to find her brother. It was a thought that had been circling covertly for the last hour, and which, now revealed, was at the root of her agitation: she was looking for the tall man from the lobby, the man from the adoption home. And, to her surprise, nearly centered within her field of vision, there he was.

In the faint glow of the theater, he was even more striking than before – and she was, once again, arrested by his expression of deep concentration. What was he sheltering behind those eyes? What kind of thoughts? Ann, wanting to turn away, watching herself watching, was captivated by her willingness to be beguiled by a man she was never going to know.

It was here that larger powers entered into the conspiracy to keep Ann riveted: the lights dimmed nearly to black, and a beam from the projection booth lanced out over the audience and then, like tiny beads of rain, the first delicate drops of Avro Part's "Spiegel Im Speigel" began to play – a piece she knew by heart because it was featured in one of her favorite films, one which she'd listened to countless times whenever she had felt alone or wistful. Then, on a lowered screen, images of Uncle Aaron – from his childhood, his adolescence, and his nearly 30 year career – began dissolving, one into the other. But even then, this was not where her eyes were fixed.

It was on him. Just him. It was the way the music and imagery washed over the face of that man, sitting intent and focused – it was the way the delicate interplay of the piano and violin seemed to find almost perfect accord with him. It was the way the subtlest tremors on his brow kept her spellbound.

How long the moment lasted, however many minutes, was not nearly long enough. Suddenly, the room shook with applause, and Ann found herself among a swarm of activity: a troupe of stagehands rushed past her to strike the podium, cos-players began lining up to go on for the next vignette, and Caroline Morris, electric with the success of her tribute and the memorial montage segment, came sweeping by and was immediately besieged by the fan club. Ann needed space. She moved away from all the flurry – traveling further backstage, past the pulleys lining the fly system, out through the rear stage door, past the dressing rooms, and into the scene shop where Brenda was just coming inside from the loading dock.

"Oh! There you are!" she called out to Ann. "Good news! We found our crate! It's in a delivery truck that's stalled about three blocks away from here – if you can believe it. I just sent out a bunch of guys to carry it the rest of the way."

"Wonderful," said Ann with performative relief, with thoughts still stuck on her view from the wings, staring out at an impossible future. But then, though she had hoped to find a minute to grab a cigarette in seclusion, Brenda's drive towards keeping everything on schedule snapped Ann back to reality and her own responsibilities towards ensuring that the evening ran smoothly – which meant dealing with her brother. She would have plenty of time to daydream later.

Hearing the action of the main theater playing over the scene shop intercom, Brenda noted, "They've started screening the episode, we're almost there," which Ann knew was her cue. Nodding, she confirmed she'd check on Jeff to make sure he was ready to go, and walked off toward the main lobby and the conference room where Brenda indicated her brother and his friends were still sequestered.

Throughout the theater, the sounds of the classic episode featuring one of Professor Puck's seminal adversaries, Crazy Cook, began playing to ecstatic hurrahs. As Ann moved along the service hallway back towards the front lobby, she had to laugh at how clearly she could see the psychedelic sets and costumes just from hearing the soundtrack. How many times had she watched the opening teaser with the giant pie arriving at city hall? The rubber bats breaking out from the crust and swarming the mayor's office?

"Bats! Thousands of them!" the Chief of Police was shouting.

"Great thunder!" cried Mayor Pingus. "They've got Miss Weatherton!"

A calamitous shattering of glass, followed by the chilling scream of the Mayor's secretary, called to Ann's mind the nightmare-inducing shot of Miss Weatherton being carried across the sky by a cluster of bats, while a second mass of the creatures flapped in place, spelling out with their bodies the phrase, "Your goose is cooked, Silver City!"

Ann had to shake her head in dismay – whatever she might have hoped for by involving herself in the memorial was being quickly negated by the relentless insanity of it all – and she found herself half wishing for the intervention of a supervillain.

The demon thrummings of bass violins and the crack and flash of lighting scattered these thoughts – and as the audience broke out into a joyous sing-along with the opening theme song, Ann barged into the conference hall, nearly running right into Jeff, who, thankfully and to her great relief, seemed to be rehearsing his speech.

"Come on, you're up in 25 minutes," she said, grabbing him by the arm, and leading him out the doors. "We need to get you backstage. And I want to hear exactly what you are going to say."

Jeff seemed resigned to having his sister take up the reins and lead him to whatever horror awaited – but, just before being dragged out, felt one last obligation to Diane, who was still seated next to Dirk, tending to him affectionately. "I gotta go do this,"

Jeff called to her, "But I don't want to get separated. You and Dirk meet me back here after the show!"

Diane nodded and, as Jeff disappeared out the door, returned her attention to Dirk. Somehow, his condition was getting worse and it was taking every bit of whatever acting talent Diane might possess to sound as though her words of encouragement were sincere.

"You have to start pulling yourself together, buddy," Diane said to him at last, comforting him with her arm. "We're going to need you as focused as possible to get you out of this."

Dirk, despondence and misery smearing his face, turned back to her and with his words mashing together said, "Even you don' believe that. You know I'm doomed..."

"That's not true. You heard Jeff. There's still all kinds of avenues for us to take. But we can't if you're falling apart."

To this, Dirk simply dropped his head into his hands and moaned something about his mother.

"What, Dirk?" Diane asked gently. "What did you say?"

Lifting his head slightly, he said with a meekness that broke Diane's heart, "This is gonna to kill my mom."

"No, no it's not because—"

"She gave me up, you know," he burst out, with a strength that startled, "when I was little. When I was three."

"No, I – I didn't know that," Diane replied.

"You wanna know how someone gets as fucked up as me?"

"You're not fucked up, Dirk," she said with another caress. "Weird and demented? Absolutely. But not fucked up."

Dirk went on, rambling in broken sentences about a young teenage mother who had been forced to give up her son. Looking

out towards some faraway spot, he seemed to rally in the telling
and find some kind of comfort in recounting the story to its end.

"Yeah?" Diane said, leaning into him, having no idea what to
say.

"And then, we found each other again. When I was at my
worst. We found each other and she pulled me through."

Diane knew that Dirk had struggled for several years with a
drug addiction, but this was an extra wrinkle of which she had
been completely ignorant. She asked him to tell her about it –
and he told her, in pathetic detail. To the sounds of the Groovy
Gang trying to escape from gingerbread henchmen – and Crazy
Cook and Professor Puck dueling it out with giant spatulas –
Dirk detailed the story of a little boy who suddenly found himself moving from foster home to foster home, then surviving on
the streets for a time, and then somehow, impossibly, putting
himself through animation school and finding a place in a world
that had done everything it could to destroy him. And then there
had been that final twist of a happy ending – the reunion with his
mother who had helped him over his last hurdle. But in the effort
to convey the tangle of events that had transpired over the last
week, in trying to make sense of how his tough luck had returned
with a vengeance, Dirk's head fell back into his hands and sobs
broke up his attempts to communicate.

"You're not going to prison, Dirk," she told him again, and
found she was now really believing it – whether from her affection towards him or some kind of instinctive protectiveness,
her knack for digging in her heels for underdogs had now fully
embraced Dirk. He sat there, rocking quietly back and forth
before going still – and for a moment, she thought he might be

asleep. But then, in the tiniest whisper, he said, "Just promise you'll watch out for her..."

"Dirk. Listen to me. I don't know how we're going to get you out of this, but you are *not* going to prison. And these charges are not going to stick. And your mother's going to be just fine."

She helped him wipe his eyes, and her newfound sense of surety seemed to lift his spirits, if only a little. She told him that he had not only his mother on his side, but two friends that were not about to abandon him. After all, she told him, did he think they'd let just anyone ruin a perfectly good evening like this? He cracked a frail smile on his face, and he seemed to revive further.

"What I can't understand is how you've managed to get so drunk," Diane mused, perplexed at the potency of a drink he must have had hours ago. "You haven't been near a bottle since we left Jeff's place."

"Well," said Dirk, pulling a flask from his breast pocket, "I guess this stuff is stronger than I thought."

"Oh!" Diane grunted in annoyance, swiping the flask, and in her sternest tones declared, "I'm going to go and dump this stuff out. We need to get you sobered up."

"If that's the case," said Dirk, reaching into his opposite breast pocket, "then you better take this one, too."

"Oh, for goodness sake," she said. "Are you sure that's it? Do I need to pat you down?"

As Dirk shook his head and spread his jacket for inspection, Diane was caught by the sounds of Professor Puck shouting his signature line, "Remember friends, the truth shall prevail!" followed by a rapturous response from the audience and then the swelling end credit theme blasting from the intercom. She hadn't realized how much time had passed. And now, she had a quick, important decision to make. The thing was, and she hadn't exactly said this to Jeff, but something she had been especially looking forward to was seeing Jeff's speech. It wasn't that he was the world's best orator – he wasn't – but for some reason being under pressure and under-prepared often brought out his best. Witnessing Jeff struggle against these factors was an opportunity she was not going to miss.

"Dirk," she said, "Jeff'll be on in a minute. Will you be okay in here?" To which Dirk nodded, laying back across the chair seats, his eyes heavy with sleep.

"I'm going to step out for just a sec and watch him. Then I'll be right back," she explained. "And I want you to stay put. Do *not* go wandering off!"

"Yes, ma'am," Dirk managed to get out, before his eyes fell shut.

CHAPTER 15

There were any number of regrets Ann knew she would carry with her to the great beyond – and asking her brother to give the eulogy was clearly going to be one of them. They'd huddled outside the dressing rooms – far enough from the back of the stage so as not to disturb the proceedings, but close enough to get Jeff on without any delay. Looking over the notes he'd managed to thumb into his cell phone, it was also clear to them both that any attempt towards oratorical weightiness – or even *mediocrity* – was not going to be the order of the evening. No, what they were dealing with here was harm reduction.

"Okay, take it again," Ann said, exhaling audibly and trying not to get too flustered as Jeff looked down again at an opening sentence he must have repeated to her fifty times in the last twenty minutes. "And please concentrate," Ann demanded. "Now go."

"How do you measure the life of a man..." Jeff intoned, no longer trying to hide his look of defeat.

"Wait a minute," Ann interrupted. "I thought we decided to cut that."

"No, I thought you said to keep it in."

"It doesn't matter," Ann interrupted again. "Keep going."

"How do you measure the life of a man?" he continued, not noticing Ann's jaw clench at his restart. "How do you put a price on his gifts of love? These are questions we can never answer – we can only ask them."

"Okay, great, we don't need to go over the whole intro. Let's skip to your first important point."

Jeff nodded, just as relieved as she was to skip as much as possible. "Um, let's see...then I start talking about his impact on the world of television."

"Yeah, okay, good, we want to get the obvious stuff out of the way. Then what comes next?"

"Um, then I talk about his charity work."

"Great. And, remember to make it sound like you are *familiar* with them."

"Yeah. Sorry about that."

"And Jeff, look up from your phone when you're talking."

"Huh?"

"Jeff, you work with actors all day long – think about what you'd say to them."

"What? Oh, yeah, right."

Ann's exasperation was cut short by a battery of fan club members, lugging a massive crate, jostling into the narrow hallway – and Ann and Jeff having to retreat to opposite walls to allow them passage.

"Sorry, folks," the man leading the entourage offered, trying to keep his voice down. "Do you know where Brenda is?"

Before Ann could hazard a guess, in came Brenda – looking about as harried as Ann herself was feeling and in clipped tones commanded, "This needs to go to the conference room, what are you bringing it backstage for?"

"Sorry, Brenda, we got lost."

"You need to go back out through the loading dock and around to the front entrance," she said, stabbing her finger towards the exit, "like I *told* you."

Jeff looked over at his sister and bit his lip to stop himself from chuckling. The whole day, the whole past couple weeks had been so absurd – a train of thought which was cut short by Brenda turning to them with, "Sorry to interrupt again, Ms. Tanner, Mr. Tanner, but you're on."

Their path cleared, Jeff followed his sister backstage and he could hear the packed theater, could feel the mass of people hungry with expectations – those same sounds he'd heard a million times at a million premieres. But those audiences, who had clamored in the past, had been different. Back then, he'd been feeding them with the kind of fast-food entertainment crap he could shovel by the metric ton – and which they'd lap up without fail. But this was different. The expectations were totally foreign to the cut of his tools.

They want something more tonight. They want –

Brenda, now center stage and nuclear with the glow of spotlights, was turning towards him – and he only just then realized she was gesturing for him to walk out on stage, had announced his name to the theater and that it was *he* that was the reason for the storm of applause.

"My sister's going to kill me," Jeff said, suddenly finding himself at the podium, his voice echoing out across the audience. Adjusting the mic for a second time and looking out into the wings, he instantly spotted Ann, still there, staring back. "You see," he said, "I've known about this speech for over a week, even had a bunch of notes cobbled together." He slipped his phone into his pocket and rested his hands on either side of the lectern, and then added, "But they're no good." Looking back at Ann, he only needed to know that she was there, that she was watching and listening.

Something was happening to her brother, Ann could feel it.

He's opening himself up to something, something important, something –

"You see, my sister is a phenomenal writer," he began, "and a far less famous one than she deserves to be." The words now flowed. In the eternity of time that Jeff had spent that evening considering his life and where things now stood, everything boiled down to a decision that had to be made. And in his walk from the wings to the center of the stage, he had made it.

"I'm not a writer. I'm a producer of crappy films.ᐟ.."

Ann held her breath. Through their mystical conduit, she knew Jeff had come to some kind of profound decision, but what it was, what leap he was prepared to make was still hidden from her.

Is it his work? What has he done?

In seven steps, Jeff had judged a world of possibilities.

He had weighed all the expectations he'd been buried under – his quixotic rush to save his friend Dirk, his mania for a film project with no chance for success, his senseless expectations of himself. And, at the conclusion of those seven steps, he had chosen to rise from beneath all of it.

I know what I need to do. I know I –

"My sister has the real talent in our family," Jeff said, then turning profile to speak directly to Ann, standing wide-eyed in the wings, "I never really told her that before, but Uncle Aaron knew it. And as I struggled to come up with something to say tonight, I kept finding all kinds of reasons that things beyond my control were getting in my way. But, if I'm honest, it was because I didn't want to let her down..."

No! That's what it is, he's giving up, he's –

Ann saw that Jeff was unburdening himself of everything: He was free. And he could finally breathe. He was free of the debt he owed Uncle Aaron, he was free of all those public expectations, and, most of all, he was free of trying to be a film director he wasn't. There were, potentially, things he might regret abandoning down the road. But those worries, too, she saw him cast aside. Once more, through their secret connection, he told her everything he'd needed to say – and that was all that mattered.

But, rather than relief that her brother had let go of so much that had been painful, all Ann could see was the shattering of some secret, trembling beauty, hidden far within, that had always pulled her towards him.

"So," he continued, "to stop myself from mangling my way through something you'll be glad I spared you, let me just talk about a few things I am reminded of that I learned from my uncle, if you will indulge me..."

Jeff and his sister would, for years to come, look back on this night and this moment; and what would strike Jeff most was his original intent – how in that very moment, he had had every intention of explaining, through his speech and, imbedded through that speech, in which were woven those revived connections to Ann, his new-found freedom, his acceptance of his role as a maker of circuses. He had intended to share a forgotten part of Uncle Aaron's past, which he had remembered as he had paced about the conference room. As he had moved about, passing poster after poster, looking at the advertisements for all those early films, he had remembered being told about Uncle Aaron's arrival in Hollywood. Like thousands of others, the young man had landed on the outskirts of the dream factories, with no one and nothing but faith in himself to sustain him. He had gotten by for years doing part-time jobs and some cab driving. But then came that rare big break – a featured cameo as a waiter in the comedy, *We'll Bring the Daisies*.

The film had underperformed, and the two leads were quickly forgotten, but Aaron Arbuckle as the waiter trying to remember who had the soup, who had the soufflé, and who had the spaghetti, became an instant star. What followed had been a solid decade of consistent character work – often as the film's comic relief. What might have gone on for another twenty years was interrupted by Uncle Aaron's burning desire to develop and star in an action/adventure TV show for all ages. A small production company had shown interest, but everyone at the time had warned him that the work would brand him forever as a "TV actor," ruining any future work in features. The studios had wagged their fingers, his agent had threatened to drop him, his friends had scoffed behind their backs, but Uncle Aaron had pressed on – and now it was all a part of television history. Still, the prophets had been correct. The long-running show had ended his film career. But, there was nobody, Uncle Aaron least of all, who would have said it was a mistake. Except, perhaps, his former agent.

The speech should have then proceeded smoothly, or so Jeff had thought. The tale of Uncle Aaron's beginnings he had intended as a way to let his sister know that tonight was not about Jeff himself, not about his own problems – no, tonight, he had accepted he was not the talent he wished he was, that *Summer of the Rainbows* was a joke which he would no longer suffer – rather, tonight was about Ann. It was to be about how much he believed in her and had intended to wrap their mystic language around it and apologize for shirking his duty as a brother and not supporting her gifts. He wanted to tell her that he had *always* known the kind of talent she had. And, with these confessions, he would finally fulfill duties long neglected – and, perhaps, give her the lift he knew she needed. Except that is not what happened.

At some point, Jeff would be knocked wildly off course – as he again, and quite to his surprise, suddenly recalled his moment of epiphany. For the third and final time, the shroud within parted, and he remembered the painting. And, he remembered *believing*.

Just as he had felt the last time, during that frenzied night of writing, he was astonished how he could have ever forgotten what he had seen. But then, just as quickly, he understood why: to describe the painting was impossible. Any effort to explain the subject of the work would have been meaningless – except to say that it was purity itself, and that gazing into its depths had opened unimaginable things up in him. And, with a bright flash, like sunlight on burnished chrome, it had transformed him – and he had been able, for those few precious moments, to stare undaunted into all his heart's desires, stretching out before him, clear to the horizon.

And, for the first time in a long time, he knew, really *knew*, exactly what he wanted. And he was not afraid.

What would surprise Jeff, and Ann in her brother's reaction, was that his sister would later attest that she had still clearly sensed his original intentions, despite his belief that he had failed to fully express them. Ann would relate that, as she watched and listened to Jeff on that stage, she had been swept along – away from her initial exasperation, to alarm that he seemed on the brink of abandoning some essential part of himself, then to seeing that a shift had occurred, just as he was describing that glorious eleven-year run of Professor Puck. As he was trumpeting the will of an artist who stood firm against an entire industry united in their lack of faith, she saw it happen. He paused and seemed to suddenly brighten – as one might at discovering a hummingbird resting on a branch close at hand – seemed to be recognizing something he had forgotten, and then, although it would have gone unnoticed to those who did not know him, began a new tack. Jeff began talking about faith.

Yes, he was using the incidents and arc of Uncle Aaron's life to express it – but he was no longer speaking of their uncle. Ann was certain of this. He was speaking of universal duty and the debt we owe to our soul. And the entire theater was swept along with him – the Aztec Orpheum that night, for a quarter of an incandescent hour, became a church.

"My uncle understood something that too many of us ignore," Jeff was saying, his oratory building, intensity upon intensity: "He understood that if you are one of those very lucky people who finds themselves with the opportunity to seize a dream, you have a duty to every one of those millions of variables and confluences, to every fellow human being who, knowingly or unknowingly, contributed – in however small a way – to bring that moment into being." Ann watched as her brother became merely a vessel for his vision, possessed with some kind of supernatural splendor, and he called out: "He also understood that these moments are gifted to us unceasingly, which we could forever reap – but for our willful blindness to them!" At this, the crest of his oratory, the audience rose to their feet as he shouted, "Because, forever more, the *truth* shall prevail!" – as their rapturous applause washed over him with the cleansing heat of a blast furnace, the window that had opened to him once more – that glimpse into the infinite that he had first witnessed up in his uncle's studio, that gift from his uncle's painting – just as quickly, snapped shut.

And, with that tiny death, he was spent – but filled with a number of certainties. Resting back against the podium and accepting the standing ovation from the audience, he knew he had been wrong in his decision to abandon his project. He'd seen that the demon of failure has a vastly more terrifying cousin named "regret" – and he knew that, win or lose, he was no longer going to doubt the endeavor, or himself. There would be no regrets. He knew, too, that there was no possible way that he

CHAPTER 15   185

could ever abandon one of his closest friends – this had come to
him while building to his crescendo and, in a moment of tele-
scoping intensity, had become hyper-aware of Diane, standing
in the back, and looking at him with unbridled admiration, and
with a heart that would break if they were to cut Dirk loose. It
was, all told, a feeling of incredible fulfillment – but, Jeff had also
been made aware that that window from which that unassailable
confidence had come to him would never open again. By the
time the applause ended, he had already forgotten what it was
he had seen – and how he had come by these certainties. No, he
was now on his own. Nothing but the memory of his rapture
remained – and that would have to sustain him to the end.

   Ann had discovered things too. Her finalizing of Uncle
Aaron's will and involvement in the memorial had kept her quite
busy and distracted – and she recognized now that she had been
witness to some kind of decisive event in her brother's life. She
also knew that, whatever it was, tonight he had confronted it in
a struggle that had unlocked brand new horizons for him – the
unsealing of which had released an energy powerful enough to
bring 900 people to their feet, and, basking in the intensity of it
herself, to bring a sister the strength to face the riddle of her own
life. Something in the way Jeff had spoken of Uncle Aaron had
taken her back to that great white void, into the color that reflects
everything, into that space where she must never be afraid to go –
and where all the answers lay. Listening to him then, as she stood
hidden discreetly in the wings and, with a tilt to her head, turned
to stare at the face of the tall man in the audience, shining now
with the reflecting passion of Jeff's stirring oratory – flickering
images of Brenda and Paul broke in upon her reverie and she

slipped back into that purifying realm and saw, in stark contrast, exactly what it was that she had yet to do. Like her brother, her life must be her own.

CHAPTER 16

As they would all say for years to come, the night was a triumph. The lobby reverberated with the celebratory ruckus and laughs and glinting eyes of patrons, each one aware and transmitting to the others that they had witnessed something spectacular. And they still carried, within each of them, a small fissioning piece of that energy which they clung to and paraded while it still retained its vibrancy. Many would point to Jeff Tanner's closing speech and the way in which he had brilliantly combined a tribute to his famous uncle with an intimate and inspirational plea for fearlessness as the real marvel of the evening – and, also, how they would remember it as a transformative moment in their lives. Yes, they would all agree, the night was a triumph. But, it was also true that, in the end, the evening would not go off without a hitch.

As the audience continued to pour from the theater back into the lobby, and Jeff was swarmed by attendees congratulating him on his address, he saw Diane pressing her way through the crowd, a slight look of panic in her eyes, clearly intent on speaking with him.

"I can't find Dirk," she panted, successfully prying her way next to him and apologizing to his gathering fans for the interruption.

"What do you mean?" he asked, still not fully grasping the extent of her message.

"I left him in the room for just a second to come and watch you," she said, trying to speak calmly while pulling him off to the side, "but then I went back to get him and he was gone."

"Are you sure he's not still here? It's a pretty big theater."

"I've looked everywhere," Diane said, shaking her head. "One usher says she thought she saw him leave."

Diane always had a clarity of communicating when the shit was about to hit the fan – and was especially adept at discretely intimating the approach of bigger problems in public settings.

"Did you try his cell phone?"

"Yeah," she said, holding it up. "He left it on the floor."

"Alright, how much time are we talking here?" Jeff asked, finally grasping the full extent of what they might be facing.

"Everyone setting up in the auction room said they'd all been in there for the last ten, fifteen minutes – and they said the room was empty when they got there. He must have wandered off sometime during your speech."

"What do you want to do?"

"My guess is, he's probably trying to walk home. Maybe he's just at the car, but we should get going and look for him."

"Alright. I'll let my sister know we're going to have to cut out."

He'd done it once again. As she'd hoped, that some-
times-jerk of a big brother had pulled another victory right
out of his ass. And, if maybe she'd overplayed her anxiety
about it all coming out alright, just to spur him a bit as she
knew she could, well, then it had been worth it. She met
his news of having to leave early with grace and a hug, and
even embraced his friend from work. Diana, was it? She knew
Jeff could see his sister was glowing and they made plans
for getting together the following evening. But now, as he
said one last goodbye and rushed out the front doors, Ann
had other things on her mind. The charity auction would be
starting soon, and she wanted to stay. She was still feeling the
magic of the night and she had a strong sense that the auction
would take the spell they all were under to a whole new level.
There were other things at play, of course, but, for now, Ann
was merely content to feel herself immersed in possibilities.

It was almost 10:30 and people were making their way into the
conference hall to peruse the items for the 11 o'clock gaveling.
As Ann began moving with them, Brenda came rushing up and
the two fell into each other's arms, both clearly high on the
emotions of the night. There was so much to say, but they found
themselves skating along the more frivolous moments of the
evening, content to let their deeper feelings rest unspoken – their
mutual awareness was more than enough. Paul stopped by for a

quick congratulations and then broke off to manage his duties as the lead auctioneer.

Just as Ann was about to relate her enthusiasm for the charity auction and ask how much they might be able to raise from the hundred or so people who had opted to stay, her eyes moved, just by chance, to the front windows – and there, out on the curb, loading the children back onto their bus was the tall man.

Brenda continued talking about the insane chain of events that had befallen the crate of props and costumes on its journey to the theater, without noticing that Ann had stopped listening – or that she had become lost in an attenuating tunnel, watching the tall man from the Children's Convalescent Center place the last child onto the bus, step in himself, close the doors, and then drive away.

"So, as I was telling Paul," Brenda's voice returned to Ann's awareness, "it would be the cherry on the cake for you to an-nounce some of the big items for us. The fans would be thrilled to know we not only have Mr. Arbuckle's nephew, but his niece here as well."

"Oh, I – I'm so sorry," Ann began suddenly, almost not rec-ognizing where the impetus to speak had come from – but she turned back to Brenda and while massaging her forehead said, "It's what I meant to tell you. I'm starting to get a migraine. I'm so sorry – but I'll be no use to anyone. Once these things start, the only thing for it is to go straight to bed."

Too sincere to detect any amount of deception, Brenda imme-diately offered all manner of assistance getting Ann home. "No, no," Ann reassured her, "You and Paul deserve to have a won-derful rest of the night – and I want *all* the details tomorrow."

They hugged a final time and Ann left – mired in her thoughts. Walking to her car, she severed, unawares, her connections to the magic that she had felt certain was on the verge of blooming in full. And had she stayed, had she trusted the voices of possibilities, she would have discovered she was right, because something even more extraordinary happened that night – something that was to profoundly affect Ann and her brother's life, though they would not be present at its inception.

Asked to describe what they remembered, neighbors sleeping in lofts near the theater had testified that there must have been, well after midnight, some kind of an explosion, some kind of disaster, although this was obviously not the case: those re-entering the building the next day found it untouched. But how to explain the screams and shouts in those early morning hours? The mob of costumed characters seen running from the theater doors and off into the shadows? Had there been violence? A murder?

The truth of what had actually happened at the Aztec Orpheum that night was only discovered much later, and then in scattered pieces, put together by Ann and Jeff and several others closely connected to the incident. As they later learned, the auction had started as planned, and the bidding for each item had gone higher than the next. Treasure after treasure had been brought before the gathered fans – rarity after rarity had stoked a rising mania for acquiring what were quite possibly the last physical remnants of their beloved show.

But around one in the morning, well after all the high-profile pieces had been sold and a majority had left exhausted but happy – there still remained a dedicated group of around twenty, fully committed to bidding on the various items that had yet to be presented. Those valiant holdouts were treated to a menagerie of small, almost trivial lots, most of them worse for the wear, broken, or with missing parts – but still legitimate relics of the the show, just the same: a cracked salt shaker that had seen less than ten seconds of screen time, a scuffed pair of shoes worn by an extra, and glasses, created for the Professor but never used, with the lenses long since gone. Then, according to witnesses, something was pulled from the crate that no one had realized was there, something wrapped in a dirty sheet, something that Mrs. Doss had, she later confessed, been determined to evacuate from the house – something that had been overlooked by the auction organizers, and, once discovered, was set center stage and its sheet removed for all to see: a small but exquisitely wrought painting.

Despite not being from the TV show – which seemed obvious to everyone, even to those who would not have described themselves as "hard core fans" – the object immediately gripped the room. The subject of the painting was, in itself, unremarkable. Yet it was freighted with such tenderness, so carefully and thoughtfully had its imagery been arranged, that it was impossible for those in attendance not to be touched in an intimate way. As they stood, held fast in its fragile power, there seemed to be a flash, like a glint of light just to the side, and then colors – exploding outward, enveloping the world in brilliance.

And, all at once, they found they could look upon their heart's desires and were unafraid. Suddenly, they *believed*.

CHAPTER 17

Wilfred Weiner had every reason to be pleased with himself. Except one. And that exception he would learn to live with. He hadn't always been pleased with himself. No, his thousand or so employees would most likely be shocked to learn that he had not always had the strength of character to deal with the ambiguities which he now knew were the hallmark of a leader – and the critical ingredient to success. In fact, in the beginning, he hadn't wanted to lead at all. He had wanted to dance.

They had mesmerized him – those people that could float and fly across a stage, in vibrant, billowing costumes. Sometimes by themselves, but usually, with a beautiful partner in their arms, they swirled and dipped and leapt about his TV screen to lush orchestrations and with a grace that defied reason. He had studied dance as a child and had been surprised and delighted to find that he possessed a real talent for it. Later, encouraged by a mother who believed that her children should be sanctioned in their interests, he attended a respected dance school and moved to New York City to begin a career on the stage.

But, as these things so often happen, the praise of friends, family, fellow dancers and instructors did not translate into the professional sphere. After a series of minor roles in off-Broadway productions that necessitated several additional part-time jobs, Wilfred threw in the towel. Two years of living hand-to-mouth had soured him on his ambitions – there would be no more sacrificing for his art. He wanted to live comfortably. And, if he was going to do work that he hated in order to make ends meet, he figured he might as well do work that paid.

With no business experience whatsoever, he landed a position as the assistant to an office manager at one of the major television networks. His duties were mind-numbing in the extreme, nothing but filing and typing and answering phones, but he watched his manager – and his manager's manager – and knew instantly that he could do both their jobs better than they could. He watched and studied and learned not only their skill sets but the details of their lifestyles – the cut of the suits they wore, the cars they drove and parked in the company garage, and, most impressively, the apartments they opened up once a year for company Christmas parties. It was at one of these holiday fetes that he first put into action a thought that had been cycling around his brain, and which, he believed, held the key to his advancement at the network.

The premise of the idea was simple: if he exceeded the abilities of those above him, was it not in the best interest of the company to promote him? Was failing to do so not an injustice? And, should his advancement not happen, was he not obligated to put the company's needs first and be excused for employing whatever means necessary to rectify that injustice? As fate would have it, an opportunity arose to test this deeply philosophical question. Towards the tail end of a long night of yuletide revelry – whereat

his manager had foolishly fallen asleep on the living room sofa –
Wilfred chanced upon a cell phone which had been accidentally
left in the bathroom next to the sink. The decision of whether or
not to maximize this turn of events was solely contingent upon
whether or not he could access its contents. And, again, fate was
on his side: the phone had not been locked and, opening up the
text messages, he saw at once that it belonged to none other than
his superior. Thumbing through its contents, he found himself
thrice blessed: there, in a chain of numerous back and forth
messages between his boss and his boss's boss, Wilfred discovered
a conversation graphically insulting to the VP of their entire
division.

And he forwarded it. To the VP.

With nothing but the swish of a finger – and without anyone
being the wiser – Wilfred was responsible for eliminating two
career obstacles and clearing a path for his move into management which he achieved almost immediately thereafter.

Once in that realm, once accepted into the world of the deci-
sion-makers, his ascent accelerated. From his managerial height,
not only did he achieve even greater clarity as to his corporate
ambitions, but he also came to see his previous artistic endeavors
as foolhardy. Now that he was behind the curtain, so to speak,
now that he was privy to the decision-making processes of a
major TV network – where entire careers were assessed and
ultimately adjudicated – he saw the epic truth of it all: everything came down to money and luck. Writers were not hired on
their merit, but based on the profits from their previous scripts.
Directors were not valued for their virtuosity but by who had
demonstrated the greatest compliance with executives.

And actors and other performers were the biggest joke of all. While a sliver of talent could – albeit rarely – be seen to tip the scales in the hiring of the production team, actors would be chosen for almost any reason *except* that. What infuriated him most was how blind they all were to this fact – how haughty they became with success, how elitist and judgmental they were towards their fellow artists who had not yet "made it." With their headshots and agents and self-created worlds of disgusting masturbatory narcissism, he saw how alike they were to all those lesser-talented dancers – dancers he'd watched land lead after lead in countless auditions while he'd been pushed aside and relegated to slots as a "member of the company" – risible jobs barely above "movie extra." Over time, Wilfred discovered that his distaste for the riffraff of his former life grew from mild irritation to full-blown loathing. This hatred corresponded, in almost direct proportion, with his professional ascent. Swiftly, he moved from manager to director, and from director to regional VP.

As his power grew, he began taking an impish delight in inserting himself, when he could, into the audition process – and seeing to it that his belief in the irrelevance of talent held true. He began taking a perverse glee in surreptitiously promoting those least suited for roles – and scuttling the chances of those with real promise. And did the moral framework of the universe punish him for these thoughts and actions? Hardly. In another three years, he was transferred to Los Angeles and made executive VP of their motion picture division: Family Films, Ltd. In another two years, he was made president.

This should have mollified him. He had a seven-figure salary, his bespoke suits were envied, his car was worth more than most people made in ten years, and his home was majestic. But, into this paradise that he'd built with the force of his ambition and the ceaseless toil of his own hands, slithered a prick worthy of such contempt that Wilfred was all but paralyzed with rage over what to do about him. The person in question was one of the star animators of the company – who had, so the stories went, turned around several disastrous films and was responsible for nearly all of their most popular characters. This little shit's pivotal role with the financial standing of the company gave him wide latitude – and that bastard knew it. His pranks, jokes, and mocking references to Willard's last name attested to that. He'd seen the supposedly "secret" memes, sketches, and animated shorts deriding the company in general and himself in particular produced by this asshole. He'd clearly understood the naked contempt in which his leadership was held by the animation team – how they viewed him as nothing more than a seat-warmer and yes-man for the board of directors. He'd seen all this and had vowed revenge. He would make all of them pay eventually – but especially their ringleader, Dirk Jarvis.

But, if Wilfred Weiner had learned anything in his rise through the corporate hierarchies, it was that discretion and propriety were the two iron-clad principles by which any successful executive must operate. He'd also seen how the board of directors found Dirk amusing – and, he suspected, shared more than one of that cretin's demeaning views. Like so many of his previously successful career moves, Wilfred knew that his hand in the destruction of Jarvis must remain invisible and that the plot must be meticulously planned and executed. Let them all think he was a harmless corporate toady. One day, they'd see the truth – and realize he'd been playing them all along.

Despite all his secret devilry, Wilfred Weiner had remained – from the outside – a model corporate citizen and had prided himself on following a code of moral conduct that kept him scrupulously within the law. And if, here and there, he had needed to bend or expand his definition of those moral parameters, it had always been with an eye towards what was best for the company and for the majority of the employees. On this, Wilfred was sure, no one, not even Dirk, could find fault. And so, when in pursuit of measures that would provide maximum benefit for that majority of employees – and, obviously, for himself as well – it had become necessary to move funds from one particular bucket into another, he had done so without a single compunction. Leaders at his level of consequence – Wilfred accepted as practically natural law – had earned the right to determine when and if arbitrary codes of legal conduct were momentarily dismissible. But, on this particular occasion – and for the first time in his career – Wilfred miscalculated. But only slightly.

Monica Claggart, an assistant producer in the animation division and his mistress and co-conspirator, was the first to sound the alarm about the potential complications and to advise counter-measures. So when the New York offices, under fresh leadership, had signaled their intention for a complete audit of finances following their recent takeover, the president of Family Films, Ltd had been ready for them. But here it was that Wilfred Weiner confronted the first real moral dilemma of his life. Yes, in their siphoning of funds through their liberal interpretation of what the company owed the two of them, Wilfred and Monica had used Dirk's computer passwords to access various accounts and yes, on the surface they had done what many would have condemned as highly unethical. But a crime is only a crime if anyone is hurt. And all they had done, at least up to this point, was to move abstract values from one computer server to another – and the name on the account (allowing them to do so) had been totally ignorant of the assistance he'd provided.

But now, should the audit discover their unorthodox actions, the conceptual would become real, and a real person would very likely be harmed. If it had been anyone other than Dirk, Wilfred would have weighed the ramifications of staying silent. But, it *wasn't* anyone other than Dirk. The confluence of events which had placed his mortal enemy right in the crosshairs was nothing more than the universe signaling its concord with the underlying purpose of using Dirk's name to begin with. And, with Monica willing to present herself as an eye-witness to the crime – after Wilfred's clarifying just how personally advantageous it would be for her to do so – there no longer remained any compelling reason not to allow for this one moral infraction, which he had earned for himself many times over. Yes, Wilfred Weiner had every reason to be pleased. And, this was the one exception he could easily learn to live with.

Better still, now that the act had been discovered, and Dirk had, surprisingly, exhibited a host of guilty behaviors, including fleeing the scene of the crime, the story of his betrayal had taken hold and the employees of Family Films Ltd, including those closest to Dirk, were all turning against him.

These were the thoughts that Wilfred Weiner sat brooding over in his plush corporate office. From his vantage point on the 63rd floor, the nighttime cityscape of Los Angeles glittered before him – and he wondered which of the tiny flickering lights might be harboring Dirk, the asshole – wondered if that lowlife had any idea of the noose slowly constricting around his neck.

Had he not been so deep in thought, even with his back turned to stare out at the city below, he might have noticed the line of red pith helmets crouched behind the planters in the executive lobby – helmets complete with radio tubes projecting like bug ears, some hand-made, some authentic and some purchased at a recent auction in which a host of extraordinary things had occurred – might have noticed the stealthy opening of his frosted glass door through which peaked the strangest collection of costumed characters: Miss Sharp, Mentar the Great, Pollyanna Pipsqueak, Green Gecko, Freaky Face, Dr. Monocle, Esmerelda Diablo, and Count Von Vershlagen.

Perhaps he would have heard them enter his office, sneak up and surround him. But as it was, the first and last thing he saw, before passing out, was the giant gorilla coming towards him with the robot eyes.

CHAPTER 18

Jeff smiled. He was still able, from time to time, to watch auditions from the perspective of a first-time director or, rarer still, from that of a total newcomer to the business of filmmaking. And in those moments, it never failed to startle him with just how bad the raw elements of a motion picture could seem. No matter. He could see. Best of all, his cast was coming together – and he had, quite possibly, made a discovery.

Carol Beth turned to her mother and screamed: "I ain't havin' this baby!"

"Carol Beth!" the other shrieked, lifting herself up from her sickbed. "You shut your mouth!"

"I wouldn't bring no child into this stinkin' world," Carol Beth sobbed. "There ain't nothin' for it. When was it that hope done packed its bags, mama? When daddy left us? Was that it? Or when that no good husband of mine disappeared? Hell, there ain't never even been a rainbow in these parts since I don't know when!"

"You're wrong, Carol Beth!" her mother implored, falling back onto her sweat-stained pillow. "Hope cain't leave – why it's here all 'round, you just have to take the time to see it, that's all. And let me

tell you somethin' about rainbows – the only place they ever really live...is in your heart!"

Yes, without the practiced eye of someone familiar with the innumerable steps leading to the finished product, without the ability to mentally extrapolate how the editing process, sound design, color correction, and musical score would all work in tandem to create a whole greater than the sum of its parts, these isolated puzzle pieces were next to meaningless – and so often led to despondency and resignation in the novice.

But Jeff was an old hand at this. Of course, there were always moments of doubt – an essential quality of any healthy artistic mind – but these moments were fleeting in the face of his decades of experience. These auditions, which Jeff had been obliged to rush, were actually going spectacularly – and the dialogue, which he'd been confident in already, was coming to life in a way even he hadn't expected at his most enthusiastic. Looking around at the glances of his production team as they watched the various actors screen test with the excerpted scenes, he saw the silent signals of their growing excitement for the project as well. What had changed? How had things gone from disaster to the buzz of the studio? His epiphany last week at the Aztec had certainly been a personal turning point – but what about the others? Everyone, it seemed, had been swept up in his passion for *Summer of the Rainbows.*

Even Ann seemed to be sharing his excitement. Following the memorial, she'd become even more enthusiastic than usual towards his career – and was especially pleased that he'd resolved to pursue his pet project after all. For herself, she'd decided to stay in LA for a few more weeks. The pending offer on the house had been rescinded, and she maintained that she was finding it easier to concentrate on revising her book in this new setting. Jeff sensed there was more to it than that – she'd been rather cagey when he'd tried probing around the edges – but there was too much on his mind, and he was too glad for her company, to pry further.

His ardor was cut short by another thought: Dirk. Then there was Dirk. He'd completely vanished off the face of the earth. Diane was in full-blown panic mode, and was resolutely determined to find out what had happened to him. There were suggestions, from some corners, that he'd done himself in – that any day now his body would wash ashore or turn up in some ditch. Diane was not quite there yet, but Jeff could see she was starting to run out of plausible alternatives. But something told Jeff that Dirk was alright. Something told him he was just fine – and that he would pop up any day now. He had tried to explain himself to Diane and the reasons for his confidence – but she had presumed he was only placating her and grew even more irritated. Nevertheless, he had a movie to complete and Dirk would have to make do with Diane manning the lookout for him all on her own.

"Thank you, both!" Jeff called out to the two actresses up on the small stage of the rehearsal room. He and his assembled production team, sitting at the opposite end and shuffling headshots along with cold cups of coffee, exchanged approving glances. "Barbara, thank you, that was wonderful," Jeff continued. "And Stephanie, if you'll stay, I'd like to have you read for Carol Beth again with the next actor."

"For sure, Mr. Tanner," the young woman named Stephanie replied. Jeff smiled back, not caring at all that it was obvious he was smitten with her. Once again, he couldn't believe how everything was falling into place. His experience giving the eulogy for his uncle had dropped the scales from his eyes and the true brilliance of his idea had been restored – but it had done something else. He now knew that it had been up to him all along. He didn't need inspiration to strike from some mystic realm. Everything he required, had ever thought he lacked, resided in abundance inside himself. What had been laid bare was that it had been entirely Jeff Tanner that had allowed his doubts to overwhelm him.

It was also clear that his colleagues' transformation had been due to his own attitude and their perception of it. He had been subconsciously communicating his dread of the project the whole time – and their reversal had been entirely dependent on his. Even Murch, who had reluctantly thrown in his support, was wielding his "pussy picture" epithet more as a term of endearment than of derision. Was this what Uncle Aaron had been trying to tell him? Was this the point of those ritualistic dinner table debates with Ann – not the specific answers themselves but that *choice* was the great constant of our lives?

When they'd been forced to return to Illinois and to cut short their retreat from the world, he and Ann had found themselves back in school and back with the more provincial side of the family where all those choices had seemed to dry up. The Tanner clan, unlike the Arbuckle branch, made it a point of pride to restrict any future plans to only those options which minimized risk. Uncle Aaron, rather than being celebrated for his success,

was more often than not held up as "irresponsibly lucky" –
and how disastrous his fortunes would have turned out had
his number not come up. What would he have fallen back on?
Can you imagine where he'd have ended up with nothing but
waitering on his resume? Jeff had listened to these aspersions
with a respectful silence – yet thinking all along that when the
time came to break free, he'd be casting his lot with Uncle Aaron
and a chance to have it all.

Ann had not been so unperturbed. Back then, he'd sensed
that although she still nurtured her dreams – the ones she'd
once so freely shared with him – unlike her brother, she had
chosen to hold them close to her chest. It was just a fact that
she had been born more sensitive than he was – and he had
watched her crumble, day by day, under the constant drumbeat
of the Tanner family's stultifying convictions. He knew that she
had continued to write as a young girl – and even suspected
that she had been sending her stories to Uncle Aaron – but she
had stopped sharing her work with both Jeff himself and with
their new family. And, neither he nor they had ever asked to see
them. Had he possessed just a drop more compassion, he would
have stepped in and told her everything he'd finally been able
to express the night of the memorial. But, at the time, the wall
between them had to be maintained; he had been certain of that
though he had not known why – nor would he ever have dared to
explore the question. He and Ann had kept their separate spaces,
and though he had pretended disinterest in her writing, he had
thought often of the stories she *had* shared – of the girl with
the butterfly ring that could transport herself to distant lands –
and admired how Ann, in spite of her yielding publicly to the

Tanner dogma, had steadfastly continued to do in secret what Jeff, himself, could only relegate to a hoped-for future.

That future was now. Those conflicted feelings towards Murch and his career, those murky tangled threads that had ensnared his thoughts with the death of his uncle and the arrival of Ann to California – had all slipped free of each other and revealed that *this* was his true self. This project, written with passion and guts, forgoing any vulgar box office considerations, was himself at his finest. But what most astounded him was the way in which, now that events had been set in motion, everything so easily fell into place. Take, for instance, the casting. At first, offering the role of the grandmother to a multiple Academy award-winning (and, normally, astronomically expensive) Marilyn Dunne – which all but assured any film of an audience – would have doomed their budget. But, as fate would have it, Dunne had fallen on tough times, having pulled herself through an addiction to pain-killers, and though back on her feet, was finding it difficult to secure lead roles. Jeff, under normal circumstances, would have considered her still too much of a risk – but with his restricted budget and with Dunne willing to work well below her typical fee, this time, he accepted the challenge. Filling out the rest of the company with unknowns – Jeff was pleased to learn – added an entirely new level of excitement to the production. Already, it had paid off.

Stephanie Strane, with whom Jeff was becoming more obsessed every day, arrived like a thunderclap. The biggest thing on her resume had been a two-month stint as a runaway prostitute on the daytime drama *Search for Hope*, which, although demonstrating a command of the art, was hardly the vehicle to bring her to the attention of the American public – nor any indication of the full breadth of her talents. But her reading of the lead character of Carol Beth had instantly riveted the production team and even though they'd continued to have numerous actresses read for the role, it was a fait accompli that Stephanie had the part. Even *she* made little effort to hide her understanding of that fact as she continued to be brought in to read with other actors. By the third day of auditions, it became evident that all the additional roles would be cast in relation to their chemistry with her performance – which she somehow managed to keep perpetually interesting. Within the week, it was universally accepted that the film was going to make Stephanie a star. Everyone was high on her. Everyone except Diane – who seemed to be strangely hostile towards her. Not in matters of her talent, of course, which Diane agreed was formidable, but – perplexing as it may sound – on account of her *hair*: as Diane laid out systematically and with irrefutable proofs, Stephanie favored *side* pony-tails.

"What does *that* have to do with anything?" Jeff had asked incredulously.

"Jeff," Diane had urged, staring him dead in the eye, "any woman comfortable wearing a side-ponytail is bat-shit crazy. How do you not know that? And, what's worse, they're SO bat-shit crazy they have no problem announcing it to the world!"

"You've lost your mind."

"And you've been warned," she had said, turning on her heels and leaving without another word. She'd apologized the next day for getting a little heated and for suggesting things about someone she really knew nothing about. Jeff had told her not to worry about it. It was obvious that the pressures of Dirk's disappearance was getting to her – and although she subsequently treated Stephanie with respect, Jeff knew she remained wary.

"Okay, ladies," Jeff announced after the next auditioner had been brought in, "would you please turn to page 34? Stephanie, this is the one from earlier this morning."

"Is that the rape scene?"

"No, where your baby dies of SIDS."

"Oh! That's right! Well, okay, but I don't think I have the tears left!"

Diane entered moments later – just as the scene finished and Stephanie, contrary to her stated concerns, had just pulled off another unparalleled performance – at least according to the look on Jeff's face. Diane squelched her instinct to comment and consoled herself with the thought that if there were any acting accolades to be handed out, it would be for herself – and her bravura ability to hide her revulsion for that woman: there was no way she was going to let anyone, least of all Jeff, see her being this petty, and, second of all, she had much more important matters to contend with.

"I just finished talking to that stupid detective again," she confided to Jeff at the first break in the auditions. "We'll never get anywhere with that moron. You'd think I wouldn't have to tell him to maybe check with Dirk's *mother* to see if he's contacted her – but apparently I do. But listen to this: several people who live near the theater said they heard all kinds of shouting about two o'clock in the morning. And one lady, who owns an all-night laundromat, says she saw a bunch of people in costumes pile into a van and drive off. I don't know why, but I'm convinced Dirk was with them."

"But you searched the theater. You said he had left."

"Yes, but come on, Jeff. There's a million places he could have been hiding – or maybe he came back after we'd gone. There's too many variables for us to be certain. And there's more. I talked to your sister this morning. Those two kids from the fan club that had been helping her organize the whole thing? They're missing too. She's tried calling them over and over and there's no answer."

"Okay...so what do you want to do?"

"I don't know," she said and then, leaning in with a fervid whisper – and a look that emphasized the ominous turn she was convinced events had taken – added, "But something bigger is going on here. I'm sure of that."

It was not often that Jeff found it a challenge to maintain his composure – but Diane morphing into Mrs. Sherlock Holmes before his very eyes was too much for even his considerable talents. Forcing his reply through paroxysms of laughter, he suggested that she track down a calabash pipe and let Watson know the game was afoot. Diane, strangely, did not share his sense of the moment's hilarity. This was communicated effectively enough with an aggravated sigh and a quick exit – right after flipping him off.

CHAPTER 19

Ann had not wanted to be there. Not at first. What was she doing, sitting in her car in the dark, waiting outside the Children's Convalescent Center? What was it that had brought her here forty minutes ago to wait in silence for so long? But despite it all, why was this the one place she'd rather be than any other? Maybe because here, right here, was contained one of those beautiful, thousands of fresh possibilities that had recently opened for her – now that Michael was out of her life. Saying it and feeling the realness of it was more powerful than she had anticipated:

Michael was gone.

Yes, she'd messed up last week when he'd called and caught her tipsy. She'd folded. But she'd taken another swing at it, and this time, she'd triumphed.

And, what's more, their split had been ridiculously easy.

As she stared out at the front entrance to the facility watching strangers come and go, knowing that each unidentifiable face was like a countdown, her final conversation with Michael kept looping through her thoughts and contending with the purpose of her vigil.

"Michael? It's me."

"What's going on? How is California?"

"It's great, but listen, that's not why I'm calling."

Enough! She said to herself. Enough of Michael. Time to focus on the present.

And in this present moment, there was someone else that had begun moving into the center of her consciousness – and he'd said seven o'clock, and it was just that now. He seemed like the punctual sort, unlike Michael, so it could be any second. Perhaps she should get out of the car?

No – better to wait and then walk towards him as he was exiting – to avoid the perception that she'd arrived early and had stood around waiting for him.

Which is exactly what she had done.

The phone call with Michael had made her all the more eager to dismiss the rising embarrassment over this unfortunate fact.

"Ann, do you want me to fly out to see you?"

"No. I just want you to listen – and take what I have to say seriously."

All those years of suffering under his oppression – all that wasted time and, as it turned out, she'd been able to end it in the span of five minutes.

"OK, Ann. What is it?"

She'd picked up the phone, dialed, and now here she was, a free woman. And those crowds of women, those masses of fellow sisters who looked to her were finally quieted – had subsided into serene approval, all of them nodding and smiling and knowing she'd delivered on the promise of her words. The work she'd poured herself into was no longer the product of a counterfeit persona. And Ann was fortified knowing that *this* was her true self. This was what lay beyond those years of fear.

But where had the woman come from who had cut straight to the point and said, "I want out"? Had it really been that electrifying instant, standing in the wings of the Aztec, listening to Jeff's speech – or had that woman been there all along, and only needed one final nudge? And where had the man come from who had said, "Okay, I understand. Give me a week to find a new place"? That was the real kicker. Not even an attempt at feigning disappointment. But her own reaction had been the real eye-opener. As much as she'd told herself that it was nothing more than a relationship of convenience, it was obvious there had been a part of her hoping that it was more. Well, screw it.

Through the multiple glass doors leading to the reception desk, she spotted him. He'd propped himself against the counter to sign some papers, turning his back to the entrance, and she instantly calculated that exiting the car now would position herself perfectly in his line of sight – and, as an added bonus, as soon as he turned around, she would be in the act of *striding* towards him. Ann had enough self-awareness to know that first glimpses of her body in motion – and head on – tended to flatter her figure more than a static position.

Her heart began pounding and, again, she was flooded with shame – and then had to remind herself that none of this was her fault. She would *never* have made any attempt whatsoever to contact the tall man who had entranced her that night at the Aztec. In fact, it had always been a long-standing point of pride that she had never once "gone after" any man. But the fates, it seemed, were determined to foil her resolve. Around noon – the day after the memorial – and shortly after her final conversation with Michael, Brenda had called.

"Ms. Tanner?" the voice on the line had asked, sounding as though deep within a dreamy fog.

"Who is this?" Ann had replied. Although the caller ID showed exactly who it was *supposed* to be, it sounded nothing like her. "Who is this?" Ann asked again and more forcefully. "Where's Brenda?"

"It's me, Ms. Tanner. I'm right here."

"What's happened? Where are you? Is everything alright?"

According to Brenda, everything was more than alright. In fact, Ann was informed that they were going to "save the world" – but first, there were some things that needed to be done. Before abruptly hanging up and in a rather jumbled outpouring – and with what sounded like someone occasionally yodeling in the background – Brenda communicated to Ann that the money raised from the auction (some $10,000) needed to be picked up from the theater (where it had been left) and delivered to Thomas Naidoo, the director of the Children's Convalescent Center (the tall man from the memorial) and that should Ann hear that she and Paul had gone missing (or any other such strange rumors), she was begged to say nothing of this phone call – and must believe that they had gone off, as she repeated, to "save the world."

Stopping by the theater the next day, Ann had found the deposit bag easily enough and, having been given no further information, had no choice but to call the Children's Center herself and ask Mr. Naidoo how she could most conveniently get the donations to him. It had, let the record show, been *his* idea for her to meet him in person for the drop off.

As he continued leaning over the counter, she strode towards him, affecting an expression of carefree nonchalance. In those last few seconds before he turned around, she felt pride in the fact that she hadn't violated any of her higher principles in coming here. No, this was a situation that she had been *maneuvered* into. And besides, considering all that had been just handed to her, considering the personal life she had committed to totally rebuilding, the far *worse* crime would be failing to maximize a golden opportunity to meet a great guy. Or something like that.

Just as she approached the lobby entrance, and just as Thomas Naidoo straightened up from his paperwork, an elderly gentleman appeared from out of nowhere and thrust open the door directly in Ann's path – and, in an attempt to avoid colliding with him, she initiated a sharp tilt to the right which caused the strap on one of her two oversized purses (which she would, endlessly thereafter, ask why she had been compelled to carry in the first place) to disengage from her shoulder and become entangled in the handle of the man's umbrella – which stuck out from beneath the corner of his arm. The result of this unfortunate encounter was that Mr. Naidoo, rather than seeing Ann's attempt at a runway walk – was presented with her rear angle, stumbling awkwardly away from him, and trying to extricate herself from an enfeebled and scowling senior citizen.

"Are you alright?" he asked, rushing up to her moments after she'd finally broken free.

"Yorse!" she said, trying – and failing – to successfully stop herself from saying "Yes" and, instead, switch to the more eloquent, "Of course" – and then, in a hasty attempt at recovery, sputtering out both answers again in an only slightly less mangled fashion.

Unphased, Thomas Naidoo helped to re-adjust her purses and, smiling affectionately, held out his hand and introduced himself as the director of the Children's Center. It was all Ann could do to recover, collect herself, and respond.

"Hi, I'm Ann, it's very nice to meet you" she said, reaching out and wondering why her arm looked to be bending in all the wrong places.

"Yes, I know," he said with an unnervingly firm handshake. "I recognized you right away from the memorial."

"Oh, really?" Ann asked, his admission opening terrifying possibilities – and not at all certain she had tamped down on her sudden enthusiasm adequately enough. But, she needn't have worried. Thomas was unbridled in his enthusiasm at meeting *her*. Apparently, Paul and Brenda had regaled him with stories of her charm, her generosity of spirit, and her willingness to do whatever was needed to assist with their charity auction – and he piled his gratitude at her feet like an offering.

As she looked up into those eyes that shone down on her and those magnificent expressions that moved with hypnotizing dexterity across his face, Ann would not have been able to say that the experience exceeded her expectations – because she had envisioned them perfectly. Somehow, in her formulation of who she supposed him to be, and though filling the myriad gaps left by their all too brief encounter with idealized traits, Thomas Naidoo, in the flesh, met every one of her impossibly high standards effortlessly. He was funny, he was clever, magnanimous and eloquent – and despite being laden with these gifts, he kept her locked at the center of his attention, making no effort to disguise that he had inquired about her, and never once indicating that he found her anything less than beguiling.

"I'm so sorry that you'll be heading back soon," he said in his soft baritone.

"What?" Ann asked, pulling herself back from momentarily fancying what dating, marriage, children, and retirement might be like with him – and only just realizing he had been asking her something.

"Don't you fly home to Boston soon? Brenda said you were only here through the auction."

"Oh, well, actually," Ann said laughing, "it looks like I may need to stay a little while longer."

"Really?" Thomas asked, smiling broadly.

"Yes, um, it's proving a bit more difficult to wrap up the estate than I thought. We had a buyer, but that fell through. And I really don't want to leave until I have a firm commitment for the house."

"I see," he said, raising his eyebrow comically.

"I've still got several months before school starts, so, I figure I might as well be here," she added, again adjusting her two oversized purses which seemed intent on disrupting her concentration.

"Well, if you're around, I'd love to talk to you more about the Center. Perhaps we can meet later this week?"

"Sure! That sounds fantastic."

"How about dinner?"

"Even better!"

"My wife and I would love to have you over. I've told her – "

"Oh!" Ann gasped, dropping both purses.

What happened next was one of those consummate examples of living theater – microsecond performances of such sheer brilliance that, could they be shared with the world at large, would compel matchless accolades – but which, sadly, must forever remain unknown to all but the actress herself, whose sole consolation is the avoidance of a clear disaster – especially after shouting a stunned "Oh!" (while stopping herself at the last possible moment from adding "Why didn't anyone tell me you were *married!*") while at the same time formulating an ingeniously simple lie to explain away her humiliating reaction.

Thomas, ever gallant, immediately proceeded to scoop up Ann's bags and return them to their owner.

"Are you hurt?" he asked, his face gripped with concern owing to Ann ensuring that he noticed she was gently rubbing her side. "I'm so sorry," she said with a laugh, "I use a safety pin to hold one of these straps on!" Then, turning the offending fastener towards him (which she had discreetly unclasped), "It pops out at the worst moments."

As she continued to conspicuously nurse her injury, Thomas asked again if she would accept his invitation to dinner – and the Ann that had mastered the art of faking a fully collected exterior swung into action.

"Well, I'm totally open to it," she said, relaxing into the response. "I just need to check my calendar."

"I don't mean to pressure you."

"Oh, no!" she said with waves of calm while taking her keys out from her purse, "I was just hit with the thought, here I am making plans and, you know, my schedule's so crazy, I'm really not being responsible. I've got the house to worry about – and a book I'm editing, which I forgot to mention. But yes, if it works out, for sure. I'd love to."

"OK, great. I'll call you tomorrow."

"Wonderful. And like I said, if I can swing it at all, we're on!"

He thanked her again for all she had done, for the generous donations, for taking the time to stop by and meet him, and with hopes they would see each other soon. Ann bid him farewell and left him there, as he was, and feeling those dark searching *married* eyes following her to her car.

On the drive home, her sole comforting thought was that she needed to write. Her next chapter had taken form and she would get all this garbage out and on paper. At least Jill would be pleased. Oh, and while she was at it, fuck Michael.

CHAPTER 20

The first thing that had come to him was that he had been dancing. Before the awareness of the restraints or the masses of figures surrounding him in the shadows, Wilfred had been flying. In great synchronous leaps, he and his troupe were vaulting deer – bounding across an endless field of billowing grass. High above, in the bright blue dome of the sky, birds swooped in sympathetic ecstasy. On and on he and his brothers danced, traversing miles of rolling hills and off through meadows of perfumed flowers. And their wild, uninhibited cavorting was more than rhapsodies of joy – it was their tribute to this Eden which sheltered beneath the munificence of a radiant sun.

Then, night had fallen – and the stars that coruscated themselves in a great arc above him began their own far-off dance. Closer and closer they came – and then the stars were tiny wisps of candle flames. Candles! Hundreds of twinkling candles burned all around; and shapes moved in and about, whispering his name, as mourners to a grave.

Still groggy and with a voice barely contending with the darkness around him, it seemed as though the candles were gliding past him – or was it *he* that was floating through them?

"Am I....am I dead?" he breathed.

"Yes!" came the commanding answer – and he felt himself rising, being tilted to a nearly upright position, yet still he was bound, held tight and immobile against a hard surface. From his new vantage, and with the sleep slowing draining from his mind, he could just make out the faint outlines of what seemed to be a large chapel – and before him an alter and on it, the source of the voice which had addressed him: a cloaked figure that towered before him and before dozens of congregants who Wilfred could feel surrounding him in the murky light.

"You are most certainly dead, Wilfred Weiner!" the voice of the hooded specter called out again, raising its hand to point at him in accusation: "But we did not kill you. You did that to yourself – and long ago!"

From deeper within the darkness, a pipe organ sprang to life – its notes peeling out with trembling insistence, scampering up and down the register with a heightening frenzy. The voices of the congregants joined in the frenetic hymn, adding their own ethereal might, burrowing into Wilfred's horrified, widening eyes. But something was wrong. The voices were shifting, moving off from their harmonies and, slowly, deliberately, oozing over to half step dissonances and atonal intervals – and as the tempo accelerated, the clashing discordant chords slammed against Wilfred's mind, and the very room itself rolled and swayed vertiginously, sending him to the brink of nausea.

Backed by this unholy chorus, the dark priest leapt down off the dais and began drawing closer, raising his hands in supplication to the black arts swirling about him.

"Welcome, honored guest, *to Hell!*" he cried out, and then, shifting his tone to one of near euphoria, he proclaimed: "But tonight, Wilfred Weiner, you will be REBORN!!"

The figure began moving among his followers, urging their singing on, repeating his assertion that their prisoner would be "reborn" – and Wilfred was convinced he had fallen into the hands of a madman. Little could Wilfred know, but this night had, in fact, already been the scene of *many* rebirths.

This gathered band of shrouded outcasts had themselves collectively witnessed a moment of profound revelation, not long ago – at a memorial to a beloved saint, Aaron Arbuckle. Beholding his final masterpiece, they had experienced a transformation – a last gift by that departed angel – a transformation that they, to every woman and man, were still deep in the throes of: they had all found they could look unflinching at their heart's desires and, for the first, wield the power to manifest it. For most, it was fully incarnating what the world had told them could never be more than a fantasy. The characters they had longed to be, they *were*. But, for one of them, it was the bringing of them all together for the premiere of a long-gestating opera.

Yet not one of them had been more transfigured than the still tipsy man who had crawled out from beneath the auction stage where he had gone to escape his troubles, who had emerged desperately in need of camaraderie, who had been immediately embraced by this group of fellow loners – gentle souls who had, over the next half hour, become spellbound by this strange man's heart-wrenching story of his ruination by a corrupt and evil corporate villain. Then, this stranger had stood boldly alongside them when the final moment of truth had come – at the unveil-

ing – when the shroud had been swept aside, and they had, all
of them, stared straight into the majesty of the last item up for
bidding – and when, from within it, had exploded that fusillade
of colors, arrows of fissioning sparks, he had been seized, right
along with them, by its inexorable magic.

And, like the others, he saw what he wanted most. He wanted
justice.

None of this tale would, of course, have meant anything at all
to Wilfred Weiner. But the cloaked priest – who had returned to
move within inches from his face – cast off his hood, revealing a
person with whom Wilfred *was* more than familiar.

"You!" Wilfred cried out – as, from the shadows, the congregants rose, doffed their robes, and leapt up onto the stage wearing all manner of strange costumes. There were spacemen and
werewolves, winged pixies and chrome-plated robots, lizard men
and leering witches – but among all these there also seemed to be
a handful similarly dressed as children and, standing guard over
them, a hulking gorilla with nightmarish robotic eyes. It was two
of these faux children who approached that deranged asshole,
Dirk Jarvis – and who began helping him into a costume unlike
any of the others: a Napoleonic jacket, jodhpurs, black boots,
and a bizarre red pith helmet garnished with a looped antenna
and two glass radio tubes – a costume change performed while
Dirk moved backwards and up and onto the stage – keeping his
eyes locked with Wilfred's.

To compound his bafflement, a stagehand dressed in black
ran up to Dirk and quickly attached a cordless mic to his ear.
It was then that Wilfred realized with stabbing alarm that this
was no death cult preparing him for sacrifice, this was no satanic

church out to confiscate his soul – the bodies gyrating in carefully choreographed union, the swelling music and voices raised
in song were not performing a requiem for the dead – No! This
was nothing less than an overture and opening number! And,
judging by the completely incomprehensible setting, costumes,
and libretto: an avant garde theater troupe – who had every
intention – as one might naturally surmise from the restraints
– of forcing him to witness their production!

The scream that broke from Wilfred's mouth was perfectly
timed with Dirk's belting out of his opening note: an extended
high F – just a hair outside of his vocal range and precisely a half
pitch off of the unseen organist's accompaniment. Had Wilfred
been aware that what he was witnessing was no less than an
astonishing example of a total neophyte completely embodying
a role (one that had been reluctantly abandoned by an ailing
lead actor) and one which Dirk had demonstrated his other-
worldly aptness for by sheer chance: an impromptu performance
of Mozart's Queen of the Night (done as an acapella yodel)
following his acceptance into the Professor Puck Society – then
perhaps Wilfred would have found something to cling to as Dirk
began trilling through his opening solo while breaking out into
the funky chicken.

Over the next hour (Or was it two? Or three? Time, for Wilfred, ceased to have much concrete meaning), as he drifted in and
out of consciousness and from stupefied submission to mindless
hysteria, the performance – which at first seemed impenetrable
– began to take on a recognizable form. Wilfred began to suspect
that he knew these characters, that he had seen them all before,
and that the story (as much of it as he could make out) was also

oddly familiar. But it was not until the robot gorilla reappeared – at which point he suddenly remembered his abduction – that he made a complete connection.

Of course! These lunatics were acting out some kind of insane operatic version of that ridiculous television show he had hated, even as a child. And, had Wilfred not succumbed to yet another 20-minute maniacal laughing fit – before passing out, once again – he might have arrived at the meaning of the greater whole. Finally, after repeated bouts of consciousness mixed with oblivion, after bringing Wilfred to the very limits of human tolerance and after he had peered more than once over the brink of the abyss, the crescendoing voices and music and dancing all came to an abrupt halt.

The stage lights dimmed and all that remained was the sound of Wilfred's exhausted breathing. How long he was left in this spent state, he could not say – but eventually, he became aware of himself and the presence of his abductors, with one cloaked figure nearer to him than the rest – which he was certain was Dirk Jarvis.

"I'll get you for this," Wilfred was just barely able to gasp. "I'll get you if it's the last thing I ever do…"

"I'm so very sorry," the voice of Dirk whispered in return. "But we're not quite done yet. The truth *shall* prevail!"

At this point the stage hands brought out something wrapped in a sheet and slowly began uncovering it.

Wilfred smirked as he deliberated whether or not to reveal his belief that there was nothing more they *could* do to him – but decided to jealously guard that secret and gloat over it as just the first step in his ultimate revenge. And, also, because being in possession of something Dirk would surely desire to know was a unique and pleasurable sensation.

Then it seemed as though the darkness surrounding him had grown even blacker – except for a moment of penetrating light – like sunlight reflected off chrome – which shook the earth and blasted clear through him.

What Wilfred then *knew* was that he must not be distracted from getting with all haste to wherever it was that he was going, to wherever it was that his feet were leading him. As his steps moved him ever forward, he felt the fatigue of all the burdens he carried – and what was this secret that compounded his hardships? His hands unclenched and as he looked at his bare palms, he began to recall that there had been something before this long journey – he had not always been walking like this, in fact, he had the vague recollection of being with Dirk Jarvis.

Yes! Dirk! He had been captured by Dirk! He remembered the church and the candles and the altar...and then something being set upon it...something wrapped in a sheet...and when the sheet had been removed...

It was a door, that's what it was! A door set upon an easel, and somehow, he had opened it, releasing blinding colors, and then he had run through it! He had escaped and now had come to this life of wandering – forever traveling this desolate void.

How he wanted to sleep. How he wanted to close his eyes and succumb, but a tingling unease told him that he must avoid that at all costs.

Ahead, it appeared before him – a great glass cell, a hundred feet tall, like a giant human aquarium, aglow with a pale, sickly light. The light called to him, promising sleep. There was restful sleep within. But also a throbbing dread.

Wilfred slowed his approach, knowing he must not yield to it. The inmates inside that giant glass prison had made that mistake. He must not be captured and thrown inside to die with them, to be slowly eaten alive at the hands of the Worm – which hung affixed to the far wall of the enclosure, its blind, writhing prostomium releasing venomous clouds of toxins while its bloated abdomen disgorged a steady stream of coagulated, acidic puss.

The smell of its victims' rotting skin hit him with all its sickening pungency and he wanted to flee from the stench – but the horror of their plight kept him petrified. Through the thick glass wall, smeared with the sallow bile of the creature, he watched all of them, mouths slack and gaping, mutely staring out from their captivity. With their clothes removed to allow the digestive juices and scum – within which they slowly trudged or lay about in soulless agony – to more effortlessly render them into this human soup, they had the eyes of the living dead. A mother, the skin melting from her face, sat silently cradling a cold, gray child. An old man, his legs dissolved to the knees, tried vainly to pull himself up against the glass. And what appeared to be a newly arrived couple stood clinging to each other, attempting to hide their nakedness while succumbing to the stupefying vapors of the tank. From this chamber of abomination, Wilfred would have gladly fled, would have turned and run and freed himself forever – but for a single prisoner who, unlike all the others, seemed to be looking directly at him, seemed to acknowledge his presence, and who began painfully stumbling towards him.

Hypnotized by the pathetic creature's plight, Wilfred approached the thick glass, a part of him feeling the need to communicate at least his recognition of this fellow human, of its suffering, to give it one last sense of connection. The two drew closer and closer – Wilfred from an overpowering compulsion and the other more from blind animal instinct – until they were nearly face to face, separated only by the thick glass wall.

Wilfred looked deep into the other's empty eyes and saw only death. But then, slowly to his horror, Wilfred realized he was not looking *into* the cage, was not looking from *without* – but was looking from *within*. And the other, the one whom he had perceived to be on the other side of the glass, was, in truth, his own reflection. The reflection of a prisoner, bereft of hope, awaiting the end.

Wilfred's mouth opened to scream, but again, a torrent of blinding color erupted around him and swallowed him whole.

CHAPTER 21

*T*here was no door nor portcullis nor gate – only open, un-
dulating, organic forms welcoming all visitors, beckoning them onward, inviting them into the nurturing arms of the
sacred temple. Here, the eye was not drawn upward – the neck
was not craned towards heaven to gaze at unreachable heights;
here, among the statuary, would be found no angels or demons
or martyred saints, no chastising monuments to the natural
instincts of the flesh; here, sculpted from warm sandstone, were
effigies of mothers, fathers, children, laborers, field hands, the
poor, the homeless – but no fist pounding the observer into a state
of religious awe, or to the precipice of artistic rapture, or overpowering with impossible majesty. Here, the cumulative effect
was not the diminishment of the visitor nor the condemnation
of human imperfections – rather, one entered the sanctuary
from above and descended down into the protective womb of
the earth, into a great sunken amphitheater that held, at its
center, a pool of crystalline water, fed by seven tranquil streams
radiating outward like spokes in a great wheel – a home of
worship embracing all who sought communion, a cradle of
total acceptance, benevolence, and love. The Cathedral of St.
Margaret of Antioch would be unlike any other.

Alice, now alone, sat staring at the architectural model which had just been accepted by delegates from the archdiocese. At the conclusion of the meeting, after escorting her guests out, she had given her staff the rest of the day off – desiring to meditate over this triumph and the innumerable lessons that seemed to be cascading from it. Three weeks ago, she had been prepared to present a completely antithetical concept to her potential clients: a cruel, towering monstrosity of granite and steel – a terrifying fortress that she had crafted to push all the correct buttons, to flatter all the accepted norms of religious design and which would have easily guaranteed her a place amongst the top tier of firms competing for the commission. Her consummate negotiation skills, she had been sure, would have provided the extra leverage to take her across the finish line.

But, that was before her epiphany. Breaking with Michael, permanently, had scorched her thoroughly; had obliterated decades of dreck coating her psyche – and she had seen that all of it, every part of her concept down to the smallest detail, had been nothing of her own. In a flurry of abandon, she had chucked the entire raft of plans she'd labored over for months, and in a single weekend, in a nearly 48-hour passion, had crafted what now stood before her – a work infused with such truth that it was impossible not to view all that had come before as anything but profane.

Well, thought Ann, scrolling through her manuscript, *that's about as good as I can make it.*

But her assessment of her book drifted – Ann could not stop fixating on her chain of bad choices since arriving in California. The whole point of ending things with Michael had been to stop thinking about him – but now that their relationship was officially over, he weighed on her mind more than ever. And she felt herself coming to another, albeit new, crisis.

To collect herself, she'd spent the whole night re-writing the Alice chapters, changing the ending from her protagonist seeing the truth only at the very end – after the damage had been done – to having the fortitude to preemptively sever things before the worst of it could befall her. And to discover, in that act of her bravery, that she had unlocked the floodgates of her genius. But, like Alice's original concepts for her cathedral, the rewritten chapters smacked of authorial deceit.

Goddammit, why didn't I wait until I got back home?

What she was realizing – and what she would have known had she taken but a moment to consider it all – was that until he was out of her house (while she stood half a continent away), until he was gone, she would be unnerved by the infinite opportunities he had to screw her over – as small a chance as that might be; he had, after all, never shown himself to be *vindictive.* However, what was done was done – and her thoughts, as usual, went where they would, agitating with a mob mentality and elbowing aside anything not promoting Michael's potential mischief.

I'm a fraud. How can I write about the answer if I don't know it myself?

Maybe, she thought, she should be grateful – because the moment she stopped panicking over her ex-lover, even more profound and disturbing questions erupted. What good were independent actions if, psychologically, she remained a prisoner? And what kind of defect allowed her to intellectually grasp what always must be done – but kept her visceral, physical self at odds with those conclusions?

She'd always considered herself unflappable. Always. But over the last year, as she warred with herself in a conflict that was swiftly taking on the appearance of an infinite stalemate, for the first time in her life, she began to imagine something she had previously found incomprehensible – for the first time in her life, in this accelerating spiral, she began to grasp the possibility of succumbing to a breakdown.

But all this, she reminded herself like a mantra, would come to an end when Michael was completely out of her life. And as for the "why" she had so rashly pulled the plug on him – to really get down to it, she knew all too well his power over her when, in person, he wanted her forgiveness, how quickly he could make her forget all this stupid agonizing. She needed time to brace herself.

Because she refused to ever forget what she had learned.

No. The chapters would have to be rewritten. Again. Maybe the answer is we're all trapped – and impossibly so. Until Ann had a better answer, Alice was not going to be spared anything her creator herself was finding impossible to avoid.

"You're a million miles away."

"Sorry," she said, looking up from her dinner plate and back into the eyes of Thomas Naidoo. "It's not the miles you're seeing, it's the cargo."

"Talk to me. I want to know."

"I'm not sure I know where to start," she said.

The restaurant had been *his* idea – and that his wife would *not* be joining them, was his wife's: *Mrs.* Naidoo had had a last-minute demand from her company to fly to Houston. And, once again, despite every reason to the contrary, despite what would put her *right back* into a romantic situation that was impossible from the start, Ann had decided to go ahead and meet him.

"Just thinking of all the problems, really," she added, then smiled, "the usual."

"You're here. Possibly for a few more weeks," Thomas said. "Is there anything wrong with us getting to know each other?"

"All kinds of things. You're married, for one."

"Yes. That's true."

"Well, there you have it."

"I don't know what's going to happen with Marcia and myself," he said after a pause, and with a look and tone that suggested he was trying to be as fair as possible. "We're no longer sleeping with each other. If that makes a difference."

"A little. I guess," said Ann. "But the larger picture is me starting something that can't be anything more than a quick fling. I don't think I want that."

"Where does it say this has to be quick or a fling? All kinds of things can happen, Ann. Isn't it enough that we're two people who've met and, even more miraculous, are attracted to each other?"

"I didn't realize that we'd established that."

"Established what?"

"That we're attracted to each other."

"Ann," Thomas said, with that smile of his and a wave of sensitivity playing across his brow, "why would we both be here if that were not true?"

Ann gave a "Who knows?" look accompanied by a slightly comedic shrug of her shoulders and then, as an excuse for not technically answering, speared a piece of steak with her fork and thrust it into her mouth.

"This will either work out, or it won't," he continued. "Why not find out?"

Now it was time for Ann to answer. It was time to push. If this was, indeed, to go anywhere, he'd have to show he was not afraid of scrutiny. "Have you ever stopped to consider that some people can't be so casual as that? Maybe I can't start something with someone I like, and then turn it off and say 'oh, well' – did you ever think about that?"

Thomas sat silently for a minute, then leaned forward, putting his chin in the palm of his hand, his head slightly tilting to one side. "Why do you believe that if we start something and it ends, that you are the only one who would be hurt?"

"Well...you're so..."

"It's because I know very well I would be hurt – that I know it will be worth trying."

He didn't miss a beat.

"Oh, wow. You *are* good," she said, laughing. "Yeah, that was pretty much a textbook answer."

The waiter approached and took their dessert orders and the conversation moved to far less taxing subjects – more as a respite to allow each of the opponents to review the previous sallies and skirmishes, regather their forces, and mass for the next engagement. Thomas was the first to break the peace.

"You know what your problem is?"

"Trust me, knowing I have problems is one of my few gifts."

"You're gorgeous – and you don't think you are."

Ann pressed her fork into the crust of her cheesecake, slowly smashing it into the plate. "Okay. Now that's hitting below the belt," she said, still looking down at her food and wondering if there was enough room under the table to go at it there and then.

"It's true," he said. "I saw that right away."

"And what about you?" Ann countered, looking back up and steeling herself for this line of attack. "What are all *your* problems? Why don't you tell me what I'm in for?"

"Fair enough," Thomas said. He looked just past her, off to the side, and again, that marvelous way his face had of communicating expressions, entranced her. It was growing increasingly hard to resist how seriously he was taking this time with her. After a moment, he came back, and there was now a sadness surrounding his eyes. "I can be rather cold. People look at what I do, they see me with those children and say how warm and loving I am. But, much of that is merely compassion for suffering in general. One-on-one, I can be overly clinical and distant."

"Now this could be where *you're* wrong. You haven't been that way with me. Not at all."

"It's not there all the time," he said with a smile, and fresh levity shone out from his face. "But, you'll see, it's there – and it may hurt you from time to time."

"I think I can deal with a little coldness."

Her last word stuck to her lips and she had to push down rising feelings. The effort brought her to thoughts of Paul and Brenda. They haunted her by floating up to the surface images of how far off the mark she had gone in her own relationships. How little she had been willing to settle for. And, by the way, where were those two now? It had been over a week since Brenda's last bizarre phone call. Where they had gone or what they were doing remained a complete mystery.

She looked up to find Thomas, arms crossed, staring at her.

"Are you done being inside your head?" he said with a suppressed chuckle.

"Oh, god, I'm so sorry," Ann replied, taking off her glasses and rubbing her eyes. "I *am* in my head. And I really need to get out of it. I'm just not sure I know how."

"How about talking to a guy that wants to understand you?"

Ann laughed – and then tried, as best she could (eliminating those details too embarrassing or revealing – which counted for much more than she would have guessed) to explain to Thomas all the quandaries in her life she was attempting to resolve. She talked of her uncle and his estate, her brother, her new book and the mess she'd made of things with Michael, which she hoped would soon be over. What she didn't mention was how Thomas's presence being added to the mix was making everything even more difficult.

As she spoke, she remembered thinking how nice it would be to find a companion who preferred to listen, who had that quality of making her feel at the center of attention, who filled that one gap that persisted. He stared back at her, absorbed, his expressions rippling in response to the subtlest nuances of her story like tall grass in a scudding wind; and Ann began to regret her wish. Now, she wanted to do all the listening. She wanted to sit back, relax into the chair, and have him tell her everything about himself. But as she worked to conclude what she had committed to, she found that another part of her mind began moving along an alternate track.

She recalled to herself a moment at the Aztec Orpheum when her attention had been captured by a little girl, hobbling across the lobby in leg braces. Ann had been gripped with a sickening sense of pity, of all the barriers that awaited that little girl that would have to be overcome – and the ones that she'd never make it over. Thomas had approached the girl just then to help her into the theater – and the way he held the child's hand, the way he looked down at her, and spoke with her, there was no pity at all, just a settled normalcy to their interactions which made you suddenly ask yourself what was so odd about the scene which had made you stare.

Thomas had started talking now, picking up the conversation and Ann wanted to engage, to peer into his past and get lost in the adventure of another life. But the images of the little girl would not let go. Ann seemed to move forward in time, Thomas's voice blurring as if speaking from another room, while she stood witness to the future that lay ahead for that child. She watched as the years passed, no adoption came, and so the girl stayed on at the orphanage, first as an assistant, and then as staff, her great consolation: the wonderful bond that had developed between herself and the man who had showered her with so much kindness. Then, she was a young woman, sitting alone on a bench in the outdoor garden of the Children's Center, and Ann knew why she had been crying. Thomas had arrived that morning with his fiancé and her life was shattered.

At the conclusion of the meal, the vision had left enough residual bitterness, irrational though it was, to allow Ann to diplomatically say goodnight for the evening, to thank Thomas for a delightful dinner, and skirt unequivocally promising to see him again. The walk back to her rental car was slow and leisurely. And, as she was still quite absorbed in a fog of contending anxieties – and not quite ready to scatter them to be picked up later – Ann decided to extend her stroll around the city block.

The high-rises were sparkling to life as each tiny window added its jewel of light to the evening sky. The sense of thousands upon thousands of lives all around her, lives she would never know and who would forever remain ignorant of her, was tranquilizing – and the pressing demand to come to some definitive answers before the night was out began to lift. Soon, a warm insignificance descended over her as she walked below those towers stacked with lives, all those people piled in dizzying heights above her, or walking or driving past, and going about their own private routines, winding down for another day. The last of her worries to leave her had been the various topics of conversation with Thomas, and even those began to evaporate until there remained just one.

Ann stopped in front of the display window of a fashion boutique, closed for the night, and stared at her reflection in a mirror set between two mannequins. She'd always been somewhat disturbed by looking directly into her own eyes in any mirror, the hyper-awareness of her consciousness being reflected directly back tended to be a little too intense. But, this time, she held her ground.

As she looked at herself – and with more forgiveness and liberality than she had in a very long time – she began to wonder if she really were seeing a reflection, wondered if she were not, in fact, actually peering into a cage, and the other, the one who she perceived to be herself, was, in truth, another person, standing on the other side of a glass wall, staring back at her with the exact same questions. At some point, although she did not notice when, a corona of lights appeared in a shimmering halo about her head and she felt as though she might be on the verge of ascending to heaven.

After a moment the vision passed, but not the lights – to which the sound of sirens and an excited crowd was added. Turning to see what she had somehow failed to notice was happening behind her and causing those lights, Ann saw, down the street, that a mob of people had gathered, cameras flashing and popping – and with police working among them to wrangle the crowd. Spotlights shot bright rays up onto the side of an office building – and, following those beams and the raised faces upward, Ann was stopped cold at the sight of a man, suspended half way up that gleaming wall, preparing to jump.

CHAPTER 22

It would be suicide to start drinking again – which was why Jeff was being so careful with how much he was having each morning. But this was not the hard, out of control, problematic drinking of panic. He wasn't Dirk, after all. He knew the signs of that and could guard against it. No, this was just the calming drinking of a man managing the normal, immense pressures of a typical film shoot. For the past three weeks, Jeff and his cast and his crew had been well under way with his production of *Summer of the Rainbows* and, without a doubt, things could not have been better. But, the time for evaluating the project as a whole was well past. As any seasoned filmmaker will tell you, the process of actually shooting a picture is all about the details.

At the start, of course, the broad brush-strokes of a film are laid out, the script weighed in its totality, the major themes and beats approved, and an overarching picture of the final product is shared by all. But then, those bird's eye views are all disassembled, quartered, dissected, and the project broken down into its constituent parts – and director, cast, and crew are all dropped right into the heart of a jungle. Deep into the chaos of infinite possibilities, the team must then find its way back home – and simply trust that the maps that had been carefully drawn are accurate and to scale. Everything, at this point in the process, becomes the purview of the microscope. Every decision a minute one, and the journey: a seemingly endless matter of stringing one tiny choice onto the next.

This immutable fact of the job had rattled Jeff on his first couple of productions – this blind stumbling towards the goal – until he began studying the life and career of Torben Pitts, maverick director of the previous generation, and gleaned one very important piece of advice. Pitts had exploded onto the scene in his early twenties and conquered Hollywood with his first film, *An Ocean of Eyes*, now widely regarded as one of the greatest movies ever made. His reign was short-lived, however, as his bad-boy exploits and refusal to conform to conventional narrative techniques alienated him from executives and the public at large. Yet, his subsequent career as a film-gypsy of sorts, traveling Europe and self-financing his own low-budget projects, in many ways garnered him an equal measure of acclaim. Not the least of which was his ability to improvise his way through the countless obstacles that his constant need for cash and on-the-fly film shoots naturally precipitated.

The most infamous example of Torben's creative genius occurred while pulling duty as a director-for-hire on a French-Iranian co-production of *Gulliver on the Moon*. After being informed that half his acting company (including his two leads) had been lost at sea while journeying to their remote island location, Torben, ever mindful of his inflexible shooting schedule, rewrote the final climactic scene for those handful of extras that were available. The result, still considered a watershed of avant garde cinema, stunned audiences with its audacity and innovation. It was a lesson that had lodged itself deep within Jeff's brain. No complication could ever arise without Jeff quoting Torben's famous motto, "If you're given a fish, don't start building a birdcage." And since absorbing this essential truth, Jeff had yet to allow any hurdle of any production to break his stride – thankfully (knock on wood), on this particular shoot so far – until this morning, that is – he had not had the occasion to employ the saying in thought or word or deed.

And this morning, in the grand tradition of the great Torbin Pitts, he would remove a particular obstacle which had suddenly occurred, with total and complete precision. There would be no birdcages on *his* watch.

But before he could deal with his big problems, all the others needed to be brought to heel, if not eliminated. The vodka shots had finally kicked in and accomplished their first job: the minor problems that accost even the most well-oiled production were blurring into the background and Jeff could, in preparation for battle, focus on those key foundational elements which, so long as he maintained their integrity, would weather any storm and ensure the film's success.

Without question, the central unifying force, the keel which was keeping everything else aligned and afloat, was his star-performer Stephanie Strane. With everyone else on the production team now focused on their individual duties, it was understandable that there was less attention being paid to the phenomenal performance he was capturing on film: her scenes with Marilyn Dunne were electric. And if Stephanie pushed some professional boundaries by having a more relaxed view of her call times or as to what qualifies as being memorized for the day's shoot, that could all be chalked up to an up-and-coming, commanding actress feeling her oats. Jeff took it all in stride. Even the dustup between Stephanie and the costume designer – Jeff had to reluctantly admit – had filled him with a sense of admiration for her brashness.

It was, however, that brashness that had created a second job for those vodka shots which, it turned out, had not been quite up to the task. Not yet smoothed over, there still remained a stubborn, minor little difficulty that was giving Jeff pause: Stephanie had stopped by his place last night, unannounced, and they had slept together.

She had definitely been the aggressor – it was only a matter of minutes before she had dropped the subterfuge of wanting to return his insulated coffee mug and had him up against a wall. But had he pushed his advantage too far? He'd had feelings for her from the start and she had seemed to reciprocate – but, now, she'd not said a word to him all day, and he couldn't help wondering if it had been nothing more than a game of conquest on her part. Now that she'd landed him, would she move on to other challenges – or would she test how far his sense of obligation would go?

He had tried to get their evening together out of his mind, but he was still vibrating with the magnitude of the experience. Yes, she was gorgeous. Yes, she was charming. All the usual temptations had been in abundance – but no more so than with any of the other sexually provocative starlets, ubiquitous in his social and professional circles. Being immune to the more reckless male responses that felled so many in his position he'd always considered one of his salutary gifts: he'd yet to meet the woman who had ever gotten the upper hand with him. But from the minute she'd pounced, merging her mouth with his, it was as if she had been explicitly tutored to gratify his most deviant appetites.

Hours later, as they lay coiled about each other, still damp, she'd confessed to a bit of embarrassment at how much she'd revealed of herself.

"Sorry if I got a little too filthy," she had whispered with her head to his chest. "I have an inner demon that certain guys can bring out."

"Not at all," he had said, laughing, and trying not to sound utterly ready to worship at the altar of her inner demon. "No problem with that at all."

"I need someone like you. Someone as hungry as I am."

It was a foregone conclusion that even under the best of circumstances nothing good could come of it. Except that Jeff could not stop thinking about those best of circumstances and so was finding himself hoping that she'd been serious. It was farcical. All he wanted was for her to swear that everything she'd said was sincere – and that she'd take her chances with him.

No.

He'd been an idiot to let it happen in the first place and any kind of relationship with the star of the picture was out of the question. It could only and invariably lead to dangerous distractions, when what he needed most was to maintain the concentration and discipline he'd battled so mightily over those first early days of the production to achieve. Yes, best to stand back, give Stephanie her space, and allow her the freedom to make whatever moves she wished – but to clearly communicate that his job as director came first. Any romantic involvement would not be practicable until filming had wrapped. There was too much riding on his piloting this production through treacherous straits.

Finally, with this minor emergency mapped out, Jeff was primed to fulfill his ultimate obligation: tackling the shit-storm which he now faced.

"I want to thank everyone for coming," Jeff finally said, his thoughts now collected and after allowing the last of the cast and crew to gather on the soundstage. He needed to eliminate all unnecessary distractions – and was, in fact, relieved to see that Stephanie had not yet arrived.

"I'm sure by now you've heard about Marilyn. But I wanted to put you all at ease: I've just spoken with her personally. She's doing just fine and she has every intention of returning to work tomorrow, assuming her doctors approve, which she assures me they will."

A round of applause and sighs of relief broke from the assembly and Jeff raised his hand to continue. "I know this has been a difficult shoot. We're having to move much faster than we would prefer. But that's not the cards we've been dealt. To paraphrase the great Torben Pitts, 'we've been given a fish.' And in that spirit, while we await the return of our beloved Marilyn Dunne, in order to avoid 'building a birdcage' – and losing precious time – we're going to break for an hour, give our amazing camera crew time to re-light for the trailer park scenes, and resume shooting from page fifty-three."

There was a second round of applause and Jeff's interpersonal thermometer, which had not failed him yet, indicated that the majority were satisfied with his explanation. After telling his First AD to buzz him once the camera crew was ready, Jeff returned to his office to strategize on the pages of the script he'd not anticipated needing to have prepared until next week. And, although another quick shot of vodka wasn't necessary, Jeff had performed admirably enough that a small reward was acceptable. After collapsing into his chair, Jeff was struck with a new thought and grabbed the receiver of his desk phone and dialed the Marketing team.

"Katie, is Diane in her office?"

"I'm sorry Mr. Tanner, she's stepped out for a bit. Can I take a message?"

"Yeah, tell her I want to go over the promotional material again. Have her find out how small we can make Marilyn's name without breaking the contract."

"Yes, Mr. Tanner."

Jeff leaned back and wondered out loud where the fuck Diane had been lately, and withdrew his flask from a desk drawer. Turning it over in his hands, he considered how he was already referring to it as "his" flask. They'd still not returned it to Dirk – but then, again, how could they? They still had no idea where he had gone to. What's more, Jeff's previous certainty about Dirk returning unharmed had begun to wane, just as Diane had seemed to be becoming more adamant that he was alive and well. Regardless, they needed to have a chat. Something was distracting her – and Jeff needed Diane fully present now more than ever.

"Christ on a clit, Jeff!" Murch's voice suddenly boomed as he barged through Jeff's office door. "What the fuck is going on?!"

"Would you mind knocking once in a while, please?"

"I just got a call that Marilyn Dunne is having her stomach pumped!"

"It's not what you think," Jeff said, standing up and crossing to his bar cabinet. "She didn't have her contacts in and thought her sleeping pills were aspirin."

"Well bitch me with a bowling ball! How are we going to explain that to the insurance company?!"

"Calm down. Everything is under control," Jeff said soothingly, taking a final swig from his flask and refilling it from the decanter. "I already talked to Allen, they're willing to give us a pass this time. They know Marilyn gets her stomach pumped like most people get haircuts. I put her on the line with him and she promised she'll be back tomorrow."

"You sure about that?"

"We spoke right after they'd cleaned her out. She sounded fine."

Murch scoffed at Jeff's confidence with an unintelligible growl and lumbered over to the bar. "Well, if she fucks up your timetable, don't come slappin' *my* ball sack – we got a hard start for *Crash Kings*."

"Yes, Murch, I know," Jeff said, easing back into his chair and trying to think of the nicest way to tell Murch to get the fuck out.

"Well, I'm just sayin'. We've put up with enough finger-fuckery on this picture as it is."

"What are you talking about?" Jeff said, now giving full reign to his annoyance.

Murch, thrown by a perplexity on exactly where to start, did not have time to even begin.

"Jeff!" Stephanie's voice interrupted as she swept into the office – tears streaking her face and stopping Murch from letting go with a complete cataloging of the exact kinds of fuckery he was referring to, Stephanie being linked to most of them.

"I need to talk to you. *Alone*," she said, refusing to acknowledge Murch's presence – or his disdainful eye-roll which he had now permanently substituted for any kind of verbal communication with her.

"Hard start!" Murch reminded Jeff on his way out with his drink. "And keep your bitches in line!"

"Oh!" Stephanie fumed as the door slammed shut. "How do you put up with that?"

"Drinking helps. Would you like one?"

"No, no. Don't get up. I'll get it," she said, stepping over to the bar and wiping her face. This was not the turn of events Jeff had been expecting. Her request to talk privately narrowed the possibilities down to two options: an honest desire to move forward with a relationship, or some kind of pretense. He did not, just then, particularly want to delve into open negotiations over what each of them wanted, but he could recognize that putting it off was only going to aggravate the tension between them.

"How are you feeling?" he said after a moment. "I've been meaning to talk to you – sorry, it's been a crazy day." He didn't expect her to believe any of that, but she would be perceptive enough to know that he was at least aware that he'd neglected certain gentlemanly responsibilities. That would, he hoped, be enough of a balm to placate her, at least for now, into accepting the need to wait until the end of production to resume their relationship – if that was, in fact, what she wanted.

But, if she had a less admirable goal in mind, if there was going to be any kind of play on her part, she'd make it in the next few moments. Jeff hated feeling this way towards Stephanie – hated suspecting the possibility of disingenuousness. And she seemed so vulnerable just then, across the room, carefully focusing on pouring out a drink but clearly distraught and exposing herself as much more of the sensitive outsider – and much less the tough-as-nails newcomer – than anyone could guess.

But this too would have to wait – following a second interruption:

"Sorry to bother you, Mr. Tanner!" intruded a voice accompanied by a staccato of raps on the office door.

"Only if it's a real emergency, Scotty!" said Jeff, with a look of apology directed at Stephanie who sighed and nodded her understanding. The eyes and nose of Jeff's First AD poked its way into the room.

"Marilyn's agent just called," Scotty said matter-of-factly. "He said she's approved to return tomorrow but she'll be bringing a wheelchair. We need to accommodate that."

"Okay. So? What's the emergency?"

"Um, she's *confined* to it. Including on set."

"You're fucking kidding me."

"No. It's the only way the insurance company would approve her return."

"But the big scene, with her running through the cornfields – it's the emotional climax! I can't have her do that in a fucking wheelchair!"

"I'm sorry, Jeff. I'm just the messenger."

"I can't fucking believe this."

Scotty threw up his hands in empathy with the situation, and, understanding he'd interrupted an equally important conversation, bowed out, closing the door quietly.

"Maybe we should talk later," Stephanie said, her tone free of any frustration with Jeff and clearly wanting him to understand if he needed some immediate time alone.

"No, no...stay. I'll figure something out. I always do," Jeff said with that "Torbin resolve" he'd learned to quickly employ when juggling multiple crises. "This is more important."

Stephanie smiled, took a drink, a deep breath, and the necessary moment to collect her thoughts. "I've been on edge all day, wondering if you were going to say anything," she said finally, making her way to the two club chairs facing his desk and having a seat. "I wanted you to know that I'm not expecting anything. I know you're under a lot of pressure and I'm not here to add to that."

"You're not adding to any pressure, Steph."

"Please. I know what people think of me," she said, staring down at her glass and, for the first time, appearing to be on the brink of floundering. "I can be a real bitch. Murch is right."

"No, Steph. Murch is an asshole. He's–"

"Jeff, please," she said, cutting him off. "Let me say what I have to say."

He nodded silently, completely disarmed by this new side of her that he had not known existed. Since her first audition, she'd exuded a total surety and command – had never once given the impression she was out of her element in any situation. But now, she was communicating with him on an entirely new level of honesty – which he was finding hard to resist. If this was a performance, she was manipulating it with a virtuosity beyond anything she'd previously demonstrated.

"I don't sleep with just anybody," she said after a moment. "And when I do, it's not meaningless. I like you. And I'm not going to apologize for that. But I get that now's not the ideal time to start anything. Still, I wanted you to know that, when this is all over, if you want to pick things up, I'd be happy to. I'll leave it up to you."

"Of course, Steph," Jeff said. "Of course I want to."

"Yeah?" she asked, now hazarding a look of relief.

"Yeah," he said.

"Okay. And I hope until then we can still be friends. Because I think I need one." She gave him something of a broken smile, letting him know that the comment had been cast off casually – with perhaps a bit of melodrama, but with nothing more implied than a parting endearment. He returned her gaze, unabashedly. She'd opened herself up to him in a way that left her utterly at his mercy. And, he wanted at that moment, more than at any other, to reach out and commit to her. She was the woman he thought she was – possessed of charismatic super-powers, but not so under the thrall of her own abilities as to allow them to overtake her. She had let Jeff know she was aware of the mask she wore with others, and that she was willing to remove it for him – exposing the real woman beneath it, beset by as many insecurities as any mortal, as scared and needy as the next, and unaccountably more beautiful because of them. She was radiant.

And Jeff wanted her. God, falling into her arms each night might be the thing he'd not known he'd needed all along.

In a rush, Jeff realized how close to the edge he had suddenly come – how close to breaking his pledge of keeping things platonic between them he now stood – and he took a clear step back. In the span of a breath, he was saved. Did Stephanie's look just then betray she was privy to his abrupt internal reversal? It had been but a fraction of a second and he was certain he'd maintained his outward composure – but her demeanor flickered subtly.

She rose to leave, imparting one last tremulous smile, and Jeff wondered if he had misread her. Then, as she moved to set her drink down, a subtle tremor took hold of her hand, the glass rattled against the desktop, and she fell back into her chair; her mouth open in a convulsion of thwarted speech – an attempt which was immediately aborted as she cast her face down into her hands and began sobbing.

"I'm so sorry," she wrenched out through the tears. "I honestly didn't want to do this."

Without thinking, Jeff was at her side, calming her, taking her hands into his own.

"I didn't mean to put you on the spot," she went on, still shaken. "You've done everything for me. I just want to make you proud."

"You *are* making me proud. I couldn't be prouder of the work you're doing."

"No. I didn't realize until today, until I heard about Marilyn, how much I was relying on her to get me through this," she said, taking a tissue from Jeff and drying her eyes. "And, actually, how much we're relying on each other."

"What do you mean?"

"I should have said something sooner," she said, calming a bit as though transitioning to matters outside of her present, selfish concerns. "I could tell she was unsteady. Jeff, she's so terrified that this may be her last picture. She hasn't said it in so many words, but I know she's worried herself sick about her big monologue in act three. We've tried going over it in her trailer – but it's overwhelming her."

"What do you mean?" Jeff asked again, starting to sense where this might be headed. "Exactly how overwhelmed is she feeling?"

"I'm only saying that she'll never ask it of you – but if you could cut the speech down, you'd be taking the world off her shoulders."

"Well, what do you think I should do?"

"I'm only saying I'm worried about her, Jeff," and the tears flowed once more.

Had she stopped right there, had she kept her finger strictly on this singular point, on the issue of Marilyn's well-being and Jeff's obvious concerns about its impact on the production, it's entirely possible – given the frustratingly constricted schedule and Jeff's definite pique over Marilyn's unstable antics – that he would have succumbed to the desperate logic of Stephanie's suggestion and, quite on his own, developed counter-measures even more favorable than any that might be hoped for by his ingénue; but some kind of deeper logic led him to cautiously add, without knowing exactly why, "But that speech is the heart of the film. It's the show-stopper. We can't cut it out of the movie."

"Well, I...I mean, it's not a perfect solution," she replied, her words proceeding with the precision of a surgeon. "Of course, the lines *could* be easily switched to Susanne or Janet...or Carol Beth. That's your call, naturally."

And there it was. The play that Jeff had dreaded. And it had been far bolder than he had suspected Stephanie would have been comfortable attempting. The exposed stratagem confronted Jeff with a whole new array of complications. If he were to acknowledge his awareness of her duplicity, or, stopping short of that, simply deny her request, there was every reason to believe she was capable of employing a new, more sophisticated, and vastly more covert scheme – or worse, outright sabotage – to get whatever it was she ultimately wanted. Too much was riding on Stephanie feeling positively about him and the picture. Too much lay vulnerable, especially on a timetable with no room for error.

But a plot exposed is a plot derailed. Better to assuage any fears she might have of her plans being compromised. Better to soothe and placate and allow her to operate under secret observation than risk losing his vantage point. He'd capitulate for now and give her what she wanted.

"Five minutes, Mr. Tanner!" the voice of Scotty called from just outside the door. "Thank you!" Jeff called back, keeping his eyes on Stephanie, then turned away for a moment, allowing her to wonder at his next move.

"I think you're right," he finally said, after appearing to wrestle appropriately with the decision. "To be honest, I've noticed her struggling as well. And, after today, I think it's safe to say those fears are well-founded. And I appreciate you recommending the cousins, but those lines really are best suited to Carol Beth."

If Stephanie was on to him, she gave no indication. She leaned in and pressed her lips to his. There were, it was clear, going to be obvious advantages to participating in Stephanie's charade – and Jeff was capable of countermeasures equally as devious as those that had ensnared him. It was time for him to be a shit as well: "Why don't you come over tonight and we can figure out how to make this work?"

"I think that sounds wonderful," she said, getting up from the chair while reminding him that his crew was waiting – and then tossing back a final alluring glance on her way out the door. It was only at the very last that he noticed she was wearing her hair dangerously close to a side ponytail.

CHAPTER 23

Wilfred Weiner was soaring. Far below, in a scene cut straight from his favorite film, an ocean of eyes looked up at him in wonder and excitement. He was the cynosure of the world – for he had revealed to them *everything*.

It had taken a lifetime, but now that his soul was clean, he finally knew, really *knew*, exactly what he wanted. And he was not afraid. When this was all over...he would *dance!*

"There is no evil but what we allow!" he called out to them, his voice booming through an oversized bullhorn. "WE are the evil we resist – and WE prevent the good that we claim to seek!" The crowd roared their approval, their shouts and fists pumping in solidarity – and Wilfred beamed with vindication. Now that he had freed himself from his crimes, now that he had confessed to them, joyfully, he could share his liberation with the world – and, most glorious of all: to dance as he once had! The weight that had been lifted made him feel superhuman – and he was certain that he could leap straight up into the stars themselves.

All this he saw, and felt, and more. He did not, however, see the woman rushing to join those tiny figures gathered on the street below, but she certainly saw *him*.

Ann had finally reached the edge of the mob, and, pushing her way through the excited spectators, managed to squeeze her way to the front of the police cordon. There, high above, a man – whom she did not recognize – suspended and swaying by a slender rope against the glass wall of a skyrise, was shouting down to the hundreds that now filled the street. At first, she had the sickening thought that they were cheering him on, screaming for him to commit to his apparent course of action and jump – but they were not. Strange to behold, they seemed to be actually listening to him.

For this was no suicide attempt – but rather a man preaching his truth to the world.

"Your cowardice is your chains! Your courage is your salvation!" the man commanded, his amplified voice ricocheting off the surrounding high-rises. Before Ann could discover exactly why someone would choose to hang off the side of an office building to advocate for *anything*, a commotion of scuffling feet, entangled bodies, and shouting burst from the front entrance beyond the barricades. A woman, dressed sharply in a tailored business suit and heels – clearly in a rage – hand-cuffed and in the grip of four policemen, was being forcibly escorted towards a waiting squad car.

"Don't be frightened, dearest!" came the voice from above. "Soon, you'll be purified! Just as I have!" The hands of a strangler could not have twisted the woman's face more swiftly skyward.

"Wilfred! You mother-fucker!" she screamed up at him. "I'm telling them everything! EVERYTHING!!"

"Yes, my darling! Exactly! Hold nothing back!" he called down, his face aglow with benevolence. "Only the truth, pure and unfettered, will save us from the Worm!"

"The Worm! The Worm!" the crowd shouted in response,

"It is the Worm that keeps us from the true path! For only in truth can the performance of life – can the art of the soul – ever soar!"

Again the crowd cheered, their fervor startling Ann who looked about herself – and was stunned to feel, without any rational reason, that the strangers about her had not gathered by accident and that many of them knew each other. And then, as Wilfred began rhapsodizing over what seemed to be a rather lengthy confession of corporate crimes – while a pair of firemen rappelled downward towards him – Ann's perception of those around her underwent a profound metamorphosis: in the way that one might walk right past a parent or close friend while visiting a foreign city – for the simple reason that the mind cannot, at first, bridge the incongruity, cannot accept that there might be anyone recognizable – Ann suddenly became aware of costumed characters scattered among the bystanders.

There, by the woman in the overcoat, was the Crystal Witch! There, by the man with the dog, was the Green Gecko and Dr. Monocle! All around her were characters straight out of *The Professor and the Groovy Gang* – and there could be no doubt that these were the very people who had attended the memorial. No sooner had she arrived at this conclusion than she spotted, at the far end of the crowd, a man dressed as Professor Puck – standing higher than the rest on the pedestal of a lamppost. And, while she could only make generalized assertions about the others, she had, without a doubt, met *him* before. It was the selfsame man her brother had brought to the Aztec Orpheum. The one who had been stumblingly drunk: his friend Dirk.

This shock was followed immediately by a thunderclap of recognition: Brenda and Paul were there! Just below Dirk, and dressed as Lucy and Stuey, they stood looking up with all the others, shouting out in solidarity. Desperately, she began working her way towards them. But as she pushed through the crowd towards the opposite end of the nearly block-long gathering, there seemed to be a greater density of cos players – congregating, as if by magnetism, about the man on the lamppost. With a fist held high, he began leading a new shout of "The truth shall prevail!" – and Ann's effort to approach Brenda and Paul was quickly frustrated as more and more joined in the chant, their enthusiasm and lurching arms retarding her progress, which was then brought to a complete halt by the exiting cop car carrying the hand-cuffed woman.

The car bisected the crowd and pressed Ann backwards while threatening to block her view. In that instant, while still in her sights – and then just barely through the tinted windows of the vehicle as it rolled past – she lost sight of her two young friends. By the time the car had gone and the breach in the gathering had been sealed, they, along with Professor Puck, were nowhere to be found.

The drive back to her hotel was a mockery of Ann's original intent to go for a calming stroll. Again, what predominated was the sense of an invisible thread, winding and wending its way through every one of her impossible dilemmas – and, ever so slowly, being pulled and tightened about herself. But where it was attached or where she should cut herself free were equally confounding – who was to say that it was not the thread itself that was actually maintaining the integrity of the whole? If her mind had been whirling before, the evening's strange turn of events were nothing but a cosmic hand reaching out to spin it into an ever faster confusion.

The desire to seek out her brother, to confide and consult with him, was stronger than ever – but since their recent reconciliation, the centripetal forces that had brought them together had flung them apart once again. Jeff, she knew, was knee-deep in his film shoot contending with avalanching problems of his own and, at least at present, she had no wish to distract him unnecessarily. Like him, she would have to conquer her demons single-handedly before they met again.

Although Ann's present state of mind was as precarious as a man suspended along the side of a building, the adrenaline of crisis did have its clarifying inverse. The view from the cliff edge brought with it a perspective that extended for miles – and she felt as though she was only now able to evaluate her various quandaries in relation to each other. Obviously, she'd decided to test the waters with Thomas – and although she'd have preferred her superego to have had some say in the matter, the vision of the girl with the leg braces was a warning so appallingly obvious she was ashamed by the unoriginality of her subconscious. Still, it had been her hubristic notions about being able to manage a relationship while keeping her feelings disentangled that had doomed her with Michael. If she chose to move forward with Thomas, she could only do so by accepting that there were no guarantees of avoiding fresh heartbreak.

What she saw most clearly was that if there was any hope at all, she must finalize and sever every last remaining tie with Michael before proceeding any further with Thomas. And that meant returning to Boston immediately. Her efforts to sell her uncle's estate – holding out for a price that she had known from the start was based more on wishful thinking than anything – had been, at its core, nothing but an elaborate tactic to put off dealing with Jill and her book and Michael. It was time to cut the string and get the hell out of here.

Tomorrow, she would call her real estate agents, tell them to accept the last offer that had been rejected, and take the earliest flight home. Once her life was back in order, she'd re-connect with Thomas and, if he (and she) were still interested, she'd return. But tonight, she would finalize the new Alice chapters. The reappearance of Brenda and Paul – however ephemeral – was pulling her away from the precipice, and was guiding her feet back to solid earth. As she parked her car and strolled up to the hotel, she felt certainties returning. She felt as though she was reaching the end of the wending string and, through her work, by hammering against the anvil of her art, she could craft a final statement on the choices and consequences of her lead character and herself – and there would be no more compromises, whether Jill accepted her revisions or not.

Just as she had begun adjusting to these new bearings, as her plan for how best to proceed was taking form and as that calm that always preceded any intention to write began enveloping her, there, standing in the middle of the hotel lobby, all the way from Boston, was Michael.

CHAPTER 24

"Carol Beth!" entreated the mother, "Now that I'm feelin' so poorly and stuck in this here wheelchair, I can't be chasin' after you like I used to."

"I know that, mama," Carol Beth answered, holding herself and leaning against the window pane, ribbons of sunlight bathing her in a golden haze. "That's why I ran through the cornfield by myself – I guess I hoped against hope that somehow, some way, I'd hear your footsteps, and see you up and walkin' again."

"Sweet pea!" replied the other, eyes wet and raw, "Don't you know, in my *mind* I was there. Right behind you!"

"Oh, mama! I knew it! I lied just now – I could sense you chasing after me in my mind too!"

Carol Beth rushed to her mother's side and, mother and daughter, pausing only for a moment to acknowledge the years of heartache and betrayal that had finally been broached, fell into each other's arms.

Jeff held back from calling out "cut."

Shaking in his director's chair, he was bent on suspending the tension as long as possible.

Surely they had all seen it. Surely they could now feel the epochal, career-defining wallop his two leads had just delivered. But the crew could wait. Let each of them reflect on how wrong they had all been – let them consider carefully if they still had the courage to turn away from him and the masterpiece he was consumed with delivering.

He had not wanted to believe it, but it was becoming increasingly difficult to deny that a scourge of disloyalty was infecting his entire team – and as he waited, seconds swelling one upon the next, he braced himself for confirmation of this betrayal. But let them wait. Was a moment's deferment too much to ask before confronting the truth?

Crews like his, those who worked as a family from one project to the next, invariably developed a complex code of communication to facilitate the smooth and efficient daily operation of a film shoot – a network which, once established, had the unfortunate complication of conveying appraisals both unstintingly generous and mercilessly honest towards the project at hand. Not openly, of course. No, this was a milieu of almost quantum-level subtleties, but no less clear – when delivered – than a music hall mob's riotous applause or flinging of rotten fruit.

That the time for a final judgment had arrived was beyond question. They'd already used up an entire day attempting every permutation possible – and, so far, his rewrite of the emotional climax of the film – to accommodate Marilyn's wheel-chair which was only her latest contribution to his growing list of impossible hurdles – in take after take, had been met with the most devastating reaction: total silence. And so he'd pushed.

He'd pushed his actresses to the limits of their abilities, shooting and reshooting, squeezing with nothing but the naked force of his will to achieve what they had just done: transform his written words into art. Undeniable art. Which meant anything less than clear and unequivocal approval from those on set could only mean one thing: *intentional* rejection. And, if that was the case, if his crew should willfully withhold their support, then some outside force had gained control – and he would be all but alone. Stephanie, in the greatest of ironies, would be his sole ally.

It had been weeks since that first explosive night at his house and that awkward next day avoiding each other on the set. But as his troubles had mounted, despite everyone's advice to the contrary, Jeff's instinct to forge an alliance with Stephanie had been astute – her commitment and passion for the picture had actually been the one thing keeping his head above water. He'd been totally wrong about her – and looked back with embarrassment at his suspicions and attempts at subterfuge. In fact, things had progressed so quickly that it was becoming difficult to remember exactly when they had recognized their feelings for each other, when they had realized this was more than just another on-set affair. In that timeless sense of existence which the business of making a film occupies, it now seemed as though they had always been together. Not that there still weren't areas of friction.

"You know who's doing this to you, don't you?" she had said, charging through the living room in search of her cigarettes.

"No. No, I don't know," he had answered from the sofa, already resigned to its failure as a total lie.

"Goddamn Murch – that's who! And you know it. Don't tell me you don't feel the same way. You're – you're totally different!"

Finding her pack amidst the bottles on the bar, she seemed to think better of lighting up, eyed Jeff quizzically, then changed course by setting out two glasses and starting to fix cocktails – then continued: "There's all *kinds* of places you could go without him."

"I know the two of you don't get along," Jeff tried to answer her, "but I wouldn't be half as successful if he hadn't been there."

"Wrong. Maybe that was true at one time – but not anymore. He's holding you down! Not to mention he's one of the foulest men I've ever met."

She came to him with the freshly mixed drinks, sidling into his lap, and wrapping her arms about him. "It's the seasons of life," she said gently. "Striking out on your own, cutting yourself loose from him doesn't diminish anything that's come before. But you have to move on. And let's be honest, I know you've had these thoughts."

Jeff all but inhaled his drink and immediately remembered that he had promised himself to cut back on alcohol before noon. But this was important. He needed a clear head – and uprooting himself from his routine this close to the end of production was too dangerous.

"Yes," Jeff admitted, "I've thought about it. A lot lately...actually."

"Listen, I know that now is not the right time. You've got to finish this picture – and, oh, Jeff," she purred, hungrily digging her fingers into him, "you've got a real tiger by the tail with this one. It's going to take you to the next level. It's going to take you to the top."

Jeff laughed, but only because those had been roughly his exact words to himself.

"But you gotta hold on," she said, seeming to understand those doubts contiguous with this level of boldness. "You gotta fight this out – and stick to your truth."

"Easier said than done," Jeff said, sighing with exhaustion and thinking of all the conflicts that awaited resolution: Marilyn Dunne was back on set, but the insurance company mandate that she remain in her wheelchair had upturned nearly every scene; Murch was on the warpath demanding more and more cuts to the *Rainbows* budget due to swelling problems on *Car Crash Kings*; and worse, the sense of community so vital to a superior final product was leeching out of his staff by the day. Somehow, not a single one of them had the capacity to remember that when the chips are down *that* is when the greatest responsibility to the team is called for. Even Diane, he was beginning to suspect, had abandoned him. It had started with their clash over Dirk.

"Have you seen this?!?" she had said, flying into his office unannounced and waving a newspaper in her hand. "It's absolutely incredible!"

Under normal circumstances, Jeff would have swept aside his work, invited Diane to have a seat, come around from behind his desk, and indulged her in whatever kind of lively (and, quite often, hilarious) discourse she had in mind – and been grateful for the interruption and the chance to decompress.

But today, her entrance was an obnoxious jolt that reawak-ened a festering point Jeff had labored to ignore. That complex, interconnected network of signs and signals oscillating at light speeds among his cast and crew – and to which Jeff had lately been brought to a heightened awareness – had become a one-way conduit. Frustratingly, the system had kept him acutely attuned to the thoughts and feelings of everyone else, but everyone else, it was clear, had stopped receiving any signals from him. Diane's failure to notice his state of mind brought from him a curt reply to the effect that he was busy.

Undaunted, Diane pressed ahead, aghast at Jeff's dismissive-ness, and slapped the paper down in front of him. There, on the front page, Wilfred Weiner, president of Family Films, Ltd, dangled from a high-rise and was being rescued from an appar-ent suicide attempt by two firemen suspended on either side of him.

"You don't think it's odd that the man who fired Dirk, who was about to run him through a legal grinder, suddenly decides to bungee down the side of a building and confess his crimes to the world?"

"No. I don't."

"You don't see any connection?!" Diane shot back, stunned.

While Jeff had not, in fact, heard about Wilfred Weiner, see-ing the article now brought immediately to mind two recent stories that had piqued his curiosity: noted slum lord Reuben Merle trumpeting his cessation of rent fees, in perpetuity, for all occupants of his East LA tenements – and the strange case of financier and corporate raider Elijah J. Wellington, who had been discovered wandering Santa Monica in the nude throwing

hundred dollar bills to sea gulls. Whether or not these incidents were connected or – even more absurdly – connected
in some way to Dirk, was a question Jeff neither cared to ask
nor could have answered. What was clear was that mentioning
any of this to Diane ran the very real risk of sending her down
god-knows what new rabbit hole.

"Diane – I'm trying to keep together a project that is rapidly
unraveling before my eyes. I don't have time for crazy conspiracy theories. *I* don't have the time – and *you* don't have the
time."

"So that's it? You want me to just ignore something hugely
relevant to a friend that's been missing for months?"

"I'm not asking you to do anything except your job."

The comment could certainly have been worded more delicately – but, it would not be truthful to say that Diane suffering a small jab had not been a part of Jeff's intent or that
he had not found it, after the fact, strangely satisfying. It had,
however, pierced deeper than he had intended and the incident
had not blown over. Two days later, the tension between them
was still in the air.

Diane, standing over the latest unspooled proofs of promo
posters spread out across the conference table, reviewed for Jeff
the work she and her team had prepared – and Jeff found it immediately necessary to suppress a compounding frustration.

"I know this is slightly different than what we discussed," she
had said with a new flatness of delivery, fringed with icy formality
– and absent any care that what she was presenting was blatantly
undermining the vision he had laid out for her. "But, I really feel
the profile shot of Stephanie by itself lacks context. Adding the

silhouette of the mother with the farmhouse pulls it all together. Do you agree or disagree?"

"Well," he had said, lingering on the final consonant, as he tried to keep the rising resentment out of his voice. The effort only further incensed him – knowing that he wouldn't be in the position of trying to keep his cool had Diane simply *done* what he had asked in the first place – "I can see what you are going for but I prefer the original concept."

"Okay," she said blithely, still unaware of Jeff's tightly clenched jaw. "We'll revise and get you the new proofs tomorrow. No problem."

"Except that it *is* a problem," he responded and Diane stopped shuffling the posters and stood up straight to face him – the tone of his voice now unmistakable. "I wanted this done today," he added.

"I'm sorry. I thought you might want to see what the person who manages the marketing for your company had to say."

"Actually, I don't. If you can make the edits we talked about as soon as possible I'd appreciate it."

"No, no," she said with unrestrained sarcasm, crunching up the posters and throwing them in the trash. "I'll keep the team on this until it's finished exactly the way you want it and I'll stay as late as I need to to have it done today. We don't need this to go out for another month, but what difference does that make, right?"

Before Jeff could decide which retort from a number of competing options best balanced his sense of fury with phrasing that he wouldn't have to apologize for later, Diane was off and down the hall. He let her go.

"Everyone has a right to be mad but me!" he thought while distractedly pouring himself another shot. The warmth of it did not so much calm him down as bring the rest of him into equilibrium with the fire in his brain. Of course the changes Diane had suggested made perfect sense! He could see that. But you would think she'd consider for a moment the kind of situation he might be in. You'd think she would consider for a moment that *maybe* he'd already had this argument with someone else. That *maybe* his request to exclusively feature Stephanie's character was a move on his part to appease for one goddamned second yet another demand made on him by an actress that had him by the fucking balls!

No! No! Attacking Steph was just what they wanted! Better to say "an actress whose continued commitment to the role he had come to consider his highest priority!" – that Diane could not be troubled to understand the kind of tightrope he might be walking – and how the slightest resistance from those he counted on threatened to topple his finely calibrated balancing act, or that it might force him into the kind of permanent animosity towards Stephanie that was horrifying to him – that all of this she could fail to grasp spoke volumes about her character. And, in the comparison, volumes about Stephanie – who noticed everything; who understood Jeff's tiniest fluctuations and who had a response mechanism of equal sensitivity. How could he not do everything he could for her? Nothing but petty jealousies – all of it. Good God! She had a right to be imperfect – and he had a right to love her in spite of that! But how could an outsider ever understand the intimate, entangled connections between two people? Who could know the things she gave to him – or the things she absolved him of as he clung to her in the night, his head buried in her arms?

As this torrent of reflections subsided, as his mind was left with the last remnants of his interaction with Diane in his office, and with Stephanie on his living room sofa, he returned to himself: the tension that he had determined to suspend, that second of delay he had demanded of his crew and the two actresses waiting for the scene to end, the whole of it began to stretch beyond sustainability – and the weight of their stares began to oppress.

"Cut!" Jeff finally called out.

Silence.

He had his answer.

CHAPTER 25

T he toilet paper dispenser pressed hard against Ann's spine, pulling her attention away from the voice coming over the phone. Outside the restroom, back at the table, Michael was waiting. Let him wait.

"I take back everything I said about you not returning my calls!" her agent Jill was saying as Ann shifted within the stall, trying to find a more comfortable position while shouldering her cell and, simultaneously, keeping the door slightly ajar to watch for anyone entering. "These new chapters are absolutely brilliant!"

Just my luck, thought Ann. *I've finally got Jill singing my praises – and it's the last thing I want to talk about right now.*

Michael's unexpected arrival in LA had been much more of a blow than Ann would have anticipated. She had not reckoned him being so determined – especially as he had to know it held so few guarantees. After all, she'd been quite clear during the phone call ending their relationship – and, despite his surprise arrival in LA four days later and his appearance in the lobby of her hotel, she had not changed her mind. She had told him flat out – again – that she had meant what she said and sent him away, back to wherever it was he was presumably staying.

But then had come the flowers. And the cards. And the profuse entreaties to meet just one more time and hear him out. For the last two weeks she'd made him sweat – refusing to even acknowledge receipt of his messages. Then, realizing she couldn't run away from her problems – and also acknowledging a sickening resurgence of sympathy which she intended to annihilate – she agreed to meet him at a place of her choosing. To account for those residual areas of weakness, Ann sought the most fortifying location she could think of – and landed on the 14th century religious icon exhibit at the Los Angeles County Museum of Art. Michael had readily agreed.

Now it was her move.

But first, she needed some critical information from Jill. The question was how to get it without revealing more than she needed to.

"Brilliant? Really?" Ann replied finally, still trying to figure out how to segue into what she really wanted to talk about. "I wasn't sure I was moving in the direction you had in mind."

"Are you kidding? This is *exactly* what I was suggesting. You've transformed a character that was utterly devoid of flaws and made her a mess. It's so much more interesting."

"Wait, wait a minute" Ann said, interrupting, drawn into Jill's critique despite herself. "You thought she was flat before?"

"Well, not exactly. Let's say a 'malnourished A-cup' – but now, dear lord, to take a stereotypical feminist hero and reveal that, in reality, she's a doormat for her boyfriend – it's just the extra kick the book needed."

"I wouldn't say she's a *doormat*," Ann offered in meek defense, glad that Jill could not see her face.

"Oh, please. Her boyfriend is so clearly wrong for her, yet she's undone by basic, primitive lust. It's tragically pathetic."

"You don't see her struggle as heroic in any way?"

"God, no!" Jill said with a laugh. "There's nothing heroic about being a simp."

"Don't you think that's a little harsh? I mean, she's fighting the only way that she can –" Ann retorted, then, stopping herself as a small crowd burst through the restroom door, shielded the phone with her hand and continued in an emphatic whisper, "Can't you see? She's on a cliff edge! She's staring into the void – she needs to take what she can get or she'll end up with nothing!"

"Of course you're sympathetic towards her. You have to be. You're the writer," Jill countered, then adding in an exaggerated sotto voce: *"And why are you whispering?"*

"I'm at LACMA doing research. Never mind that."

"Well, doormat or no, I love it. And, by the way, you were clearly thinking of someone specific with all this – please don't tell me who it is. I'm certain it's someone you've introduced me to."

Wincing from the comment – and before falling back onto a defensive quip – Ann had to admit that Jill was not the one crouched in a toilet stall hiding out from her ex-boyfriend.

Less than 30 minutes ago, he had stood in the museum courtyard with yet another bouquet of flowers in his hand. As she had approached him, already mocking his hackneyed effort to soften her up and his useless desire to have a final go at breaking her determination, as she neared that face that could blast her like a gun, she steeled herself to deliver one final refusal, and then found her steps slowing.

She was checked by his expression, one which she had never before seen: he was terrified. He was terrified and making no efforts whatsoever to conceal it.

She had prepared herself for everything but this.

In point of fact, she had reached the museum nearly an hour early, figuring that casing the location would put her at an advantage and keep her from being unnecessarily distracted – and she had made her way through the collection of 14th century icon paintings. If Ann could ever be said to have any kind of faith – or church in which to bare her soul – it would have been the worlds of art and literature. But that morning, as she stepped through the hushed and dim rooms, the pin-lights striking from high above, looking into the eyes of the saints, seeking answers, Ann found only the lifeless dead. The scenes of martyrdom and pain, the triptychs of God and his host smiting Lucifer and his minions – portrayed without perspective in the flattened idiom of the age – acted as impenetrable barriers sealing off whatever insights into the great mysteries they might contain. She left as empty as she had come.

It was with this sense of hopelessness that she had arrived at the museum courtyard where they had agreed to meet – and looked into his face and saw, for the first time, that she was capable of hurting him.

"I know I'm a fuck-up, Ann," he said after they had been seated at the outdoor cafe, his head bowed, unable to look in her eyes.

"There's more than enough blame for both of us," she said. "But this is really senseless. I've made my decision. We're not right for each other."

"What you mean is, *I'm* not right for *you*."

"If you like."

Michael remained silent for a moment, his expression shifting with some kind of internal struggle. Then, looking up, and again, making no effort to cloak a level of anguish and vulnerability she'd never guessed him capable of, he said, "But you haven't been fair to me either."

"Really?" Ann replied, the bravado of his comment finally breaking that rising and unwanted sense of sympathy. "How do you figure that?"

"I know how you see me," he said, again, looking down at his hands, "as a...a plaything."

The nakedness of the assertion caught Ann off guard – and she felt as though she had just been accused of a mortifying crime.

"I know that you think I'm some kind of a Don Juan. That I sleep around behind your back."

"I never said that."

"You don't have to. I see it. Look, it's no secret I'm a flirt, Ann, I admit that. I admit that whole-heartedly. But that's my job. I'm a bartender and I make my living by creating relationships with my customers. If allowing them to think I'd like take them to bed is going to double my tip, so be it. But I swear to you – as soon as we started seeing each other, I was never unfaithful. Not once."

Again, Ann was in turmoil, but this time she felt no compulsion to answer or indicate in any way whether his words
were hitting the mark. It was his responsibility to lay out the
facts of his case and he knew it. He went on: "And I've been
shitty to you. I have no excuses for that. I've taken advantage
of your generosity and I've not been there for you when you
needed me. But, try to understand, Ann, knowing what you
thought of me, seeing how you always kept me at arm's length,
I didn't know what to do except to try to hurt you back."

Michael stopped and suddenly the sounds of the café
around them returned, and they both seemed to acknowledge
that perhaps the timbre of their conversation should be scaled
back. "It's my fault for not expressing my feelings," he said
after a moment, now much calmer – but no less passionate.
"I have to own that. But, goddammit, Ann – you're so closed
off, I was scared to even try."

Now, he was looking straight at her – and it was her turn
to keep her eyes averted. He seemed more desperate than ever
to make a connection, to reach her with his words, and to
stop his voice from breaking: "You've got whatever feelings
you have for me so boxed up I didn't know where to begin.
I guess I thought I had time. I thought we'd work it out. But
Ann, I know you now. This is what you do. I don't know why,
but you think that you don't deserve to be loved – and you
spend your time making sure no one has a chance to prove
you wrong."

His words struck hard and Ann looked up and stared straight
back into him. She was confronting a Michael that seemed whol-
ly reborn – his face was such a portrait of torment that he could

have been displayed alongside the rest of those icons. Try as she might, she found the sight exhilarating.

"If I've substituted sex for love with you," he said with gentleness, "it's only because that's all you would allow. And, if I'm being really honest, I guess I was scared to find out you didn't want any more from me."

Ann continued staring stone-faced, but such was the state of her mind that even had she been possessed of a response brilliantly pitched to the moment, no amount of effort could have pried it from her lips – which remained sealed in panic. She was rapidly approaching a point of catastrophe and could only hope that Michael would stumble as he neared the end of his plea. Accomplished maestro that he was, it had, so far, been delivered to perfection.

"But Ann, if you say things can't work out between us, can you say that they'll be any different with someone else?" he let the question hang fire between them, and then followed it with another: "If you can't answer that, Ann, then doesn't it make all the sense in the world to give me a second chance?" His challenge provided just the proper amount of inertia to set the wheels of Ann's mind moving progressively once again – and she was herself.

Michael had expertly limned the contours of her most shameful inner thoughts and they had instantly transformed from the shadowy into a hard, cumbersome mass. And yet – as much as the accusation pinned her down, there was, suddenly, the possibility of liberation: if, as Michael contended, he was an innocent victim, if all this trauma had simply been in her own head...

Looking at the facts of the case, it was not totally impossible to believe that she was trapped in a cycle of self-sabotage. It's not like she hadn't considered that before. Could they start fresh? But, as alluring as that might be, it would entail effacing a certain number of countervailing facts – certain circumstances and actions she alone was privy to – that even his passionate appeal could never entirely justify or cause her to forget.

The alternative explanation, the one most closely aligned with what she had initially believed about Michael, still nagged: if he were lying, she thought, I'd be saved as well. Because obviously, the only possible reason that, at this crossroad, he could be deceiving her would be on account of her money. But the suspicion that he might *not* be lying was like a tightening noose preventing an easy escape.

Everything would be made so much easier if she could discover that this meeting was simply a plot to ingratiate himself into her inheritance – then all the pieces would fit neatly together again – and, best of all, *none* of the known facts would need to be disregarded. But then, how could he know about her uncle or the fortune he had left her?

Somehow, Ann had seen that it might come to this.

Without any conscious idea why, she had from the very first, kept her entire connection to Uncle Aaron completely secret from Michael. Candidly, it was not something she ever discussed with anyone. Something in the way Uncle Aaron had conducted his life, the way he himself had cared so little for his fame, both she and Jeff – without ever openly discussing it – had always treated this branch of their family tree as a secret meant for themselves alone. But, looking back now, Ann could see that she had been particularly rigorous in preventing Michael from learning of it.

Indeed, she had arranged her trip to California with the discretion of a spy, telling Michael it was nothing more than a long overdue visit to a brother she had not seen in years. Even if Michael had seen the ubiquitous press announcements, none of them – at least none of the ones she had seen – had made any mention of surviving family members. Both she and Jeff had been in complete agreement on that: any and all official statements from Jacob's office were to avoid that subject entirely. Brenda and Paul and their tiny group of organizers had been the first outsiders to whom she had made herself known in years – but even then, all promotional material regarding the event had excluded their names.

There were, she had to concede, a number of ways Michael *could* have uncovered the truth – and one in particular involving the Law Offices of Jacob Pressman and her mail. But she had to act. A guiltless Michael, if he truly was, would not wait around forever.

It was then that Ann knew she had to contact Jill.

At the first opportunity, she had excused herself from Michael and made her way to the women's restroom.

Ever since his failure to show at the Marie de Gournay Lyceum award ceremony, she'd kept from her friends the details of their relationship – and those she did disclose were vague. There were a select few who knew she had been, and continued to be, involved in some kind of way with a partner, but *no one* knew he lived with her. This eliminated many problems, but had obliged

Ann to employ some rather tiring fabrications to maintain the ruse – especially with Jill.

After Michael had called to say he was out of her house – during the immediate aftermath of their breakup – Ann had not been satisfied. Not wanting the added burden of worrying about the integrity of her home while she continued to be tied up with her uncle's affairs in California, she had called on Jill for assistance. She had told her agent a cover story about some "not entirely reliable relatives" that she had asked to watch her place while she was away – and, to put her mind at ease, would Jill mind stopping by to make sure the lights were all off, the stove not on, and to pick up her mail? This was one of the riskiest things Ann had ever done. If, contrary to his claim, Michael had not actually moved out, Jill would have been confronted with an extremely confusing scene requiring some very complicated and personally embarrassing explanations. However, she had no choice – she needed to know if he was gone.

Thankfully, Jill had confirmed that all was well.

But now – from her bathroom stall phone booth – after the pretense of checking with Jill *again* on the status of her house and on her book revisions, Ann deftly switched the subject of their conversation to the *real* reason for her call.

"Jill, listen, before we hang up, do you have my mail with you?"

"Yes. It's right here."

"There should be a packet of legal documents from the offices of Jacob Pressman. Do you see that? Is that there?"

"Um...let me see...ah...Yes, right here."

"Is it open?"

"Is it supposed to be?"

"Of course not."

There was a pause.

"Well...the top hasn't been torn off or anything like that," Jill answered, almost apologetically, "but...I've been around long enough to tell when an envelope has been opened and resealed."

Had Jill not jumped in again after realizing what her disclosure might be implying, the silence from Ann would undoubtedly have lasted much longer: "It's really none of my business and I don't know who these relatives of yours are, but I'd do a thorough check of your place when you get back."

"Yes," Ann finally said quietly. "Yes, I suppose I should."

And with that, she had her answer.

CHAPTER 26

J eff awoke in darkness. The wrap party had lasted – and
he'd stayed – far longer than he had intended. He'd been
dreaming something important – but the murk into which he
and the room had sunk blurred the recollection into an inchoate
smear.

There had been a quick glint – a sharp burst of light – that
had been powerful enough to rouse him. But that was all that
remained. At first, he assumed he was back home – that he
must be in his living room – but the particulars of the couch on
which he currently found himself were not consistent with that
possibility and, with a start, he realized he was still in his studio
office. And, also, very hung over.

A sour-sweet smell, a heavy odor of curdled booze, made him
wince and then attempt to achieve a sitting position. He had
managed the semblance of an upright orientation when his body
suddenly felt the ominous churn of nausea. Refusing to vomit
so soon after waking, he fought his way through it successfully
and landed on the compromised sensation of mere agony.

"Holy shit," Jeff whispered to himself. "I'm never drinking
again. At least...not until tomorrow." A grin broke across his face
– and though a concerted effort to regulate his breathing was

clearly going to be required to keep his stomach contents stable, he was at least sufficiently himself to laugh about it.

He had no idea what time it was. The lights were all off, but enough of a glow from the single security bulb beyond the glass office wall ghosted its way into the room to make the dominant features appear navigable even to someone in Jeff's condition.

Rising from the doughy burrow of the sofa, he shambled over to his desk and took a seat in the executive chair. The swivel caught him off guard and he teetered once more against the margins of a blackout. But, centering himself, he regained his bearings and tried to formulate some kind of plan regarding his person – and where it should most reasonably be located to in the near future – hoping that his muscle memory, at least, might benefit from this spot where some of the more profound decisions in his life had been made.

So much for *where* he was. Now as to the *when*: he had presumed that it was seven or eight in the morning – until he spotted his cellphone lying on the desktop with the time reading 2:45 am. He needed, at minimum, five more hours of sleep.

"Oh God," Jeff whispered to himself, stretching his hands across his face, "I'm *really* never drinking again."

It was only then that the reasons for his debauched state started coming back to him in fractured chunks. Ugly slabs of memory shoved forward: those new interns Lisa and Netty dancing topless on the audio crates to throbbing house music – popping strobes – the entire cast and crew packed around them bumping and jumping and shouting in unison – Murch insisting, "You stick the stink if you can't plug the pink!" – The film, the gargantuan faces of Marilyn Dunne and Stephanie, looking down from a gleaming screen – "That's a wrap! That's a wrap!" he had shouted and – Stephanie, her lips hot with rum devouring him – The taunts and the shame! All of them! – And Diane and something awfully important he must tell her – But that asshole Rusty charging towards him wanting – wanting what? Wanting what?

Then, the chaos began to subside, and, like pieces of a broken statue languidly descending to the ocean floor, the fragments of his night began to settle down around him. And Jeff could make out, by braving the largest and most lucid first, the general shape of the last twelve hours.

They'd finished the film around noon – much sooner than expected – that's right, that's how it all started – and Jeff, swallowing the innumerable slights and betrayals, had toasted the team on a job well done. Standing on a ladder and looking out over their "ocean of eyes," there had certainly been plenty for him to begrudge. But this was not the time for itemizing grievances.

If his rising to the occasion the night of his uncle's memorial had been a showcase for his oratory, this performance was the full Broadway extravaganza. Already loaded from his third cocktail of the afternoon, Jeff had bridled his true feelings and let loose the dogs of flattery. No team had ever performed so admirably – and under such trying circumstances. No effort – by any member, no matter how minor their function – had fallen too short of the mark to not now be recognized. No plaudits for his actors – no matter how lavish – seemed to quench his zeal for what he claimed they were justly owed. And that subtle network that bound them all together into a single consciousness – that had, it was true, cast Jeff adrift, forsaken him – suddenly swelled, under

Jeff's silver tongue, with esprit de corps, with benevolence and mercy and solidarity. They must excise the dark spirit that had set their house against itself!

"Do the wrap party right here! On the soundstage!" they pleaded.

"Liquor orders for everyone!" they cried.

"Get that DJ from Flavio's!" they called out.

Jeff announced he'd pay for it all. And he urged them on.

Heavier pieces were landing again, sending up plumes of debris – smaller, disconnected images – that mingled with and diffused the perception of the larger visions – the new interns Lisa and Netty dancing topless – speckled flashes of popping strobes – and Stephanie, her lips hot with rum whispering, "You want them to join us? You want to see me with another woman?" – but before all that, before the dancing and the drinking, well before the picture had even wrapped – days before – there was Jeff shouting and there was Murch shouting back –

"I am NOT shaving another week off my production schedule!"

"You stick the stink if you can't plug the pink, Jeff – you go with what you got! Derek's next film just got pushed forward and we signed him on the condition he'd be free for that. We don't have a choice!"

"Of course we have a choice – get someone else!"

"He's the fucking lead!"

"Oh, for fuck's sake, no one cares who stars in these things!"

"And one less week isn't going to make or break *Rainbows*!"

"Fuck off!"

"Honestly, Jeff," Stephanie interjected, having sat quietly in the corner since Murch's intrusion. "We can finish the picture in two weeks – we only have –"

"Why are you taking *his* side?!?" Jeff spat back, cutting her off.

"Don't yell at *me!*" she cried, jumping up and heading out of the room – but Jeff was not letting her off that easy: "You've spent the last two months riding my ass about cutbacks," he called after her from the doorway as she ran off, "and *NOW* you want me to be reasonable?!?"

"Holy shit, Jeff," Murch said, "why do you always get so involved? Fuck relationships! Just stick to fucking the bitches like I do."

"Am I interrupting?" Marilyn Dunne piped in, suddenly appearing from around the corner.

"YES!" Jeff screamed, stomping back into the office and throwing his pen against the wall. Then, spinning back to face Murch, erupted with full force: "And as a serial cheater, you're the *last* person who should be giving relationship advice!"

"Go tit-fuck your sister!" barked the other while storming towards the door.

"Well, I just wanted to say," Marilyn offered in her bubbly cadence and, stepping aside to avoid being barreled over by Murch, continued with, "I'm wondering if we can swap today's scene with tomorrow's?"

"That's not how it works, Marilyn," Jeff said – and was preparing himself for the enervating task of explaining to her *again* why disrupting the schedule created *immense* headaches for everyone – when he felt himself instantly kneecapped by a particular fact of her presence which he had just that moment noticed: "Wait a minute – why are you not in your wheelchair?"

"Oh, that's only for when I'm on set," she said, eager to talk about her fascinating medical complications. "So stressful, you know, love."

Jeff stood, his mouth gaping – and found that the only word he was capable of saying – as he fought to keep the integrity of a brain rapidly approaching a core meltdown – was a whispered, "...*what?*"

"Didn't I mention that?" she said blinking pleasantly, punctuating her question with a smile. "The doctor said I'm free to walk except when I'm acting."

It was later said that Jeff's "GET - THE - FUCK - OUT!!" was heard five floors up and all the way to the rooftop smokers' terrace.

Damage control with Stephanie and Marilyn had been accomplished with a set of diamond earrings for the former and an extra percentage point for the latter. But the fight with Murch – now almost a week old – kept reverberating through the preparations for the wrap party. They had not spoken a word nor seen each other since and Jeff realized that things were bad. As the soundstage was cleared for the event – the sets, furniture, and flats all pushed to the side or piled on top of each other – as teams were dispersed to buy booze, find a last-minute caterer, track down a DJ – and, for many, a quick return home for a change into something more festive and to pick up personal "party supplies"– Jeff kept wondering if Murch would show up, or even respond to his text inviting him to swing by.

It was not long before the celebration had exploded into a full-blown bacchanal – strobes popping, speakers pummeling – hors d'oeuvres, shots, and joints passing liberally person to person – those desirous of more elevated experiences availing themselves of the privacy of the bathrooms – and, as for Jeff, with God only knew how many drinks in him since his first of the day – as he surveyed the joyous revelers thronging to Lisa and Netty dancing half naked – he was on top of the world.

He walked among his warriors, all of them draped in the warm, pulsing dark of the discotheque that his camera and grip crew had rigged at the last minute – until Stephanie pulled him into a secluded corner with nothing but a small blue light caressing the contours of her violent beauty and whispered to him, "You want to see me with those two girls? You want to see me with another woman?" – as she slowly descended down to taste him – as his existence spiraled tighter and tighter around the shadowed alcove where Stephanie knelt before him, her lips, hot with rum – as euphorias burst outward from the chambers of his soul – as he felt, for a moment, a flash and glimpse as of doors frantically opening and shutting against a burning sun – as the world expanded and collapsed into nothingness – Jeff's mind leapt, in an astounding feat of free association, to that asshole Rusty, one of the assistant grips Jeff had never really liked.

The man had, earlier that evening, charged towards him wanting – wanting what? Wanting what?

The night had been revving at a dizzying intensity for several hours and Jeff and Stephanie, clinging to each other, had orbited between the two bars set at opposite ends of the vast soundstage

– she'd been wanting to pull him off into one of the numerous darkened recesses created by the pieces of dismantled set stacked and piled at the far end of the soundstage, and he'd been wanting only in that moment to hold things just as they were. Despite her insistence, Jeff had somehow delayed her advances. There was too much atmosphere to embrace now.

All the anger and rage that had been crippling him for the last several months were gone – and he saw that this precious creative community, this commune of artists tethered by bonds that transcended even family, had re-committed themselves to each other and, most stirringly, to his film. He saw that what had been fractured was now whole. He saw that the spite which had been twisting his mind against all of them had been nothing but a mirage – a false vision leading him astray. Basking now in their unrestrained devotion, he was overcome.

"Mr. Tanner!" came the shout and from amidst the packed and bouncing revelers Rusty emerged with two young girls, one under each arm. The purity of their free sensuality transported Jeff into yet another sphere of bliss.

Rusty and his cuties had come as emissaries to plead with him to allow the rough cut of the film – which rumor had it was on hand – to be screened for the cast and crew that night. Jeff would most certainly have declined, would have never countenanced a preview of any of his films in such a raw state, would most certainly have thought stopping the party to do so an epic miscalculation. But no sooner had Jeff begun trying to formulate a diplomatic rejection of the idea than he found himself surrounded by half of the party-goers all in ecstatics and chanting in unison, "Screen - the - film! Screen - the - film!"

Ordinarily, Jeff would not have allowed any public mania to carry him away – but that night, already surging upon a multitude of whirling influences, he abandoned himself to their whims.

What the *fuck* are you babbling about?!" Stephanie suddenly exclaimed – "And who the fuck is Rusty?!?" she added with equal fistfuls of exasperation and ire – and rising to her feet and shoving Jeff away, she screamed out a further, "Just what do you think I've been doing down there for the past five minutes?! Jesus Christ, you're a mess!"

Jeff tried to reach out to her in the inky murkiness of the alcove, but the pale blue sliver of her outline moved off and vanished into the shadows – and, just like that, he was alone in utter darkness. He had to fight to remember where in the hell he was and how he had gotten there.

Rusty! That's what it was! Rusty and the others had demanded to screen the film and he'd been swept up in their passion. Within minutes, a massive white scrim had been rigged across the far wall. With shouts and applause – everyone gathered in a boisterous mob facing the flaming screen while the roiling beam from the projector hovering like the arm of a god above them all. Stephanie had grabbed him just then, whispering intensely with a voice that would not be denied, "They'll be distracted for a while, let's go!"

To the strains of the opening credits to *Summer of the Rainbows* booming throughout, she had led him into the labyrinth of the film's broken and dismantled sets – heaped at the far end of the soundstage – which were now piled, canted, and stacked at crazy angles, transformed by the darkness into a bizarre topsy-turvy carnival funhouse. Illuminated only by what pale blue, green or yellow party lights crept through angling cracks and slits, it defied easy navigation – as floors sloped and walls leaned within shafts of pitch black. And now, the one who had led him into this maze was gone, and he had no idea how to escape. His arms reached outward and Jeff groped desperately for the exit.

That was, he would realize, his last moment of genuine happiness.

With a painful moan, Jeff looked up from his desk and remembered everything. The cellphone resting near his hand now read 3:02 am. The dark gloom of his office, the firmness of his executive chair, the distance to his private bathroom, all unchanged. But he was transformed. A colossal despair had, in that moment, folded its frigid wings about him – and above and below he could sense nothing but the endless cold of night. It was the despair of memory. It was the despair of truth. How much then did Jeff wish that he was still stumbling blindly down the crooked corridor of his smashed sets, falling and tripping, calling for help? How much then did he wish he was only prey to the bewilderment of finding himself trapped behind walls of plywood flats? Then, it was only his disorientation and sense of entrapment which battered his mind. Then, at least then, it was only his *external* reality which had lost all form and logic. Then, at least then, he still had his soul.

But he had pressed onward, fighting through the tilted, darkened passageways, striking valiantly against the ambushing shadows, following, always following, the wafting sounds of his film, the voices of Stephanie and Marilyn echoing from above, louder and louder, calling to him – and was it a trick of the mind, of countless cocktails, which led him to believe that those voices – performing scenes he had written in a similar frenzy – were also coinciding with his surroundings? Had he, as he entered the upturned living room set, heard Carol Beth answering the doorbell and the postman delivering the devastating letter? Moving through the smashed kitchen, had he heard Marilyn standing at the sink, pleading with her daughter over the phone, sobs tearing at her heart? Could he only have gone back, he would have stayed lost forever in that broken world.

But he had pressed onward.

And then, he had come out into the stilled eye of the vortex.

It was the one remaining, untouched set piece – the dying mother's bedroom – which had somehow survived that afternoon's flurry of demolition. The dirty rug, the faded wallpaper, the wrought-iron bedstead, the hobnail coverlet, the curios on the nightstand, and the sad colorless photos of unknown faces, long since departed all scavenged by an assistant to an assistant to the art director – still undisturbed and unmolested.

Against the far wall, filling the room with a billowing yellow glow, a picture window – muslin stapled across its back to diffuse the light – bloomed brilliantly. The sound from the film was now clearer than ever – even murmurs of the party attendees pattered close by – and Jeff sighed with heavy relief that his freedom was at hand. But as he stood savoring his impending liberation, there, as the soundtrack swelled around him, Jeff was granted his own private screening of a film that he had not known would also be playing that night. Although written, acted, and directed by others, it would not have been possible without Jeff's unwitting participation.

On the opposite side of the window, a group of figures moved into view – their silhouettes perfectly cast upon the muslin screen and their voices effortlessly penetrating the solitude of the room. But who they were, exactly, was impossible to pin down. Through the fog of drink, contending with the sounds from the film and the physical barrier of the set, they could have been any number of his cast or crew.

Their performance had begun benignly enough: a fragmented conversation whose only consistent theme seemed to be finding the perfect name for one of the production's hapless camera operators who had made a rather bad bet on a recent one-night stand – and returned from the experience with a yeast infection in his throat. But mostly, the group darted in drunken abandon faithlessly from topic to topic – all of them equally trivial and all of them surprisingly hilarious.

Jeff ceased his approach towards the window, fearing discovery and not wanting to disrupt the flow of their banter. It was enough to laugh quietly alongside them and listen in unnoticed – and wager who would end up with whom.

Leaning against a post of the bedstead, Jeff took the moment to relish this small island of peace before he would attempt to break back into the party – possibly, quite literally. Then, without warning, the silhouettes that moved and merged and morphed before him had their attention drawn back to the movie and their conversation followed suit. It was not long before they reached a collective consensus to speak openly of what all of them had kept unsaid over the last several months. Standing less than four feet away, almost as if they had stepped into the room with him, the figures began – methodically, clinically, relentlessly – to unburden themselves of their true feelings towards Jeff and the picture.

Had they been patently malicious people, had they revealed some kind of irrational hatred towards himself – or been the kind of misfit-fools that exist at the edges of any organization – there is certainly the possibility that Jeff would have suffered no more than mild indignation towards his team. But what sharpened the barbs of their attacks, what allowed the blade edge of each stroke to slice down into the muscle was that Jeff could not deny that everything they were saying was true.

The violence of their aspersions was so authentic that it gave Jeff the power to see both himself and his film unfiltered and unobscured. The effect was bracing. Credit some strain of inveterate defiance woven deep within that Jeff, rather than flee the assault, chose to face it head on, and, in fact, advance towards it.

Like walking into a mob armed with straight razors, Jeff pressed himself against the side of the window. He would know the truth! And he would carve himself down to nothing, if need be, to get at it. As the insults flowed, great strips of wet skin fell at his feet, exposing his tender under-flesh to scorching agonies. Each new aspersion ripped away swaths of vulnerable tissue – exposing more and more of the lies he had wrapped himself in – and soon, he was tearing at it with his very own hands.

The film was a disaster. And it appeared the entire crew shared that opinion.

Down, down, down into his tender guts he clawed. Where was it? Where was the source of his delusions? Somehow, some deceptive, insidious force had infected him with the drive to pursue every stupid, idiotic fancy that leapt from his imagination. What buffoonish muse had ever convinced him that he had the talent to write anything resembling the kind of powerful family drama he had foolishly attempted? As vicious and violent as the blows were that came to Jeff from beyond the glowing window, they were no match for the contempt in which he held himself. They were no match for the disgust at his own imbecility. Like tormenting flies to his wounds, he watched as not a single one of his colleagues tried, even once, to defend him.

Silence.

He looked up from his desk. A cold hush pervaded. The cellphone resting near his hand now read 3:10 am. Continuing to peer back into his lost evening, he seemed to have a vague recollection of *finally* stumbling his way out from the tangle of dismantled sets to find himself standing alone inside the cavernous soundstage with the last reel of the film – the giant faces of Marilyn and Stephanie looking down from the screen – still playing out their scenes senselessly to a crowd long since gone. In a convulsion of disgust, Jeff hurled what remained of his insides onto the studio floor.

How he had gotten from there to his office couch was a total blank. He felt the need to stand and was surprised to find that he could. Most of the room was still impenetrably dark, but, familiar with his surroundings, he stepped over to the window and looked out into the night.

The moon was high and nearly full and blanketed the studio complex in a gray mist. A few scattered street lamps bore silent witness to a space barren of any human presence. But not quite. Jeff noticed that a familiar Ferrari was still parked in the lot and he imagined that Murch must have received his text after all. The thought of his long-time producer and partner brought the realization that the man was probably the one true friend he had ever really had. Say what you would about him, he had stood by Jeff over the last 20 years.

If he showed up while things were still hopping, he's probably in his office still drinking. It wouldn't be out of character.

Although not fully understanding it, he needed to speak with Murch, the one person that could maybe stop him from the new path beginning to form in his mind – a path that, once begun, he knew he would see through to its brilliant end.

Jeff made his way into the outer office beneath the harsh beam of the single security light and passed among the array of empty secretarial and assistants' desks. Murch's suite was on the opposite side of the floor and reached through a series of corridors and turns – a location specifically chosen by Jeff for its inconvenience and distance to his own office. They were partners, yes, but that had never stopped Jeff from making it as difficult as possible for Murch to see him.

Jeff emerged from a series of shadowed passages and into the final stretch of hallway leading to Murch's suite. The lights were on and he could hear voices – more than likely Murch had snared one of the newer hires who had not yet been filled in by her more battle-scarred co-workers – or the conquest was some guest to the party who knew nothing about him. If he was lucky, it was only Murch and a couple of his close drinking buddies still pounding shots who would welcome a very last minute addition to their late-night club. That might do. The camaraderie of fellow hard drinkers might be enough of a deflection to push him off course. Might be enough to distract him from what must be done.

But as Jeff approached, the hopes for this second possibility quickly evaporated as the ambiguity of the voices settled into the distinct sounds of lovemaking. Jeff made no effort to investigate any further – and would have left the scene completely ignorant of the persons involved – but, as he turned to leave, he glimpsed through the glass office walls his producing partner furiously screwing a woman spread out on the desk beneath him.

Jeff turned quickly away. But not quick enough. He had not been able to see whether she was wearing her standard side pony-tail – but, as he walked silently off, he imagined that Stephanie was.

CHAPTER 27

It was a terrible, terrible thing for Ann to do. She had met Michael, despite her better judgement, and he had made his case, and, with a quick phone call to her agent, she had discovered his deception. She had also agreed to see Thomas again. In fact, at this precise moment, Thomas Naidoo was waiting for her.

They had agreed on the time and the place. But she would not be there. Right now, she was sitting in another restaurant – a different restaurant – imagining what he was thinking: he would have started with the anticipation of seeing whether she would show up as early as he had – and then, finding himself the first to arrive, standing there in that restaurant, all alone, he would find himself patiently hoping that she would be on time.

Then, she imagined, would come the efforts to ignore the disappointments, trickling in as the minutes rolled past. Excuses for her delay would follow at ten minutes: exasperation towards the deviousness of LA traffic and the impossibility of convenient parking – and why did no one ever plan ahead for these things? At fifteen minutes past: the concession that something was wrong. What would start as irritation at being abandoned would abruptly spike into alarm that she might have suffered an accident, might have been physically hurt – then the quick dial of the phone – the long wait as ring succeeding ring had gone unanswered – and then the awkward message, asking if things were alright, if she was still planning on coming, the attempt not to sound desperate or panicked or disappointed.

It was a terrible, terrible thing for her to do. But it was necessary.

In a few moments, if not already, Thomas would realize it was over, that she was never coming – and he would be out of her life for good. Which is why it was necessary, and why there could be no mistakes.

What Ann had realized over the last 24 hours was this: the tangle of threads she had been wrestling with, that fight at trying to trace each individual strand, to sort it all out, to arrive at some greater meaning – had been nothing but a gigantic deception.

There were no individual threads. There was no unraveling. It was all one massive perpetual loop, endlessly convoluted. And it must be ruptured. Its conjoined ends must be liberated – and the endless, tangled mess of her life transformed into a long, straight, beautiful line conducting her to a permanent and solid destination. But for any of that to happen, there could be no mistakes and absolutely no distractions.

Calling Thomas to let him down, speaking to him over the phone – or, worse, in person – and articulating heartfelt reasons why she could no longer see him would have left too many trap doors available for escape. She needed the doors to him closed permanently. And yes, convincing him she was a flake and unreliable was the most expedient course of action to forestall any efforts on his part. But her highest priority must be to stop *herself* from wriggling her way back into *his* life. She knew herself far too well – and was far too capable of constructing all manner of subconscious, elaborate schemes that would appear to her as utter happenstance. No, she must make any kind of reconciliation so unbearable that even at the subconscious level the idea would be rejected.

Thomas must be left behind because what had become clear to Ann over the last 24 hours was that she could not face a new betrayal. She could not face this continued chaos. She could not face waiting for her life to fall into place. The time required to unearth whether or not Thomas Naidoo was who he said he was – and not another fraud looking for a fraction of what she was seeking or, worse, sincere but with only a fraction of the character he appeared to possess, or, worst of all, everything she hoped for but with no real intention to divorce – could be a lengthy and exhausting undertaking. That was an investment Ann was not prepared to make. Ever again. What Ann wanted now more than anything was *certainty*.

And that left Michael.

Ann could now see that Michael was willing to thoroughly play the part of the passionate soulmate so long as he believed himself within striking distance of money. Exactly how much money he ultimately felt he was worth had yet to be sounded – but that Ann was possessed of enough to meet his minimum threshold was clear. Moreover, so long as Michael stayed ignorant of her awareness of his designs, it was a *certainty* that their relationship, and her life, could proceed indefinitely. And that meant stability. And that was all that mattered.

If she could accept what he offered, she could have no further doubts. He was neither creative enough nor motivated enough to handle major shifts in strategy. For the first time, Ann had the means to assure that Michael could be securely boxed in. For the first time, she had the means to keep him under *her* control. And, also for the first time, it seemed that letting go of finding something deeper in exchange for all the certainty was a fair exchange.

However, like any magic trick, illusions only hold so long as the strings remain hidden – and she knew that she must not only conceal her manipulations from Michael, she must efface them from her own memory. In whatever tomb she planned to secret these things away, she, herself, must be immured with them.

The Ann she was now, who had walked so bravely into the void that reflects everything, that place few could enter, where she'd gone and returned countless times, Ann the creator, the Ann who had stood backstage, a part of the magic, and watched all those performances – must be eliminated. A new Ann must emerge, one who would be content to remain seated in the audience and enjoy the show. An Ann who would never question who it was who was pulling the strings, or had painted the backdrops, or convinced Michael to love her. It was an imperfect solution, but it would square the circle. It would disperse the tangled mess.

And this grief that was welling within, for which she wiped her eyes again and again, she must know that too would be gone. Yes, she would, eventually, forget who she was now, would eventually forget the parts that were lies and which were the truth, but the pain would be forgotten as well, and, at least from her new perspective, she would, once and for all, believe she was happy.

She dialed Michael's number. From that booth, and with the world moving on beyond the window, Ann sat listening to the soft, steady rings as though to chimes heralding the final moments of her life.

———*ele*———

At first, he couldn't find it.

Jeff had arrived at his Hollywood Hills home at 4:25 in the morning – hours yet before the sun would come up – and still very quiet. He had gone directly to the second drawer of his night stand.

And it was missing.

The funny thing was that – despite all his panic – he had not initially thought he would need it. In fact, it had not crossed his mind even *once* since he'd awoken on his office couch early that same morning. During the entire drive from the studio, he had been preoccupied with nothing but his lingering nausea and, even more than that, wanting to go back to bed – and hoping he would be able to fall quickly into a deep sleep.

But then, for some reason, upon arrival, a memory recurred to him that he had not experienced for many, many years. It was the memory of his imaginary friend – that little boy who had kept him company during the darkest hours following the death of his parents. The images were, naturally, filtered through the long passage of time and his perspective as a child. And while the exact details may have become rather blurred and indistinct, what had remained intact were the feelings of comfort he had felt with that imaginary little boy. Even though he was fully cognizant that it was all a child's fancy, a trick of the mind, he found that even the long distant memory – merely the remembrance of it – brought him peace.

Then, he remembered something else he had completely forgotten: he had made a movie. Actually, he had just finished it. But it now seemed as though it were ages ago. So long ago that the feelings for it had vanished. Concentrating, he was able to piece together that the film had been horrible. Abysmal, really. He also could recall that he had believed himself abandoned by everyone involved. He remembered his immense despair, how the disastrous film had broken the very foundations of his confidence and sense of self. Looking back, he was glad to see that time had washed all that away. He could still see, dimly, the faces of his collaborators, faces which he now observed with love and generosity. And, he could still see, dimly, the general shape of his film, could laugh at his foolishness, and could now recall the whole debacle quite fondly.

He was also surprised at how easily he could pick up the train of conversation with his imaginary friend. Though he knew it was infantile and, perhaps, ill-advised to indulge in such things, he knew exactly what the little boy would say at this juncture. He could almost hear his tiny voice warning that those memories which now seemed to rest securely in the distance were not, in fact, permanently constrained to remain there. They could, the boy would have said, at any moment break free and come rushing forward. And, wisely, the little boy reminded him that he was responsible for certain tragedies – and of the honorable things that must be done in order to atone for them.

It was then – and only then – that he thought to look for it.

What broke his initial panic at finding it missing – and the horror that it could have been stolen by an intruder who may, at that very moment, still have been in the house – was his recalling, almost immediately, that he had hidden it away in another, better location *to keep it from Dirk*. The irony set Jeff chuckling. Taking it down from a shoebox set high in the rear of his closet, Jeff walked slowly back to the kitchen. He set it down on the table, took a seat, folded his hands, and went over in his mind if there was anything else he had forgotten – or had left undone.

Not really. His house was immaculate. Had it been a mess, he would have certainly cleaned up first. This was important. As he told his imaginary friend – feeling the satisfaction of finally being the one doing the instructing: the setting of any scene communicates as much to the viewer as any dialogue or action. 4:37 in the morning, in the kitchen, set the perfect, dramatic tone.

Equally important, Jeff knew, was how, exactly, and in what position they should find his body once he pulled the trigger.

CHAPTER 28

"My dear companions," Professor Puck extolled, "we've faced some mighty adventures of late – but you've comported yourselves brilliantly." This sent waves of hearty agreement through the ranks of the assembled heroes. Lucy, Stuey, the twins, and Banana Barilla stood front and center beaming at their fearless leader. Behind them, and beneath the blinking glow of G.U.R.U. – the Professor's massive supercomputer – a gathering of his most notable associates applauded the success of their latest endeavor.

He was glad for the focus their current emergency provided. He needed it. The Professor had had the dream again. The dream where he – most bizarrely – was an animator, wrongfully accused of embezzlement, and whose life was spiraling out of control. He had been unaccountably shaken, and he wanted nothing more than to dismiss the thought.

Thank goodness, in reality, he only had world-dominating masterminds to contend with. And, he had his team: to the woman and man, all had names synonymous with legendary tales of heroism and daring: there was Secret Sensei, master of the seven martial arts and vanquisher of the Brotherhood of the Dragon; there was Dr. Pricilla Howell, discoverer of the werewolf-rabies vaccine; and the amazing Captain Forthwright, first man to land on the sun – to list only a few of the more regular members in attendance. But even the most extraordinary among them would have scorned to suggest that any past exploit could compare with their recent clash with that criminal mastermind, Count Von Verschlagen.

Who among them would ever forget that epic confrontation atop the Count's mountain fortress? Who among them could not still see Professor Puck running along the very back of Verschlagen's monstrous Worm, spring-boarding off its snapping jaws to catapult himself out of the pit, catching the railing of the laboratory balcony (only just) and then, with blinding speed – courtesy of his concealed turbo-charged roller skates – leaping over to Verschlagen's own brainwave machine and turning its powerful rays against him? In an instant, the Professor had not only spared the Count's life but convinced his foe to renounce his history of villainy and to assist with the capture of Verschlagen's major domo – and paramour – Esmerelda Diablo.

And then, testament to the power of compassion, the Count repaid his debt in full. Calling on his indentured villagers to gather before his castle gate – with himself high upon the battlements – he proceeded to free them from their bondage, preach the blessings of righteousness, admit to a host of past and present crimes, and, most startling of all, confess that all he really wanted to do, now that he was free, was *dance!* Unseen by any, the Professor and his team had quietly regrouped at the outer fringes of the assembled crowd to admire the Professor's handiwork and the fitting conclusion to another extraordinary affair.

"There is no evil but what we allow!" Verschlagen had called out at the finish, his voice booming through the megaphone held tight in his hand. "WE are the evil we resist – and WE prevent the good that we claim to seek!" His listeners had roared their approval, their shouts and fists pumping in solidarity.

Suddenly, from the lowered drawbridge, a woman, glamorously dressed in diamonds and furs and in the grip of four village constables, had drawn everyone's attention as she was forcibly escorted towards a waiting carriage.

"Don't be frightened, dearest!" had come the Count's voice from above. "Soon, you'll be purified! Just as I have been!"

"Wilfred! You mother-fucker!" she had screamed up at him. "I'm telling them everything! EVERYTHING!!"

"Yes, my darling! Hold nothing back!" he had called down, his face aglow with benevolence. "Only the truth, pure and unfettered, will save us from the Worm!"

"The Worm! The Worm!" Puck and his team had shouted along with the exuberant villagers – all of them heralding the Count's transformation and the crooked deeds which could now be rectified. Everyone, in the end, recognizing that it is *always* the Worm we are battling and not those poisoned by its sting – and that it is far better to pity rather than hate those under the spell of its twisted designs.

All this, and more, still resounded within the hearts of those standing before Professor Puck. He eyed his heroes keenly, not so jaded by a lifetime fraternizing with the mysterious and fantastic to fail to thrill at knowing such individuals or to ever forget the immense balance owed to each and every one of them – or to fear how much more he must ask.

"Yes," the Professor went on, "our nemesis has been neutralized. And, the capture of the brainwave machine has abetted the rehabilitation of a number of other criminally diseased minds. But, I'm afraid to say our task is not yet complete."

A hushed buzz spread throughout his audience, stirred by those who could only guess at what his tone implied – and by a number of others who feared they knew precisely. Stepping over to the input control panel, the Professor threw a series of switches and the mechanical brain sparkled to life.

"Compute," the Professor commanded into a speaking tube, "using all known facts!"

"Two are still in danger," the machine declared with columns of strobing, multi-colored lights racing up and down its two-story tall mainframe. "Both within a labyrinth. Both unaware of their peril."

"Estimate parameters: time and severity!" demanded the Professor.

"The danger is mortal. The danger is imminent," came the dispassionate reply.

Before the words had ceased to reverberate about the cavernous room, the Professor had donned his red radio helmet and coatee jacket and jumped to the rail of the command center podium – the signal to all that another adventure was at hand.

"My friends, our worst fears have been confirmed," he said. "But our duty is clear."

Puck depressed a short sequence of buttons and the giant central view screen flared to life. It may have been another of his renowned theatrical gestures – it hardly needed to be stated who it was that now faced certain doom – but choosing to display the pictures of the two most revered friends of the Professor Puck Society had its intended effect. Across the room, hands shot into the air, and everyone could be heard volunteering for the mission – offering their lives to save Ann and Jeff Tanner.

Their collective cry rang out:

Puck Society! Never fear!

Puck Society! We'll be there!

The Professor, once again, was humbled by the Society's capacity for courage and, although those selected would face grim odds for a safe return, he wished he could recruit the entire company. But this would be no ordinary assignment. And those whom he knew must be chosen would draw no small quantity of strength from the collective valor of this hour. Energizing the crowd had been no mere theatrics. He had demonstrated the power of unified purpose.

And, Lucy and Stuey would most assuredly need it.

"Thank you, all," the Professor said, "but I'm afraid I must decline your generous offers. This mission requires specialization to such a degree that there are but three of us – myself and two others – who have any chance for success."

At this, expressions of consternation erupted throughout. There could be no doubt, of course, of the Professor's assertion: he never made statements regarding mission assignments lightly and would have explored every permutation possible before making his decision. But who, exactly, his calculations had selected to join him on this critical operation, baffled them all – until Lucy, still dressed in disguise as the Martian Mistress, stepped forward.

"We're ready, Professor," she said – and, with a gentle elbow to his ribs, Stuey stepped forward to join her.

"Well," the Professor laughed, "I'm not sending you as far as Mars, I certainly hope. You'd better change."

"I think we'd both better," Lucy replied, eyeing Stuey's purple and green turtleneck which had not been washed for quite some time. "And I have a feeling costume changes will be the least of our worries before the night is through."

"I was afraid you'd say that!" Stuey cried, following Lucy off towards the dressing rooms, and wondering just how he had gotten himself into this mess.

As the assembly disbanded, each back to their own pursuits and their own worlds, the Professor felt a wave of nostalgia for what they had managed to achieve together. He fought the urge to call them back, to beg them to stay and preserve the wonder of their triumph. But another voice told him to let them go. It was a distant voice, but one which he knew he dare not ignore – nor could he dismiss the premonition that this night would be his last adventure. From deep within, the thought rang out, but the Professor was much too disciplined to succumb to it. Enough!

Quickly clearing his mind of such distractions, the Professor turned his thoughts to his immediate problem. The rescue of high-profile individuals was always the most demanding, usually requiring double the effort to prevent any harm to the hostages – but time was no longer on his side. Two teams would be required. That could no longer be ignored – and he wondered if Lucy and Stuey would understand. They'd have to: Lucy and Stuey would be assigned the sister, while he would go after the brother.

He had never before sent just the two of them on a mission together, but they were absolutely ready. The Professor believed in their abilities – wholeheartedly – but did *they*? Again, he admonished himself for wasting time on these doubts. He must trust his instincts that everything would unfold as it should.

He began a quick, last-minute, rundown of what he would need for the work to come, and, scanning his command desk, began gathering up various items that presented themselves as potentially useful. As he moved further about the control room, his eyes were caught fast by the vault where Verschlagen's brain-wave machine had been secured (and a strange object it was, wrapped in an old sheet and braced to an easel).

What he had been denying – and which was possibly fatal to the mission – was that his exposure to the effects of the machine had been more extensive than he had let on. Perhaps foolish-ly, he'd kept his concerns to himself – but, now, despite his renowned mental fortitude, the Professor was forced to admit he had been compromised. He was no longer himself. At first, the symptoms had been nothing but a fleeting uneasiness – almost unnoticeable, really. But then had come the visions.

Initially sporadic and totally incomprehensible, they had, by now, become chronic and palpable. Eminently rational, the Pro-fessor had remained confident that by maintaining his grip on the fundamental principles of logic, he could weather the effects until restored to his normal self. But the episodes presented themselves as much more than hallucinations or waking dreams. No, they seemed to emanate from fathomless reaches within – from far below the subconscious strata – from a core of actual lived experience: a parallel life completely disparate from the one he knew. These moments of perception had caused him to doubt his own sanity at times. Worst of all were the spasms suggesting that Lucy and Stuey, in fact all his companions, were, in reality, total strangers.

But through it all, out of all the people he considered close friends – whose existence seemed to be slowly ebbing away – out of all the colleagues he had risked life and limb for – who moment by moment were growing dim – the one person he felt he truly did know, the one that seemed to defy erasure, was the man fate had decreed he must now rescue.

Although this man, this Mr. Tanner, seemed to present a world further removed from any with which the Professor considered himself familiar, it was the one world which both calmed and attracted him inexplicably.

At the nexus of the Professor's intense interest was a memory of this man, this Mr. Tanner, relating the story of a friend he had once attempted to save. The tale seemed classically familiar – it was the story of a person (a yodeler by trade) who had lost it all, who had been abandoned by the very world itself, who had sought self-immolation, who had been restored by the love of a mother – but who, tragically, had become lost once again.

For some reason, the tale had struck a dark, personal chord in the Professor – and though he imagined the mother nearly hysterical over the fate of her son, he felt a strange sense of confidence about the conclusion to the story: that the son would return to the mother and make their lives whole. But again, he must clear his mind of such distractions.

It was the *teller* of that tale, the celebrated Mr. Tanner – not any side characters – whose fate teetered on the brink. The fate of the man he must now save was not yet written – and there remained precious moments left to effect it. How this was to be achieved he did not know. But that was not what haunted him. What troubled the Professor most of all was hearing Tanner's voice as he related the miseries of his buddy – and the clear sense that Mr. Tanner would have gladly traded places with that lost soul.

CHAPTER 29

They would save Ann Tanner. Or die trying. And so far, the way things were going, it looked like the latter – which had set matters on edge between Lucy and Stuey. It was bad enough that the Professor had sent them off on their own. After all, had they not proven time and again that they all worked better together as a team? If not, they were proving it now. Stuey, at least from Lucy's perspective, free from the organizing influence of the Professor – and true to form – had already managed to bungle things spectacularly. That precious lead time Lucy thought she had managed to buy them by suggesting they change clothes on the drive to the hotel had been wiped off the map by Stuey grabbing the wrong outfits. As usual, they were back to full-blown panic mode.

"How was I to know you meant something else?" he said defensively. "There are a million reasons why–"

"I said bring our *night* clothes – not our *tights*!" Lucy interrupted. "Next time, *you* get the car warmed up."

"Fine by me!" he shot back.

"We look *ridiculous* in these unitards."

Lucy was, truth be told, glad for the focus their current emergency provided. She'd needed it: she'd had the dream again. The dream where she and Stuey were married, had been leading an elaborate memorial service that had filled an entire theater. The images had left her unaccountably shaken, and she wanted nothing more than to dismiss the thought.

Thank goodness, in reality, they had more than enough to keep themselves distracted – because the whole operation was collapsing around them. The minute they'd arrived and stepped into the lobby of the hotel where Ms. Tanner was being held captive – dressed as they were in full body spandex – they'd been spotted by security and told to leave. Failing to fast-talk their way out of the sudden pinch, they'd feigned a compliant attitude before making a quick escape – a move which had rapidly devolved into a cat and mouse pursuit through the fitness center and gift shop – then a swift dash around the side of the building to sneak back in through the rear entrance. But, with the hotel management now warned of their continued presence, they'd been forced to duck into a darkened broom closet to evade detection – where they currently found themselves waiting for the coast to clear.

Two guards stood just down the hall from their location, apparently awaiting further instructions. As luck would have it, Lucy found she was able watch them unobserved by peeping through a small window set in the door. Those two guards had only to move a few steps in either direction and she and Stuey could make a break for it.

But a break to *where*? They still had to determine exactly where Ann was being held. They needed to be able to case the joint at their leisure – needed time to scout any of the various places within the hotel where their charge might be located.

If only she could concentrate.

If only she could stop the strange ideas pestering her. Things were coming to her that she could not possibly have experienced, yet which seemed so real. For a moment, she could not place anything – who she was, where she had been, or what she was doing.

Is my name really Lucy?

"Try him one more time!" Stuey's urgent whisper suddenly broke in upon her thoughts – and Lucy was glad of the interruption. Unclipping the walkie-talkie from her belt, she clicked the circuit open.

"Professor! Professor!" Lucy whispered as loud as she dared. "Come in, Professor!"

The soft static from the speaker filled the blackness around them – and, although she could not see him in the dark, she knew Stuey's eyes were wide and panicked.

"It's no use – he's still not answering," Lucy said decisively, closing the circuit. "We'll just have to think for ourselves."

"That's what I'm afraid of!" Stuey replied. "Isn't the coast clear yet?"

"No – the two security guards are still there."

"Blonkers! We'll never make it past them! We're doomed!"

"Wrong," Lucy said, turning to Stuey with that steely sound to her voice that always meant trouble. "Remember: they're on the lookout for two people dressed in pink tights. But we'll walk right past them as the last people in the world they'd suspect!"

"Who's that?"

"Princess Zalenka and Ambassador Bolonsky of the royal Prussian court!"

"What are you talking about?" Stuey whined, knowing all too well when Lucy had built up a full head of steam and would not be stopped.

"Stuey, it's time for a quick change! Turn on the light and let's see what we have to work with!"

Quickly covering the window with some old newsprint to avoid being spotted, they set about inspecting their cramped quarters. The small room proved to be much more than a simple storage space – it was, in fact, a complete janitorial supply closet. From floor to ceiling the walls were stocked with aerosol cans, spray bottles, jars, tins, and jugs of nearly every chemical, cleaner and disinfectant imaginable, boxes of paper and plastic products, and tools and implements from buckets to brooms, light bulbs to trash bags, gloves to sponges, and ladders to brushes.

"Stuey, I think we've hit the jackpot," she said.

"But how are we going to disguise ourselves as Russian royalty with any of this stuff?"

"Don't you see?" Lucy gushed. "We have everything we could possibly need!"

"No, I don't see!" he replied, now quite adamant. "Even back at the Professor's secret bunker we'd be hard-pressed to figure out disguises!"

"Honestly, Stuey, you'd think you'd never done this before," she said, then, drawing his attention to a bottle of floor wax: "Look, right here – this product contains alcohol 35-A, one of the main components in spirit gum! And over here, this tub of spackle has nearly the same consistency as face putty! We just have to use a little creative ingenuity!"

Lucy immediately set to work with a pair of scissors – cutting an empty bottle of bleach into the shape of a crown.

Stuey made a last ditch effort to dissuade her, but she was ready with the big guns: "Don't you remember what the Professor said? Don't you remember who we're doing this for? We give up, Stuey, and we'll be letting *everyone* down."

And with that, Lucy's logic proved unassailable and Stuey, as usual, had no choice but to relent.

"Now hurry up," Lucy added, "and get out of that tutu."

He would not make it out alive. The Professor had resigned himself to that. But for the moment, he was safe. He'd managed to stop the bleeding and crawl into a concealed gap in the labyrinth wall. The heavy cloak of darkness – at first his adversary – had become his ally. He knew he could rest here, at least briefly. His shallow breathing mixed with the cool stone walls and the chirping crickets and he listened for the sounds of pursuit.

Nothing.

But that was a dangerous illusion. His enemies were most certainly closing in – whether he could hear them or not. Those tracking him were masters at the art of stealth and he would need to get moving before long. Yes, he could feel them closing in – and they would overtake him soon if he remained where he was. But all he really wanted to do was close his eyes. Close his eyes and sleep. Worse, the man from his dream, the one named Dirk, was nearly a constant companion now. And he feared slipping away before completing his mission.

He cursed the appalling lapse in judgment that had left him so exposed. He'd entered the maze too brashly and had paid dearly for it: peaceful clearings lit by moonlight were *never* what they appeared to be – and, after flagrantly ignoring that universal law, he'd been instantly attacked by a pack of shadow wolves. And though he had managed to fight them off, he'd not gotten away unscathed. The blood-soaked bandages were silent witness to that. He'd bound his leg as best he could – but it needed professional attention, and soon. It hardly mattered, though. The effects of the brainwave machine coupled with the creatures' poisoned fangs were rapidly tearing apart his reality.

What had been a clear line to his mission objective was now a tortured, twisting route that writhed and turned in upon itself like a feverish snake. But Mr. Tanner, the man he must save, lay at the heart of the labyrinth, was a prisoner of its encircling be-wilderments – and only by engaging with and conquering them was any rescue to be achieved. And so he'd pushed on valiantly, hacking and beating against a legion of opposing agents – adversaries that grasped and clutched and clawed – but little remained of the strength of purpose that had so fired him at the start. It was the futility of swords against a tempest – a battle with an opponent that provoked endless forays of slashing and cutting, yet was impervious to it all.

Despite the hopelessness of his own situation, his real fears were reserved for Lucy and Stuey – both of whom he held steadfast in his thoughts like a beacon. Had they not remained so, the Professor had no doubt he would have lost his resolve hours ago.

But he found that he could not abandon his own mission until he was assured of their safety. He owed them that much. They'd failed to make their last three check-ins – and he could not stop agonizing over images of their capture. It was this that gave him what little focus still persisted. He should have gone with them! He was a fool to insist they separate!

Again, he reminded himself of the need to keep moving, of the precious time he had lost already and which was dissipating by the second. But the exhaustion and delirium which he had kept at bay was simply too much for him. Then, just as he began to despair of being able to progress any further, as unconsciousness began to overwhelm, his radio helmet sprang to life.

"Professor! Professor! Come in, Professor!" Lucy's voice sounded over the small internal speaker.

"Lucy!" the Professor answered, weak but lifting his head with renewed vigor. "Is that really you?!"

"Yes! And apologies for the delay – we had a few setbacks!"

"And Stuey? Is he alright as well?"

"More or less," she confessed – and a whimper of exasperation from a voice nearby confirmed her assessment. "We're in sight of our target" Lucy went on, "and it's just as you said. She has the phone in her hand and is keying in the final sequence!"

At the sound of Lucy's indomitable grit, the Professor had to summon herculean reserves to clamp down on the emotions that began to spill over. But it was imperative that Lucy not become privy to the truth of his situation. Nothing must distract her from her goal. The voice that answered her, that conveyed its accustomed surety and strength was a fraud – but a necessary one.

"Proceed with caution," the Professor warned, "and remember, she is most likely still under the sway of powerful forces. You must ease into her world. No sudden shocks!"

"We're on it, Professor – we won't let you down!"

With a click, Lucy was gone. The Professor felt himself gasp at the release of the effort he had been sustaining. He sagged back against the stone wall. The sounds of the subterranean night returned accompanied by his sense of impending destruction. But the Professor had what he needed: his companions were safe and mere seconds from completing their task. They had done their duty against all odds – and that knowledge began to revive him. They had done their duty! Now, he must do his. It was time to move.

Tightening his bandages one last time, he pulled himself upright and tested his wounded leg. It was now relatively numb – probably not a good sign – but it no longer sent out stabs of pain with each step. Cautiously, he emerged from his covert and moved out into the passageway. The floor of the cavern began to rise steeply and the walls began to narrow – which doubled the effort required, but also confirmed he was nearing his goal.

As he continued his assent, each minute more arduous than the last, despite the meager light, he became aware of creeping foliage gradually enclosing more and more of the tunnel walls. Soon, a thick blanket of leaves completely obscured any evidence of stonework, and, before long, the ceiling gave way to the dim flecks of a starry sky breaking through the black silhouettes of treetops spreading overhead. A chill, fragrant breeze beat back the stale air and its sharpness filled his lungs. But the respite granted by the change in atmosphere was more than offset by the eclipse of any clear path forward. The overgrowth, which had previously shrouded the passage walls, now seemed bent on impeding the final stretch of his journey. But he would not be daunted.

After fighting through seemingly endless tangles of brambles and thorns, a light appeared – a portal out of his chaos. Keeping it ever before his eyes, and with one final, desperate push, he broke free and out into the clear center of the labyrinth. The light now burned intensely and he raised his hands to shield himself from it. Then, as he cautiously moved forward, the light began to soften and objects began to appear within it. There was a room and a table. And at the table there was a man.

The man was raising an object to his head.

Suddenly, everything came into focus.

And then, just as he knew it would, the Professor and his world were extinguished. Dirk remembered. Everything.

"Jeff!!" Dirk screamed, rushing to the window – and to his life and his friend.

But not in time.

The gun fired.

CHAPTER 30

The first ring sounded. Ann imagined Michael walking towards his phone – that leonine stride of his, those tight shirts he favored stretching against his potent frame. There were worse prisons in which to serve. And although she had not yet fully committed herself, already she could see the path being cleared towards her gilded cage.

The second ring sounded.

Ann tried to imagine what she would say. It didn't take too much creativity to guess. She would put on her casual, aloof act and pretend as if there were still tremendous doubt as to whether or not a relationship was feasible – pretend as if she were only agreeing to continue to test the waters – but he'd know. He'd know it was all bullshit and that she had folded. Once again. And probably forever.

The third ring sounded.

But, maybe this time things really *would* come through. Maybe she *had* been too distant with him. Maybe –

The fourth ring sounded – and suddenly, from the corner of her eye, Ann realized the waitress had approached and was standing next to her table. In a flash, she recalled how it perfectly mirrored the first time she had met Brenda and Paul. That split-second reminder of her friends and what they represented collided head-on with what she was attempting to do. If only they were really here! She felt a huge turmoil of emotion looming and her one remaining thought was to dismiss the waitress as soon as possible.

Just as she looked up, just as she was about to mouth the words, "I'm good, thanks," several competing and totally incongruous elements assaulted her all at once: looking up from her phone, as her eyes moved up along the body of the person standing at her table, as she realized there was not one but, in fact, *two* people standing before her, her phone picked up.

"Hello?" came the tiny voice of Michael.

This would, ordinarily, have been highly problematic, and would have provoked a brusque dismissal of whomever it was standing next to her in order for her to take the call – except that, in that instant, Ann was struck with the elated thought – as her eyes continued upwards – that the two people standing at her table might perhaps actually *be* Paul and Brenda!

"Hello?" repeated Michael, now slightly confused.

He did not have a chance to repeat himself a third time.

He did not have a chance because Ann's finger had suddenly shot out and disconnected the call. This had happened because Ann's eyes had finished moving up the bodies of the two people standing at her table and had reached their faces – and she had realized *she had no idea who they were.*

She would, however, have described them as marginally terrifying.

What stood before Ann was nearly impossible to take in all at once. The one on the left – a female, if Ann had to guess – was wearing a filthy mop head for a wig, a trash bag poncho cinched at the waist by an extension cord, and what looked like a lump of spackling paste on the bridge of her nose. The other, standing on the right, had a white crown cut from a bleach bottle (the handle still intact), a kilt made of duct tape and paper towels, and, glued to his upper lip, a mustache of green plastic bristles from a scrub brush. Not so surprising, they were peering down at her with as much confusion as Ann was certain she was expressing in return.

Then, several things seemed to happen in a flurried jumble. Having hung up on Michael to free her mind of at least one impossible problem, and while trying to decide whether or not to call the wait staff for help – and whether these two vagrants wanted anything more than a handout – something extraordinary happened to their faces. Or, rather, the extraordinary *abandoned* their faces – as Ann stood gaping at them, stood gaping at their crazed aspects, suddenly, none of that mattered. Suddenly, their facades seemed to vanish – and she knew exactly who they were.

"Brenda?! Paul?!" Ann cried in amazement. Her greeting inspiring an equally enlightening effect on her guests.

"Ms. Tanner?" Brenda said breathlessly, her eyes widening and with a hand reaching over to Paul to steady herself. Oddly, it seemed to Ann that they were just recognizing her as well – as if the two of them were in the process of emerging out of some kind of dream. But no matter, it was all that Ann needed. Jumping up, she pulled them both to her. Something about their presence was purifying. She could feel it. Something about seeing them again was shattering all manner of frigid, crystalized thoughts – and freeing her from something dreadful. What it all meant, she would parse out later. For now, all she knew was that she must return the favor. They were obviously in need of help and she would give it to them.

"Alright now, have a seat. Both of you," Ann said soothingly, guiding them into the booth. Sitting opposite them, just as before, she adopted her most mothering tone and asked, "Where have you been? What's happened to you?"

"What's happened to us?" Brenda repeated, again, with a faraway look in her eyes which she seemed to be fighting to overcome.

"Yes," Ann said, "you know people've been awfully worried."

"I'm not sure, Ms. Tanner," Brenda finally answered. "It's all a bit blurry."

Removing her wig – and then helping Paul out of the crown wedged onto his head – Brenda sighed and then closed her eyes to steady herself further. Paul looked on the verge of nausea.

"Well," Ann said, reaching out to hold Brenda's and Paul's hands, "I've seen bad trips before...and you've been messing with *something*. But everything's going to be alright. I promise."

Hailing the waitress, she ordered cups of coffee all around and, not ten minutes later, the warm liquid seemed to have the desired, vivifying effect. The worst of their disorientation had lifted, and Brenda and Paul tried to explain, as best they could, the events of the last several weeks. There was little Ann completely understood.

"It's all so mixed up," Paul was saying, as if sensing Ann's struggle to put the pieces into a cogent whole. "I still can't honestly tell you what was real – and what was imagined."

"But don't you see, Ms. Tanner?" Brenda implored. "Every night, performing Paul's show, the craziness would start all over again. Every night, at the end, it would be brought out on stage, set on its easel, and just as I would feel myself recovering, there it would be – the flash and the blinding colors – staring into us, and we'd fall, all of us, back into it – !"

"I want to understand, Brenda, honestly I do," Ann said but felt herself growing lost within the absurdities of their story. "But I don't know where to even begin unraveling all this."

"Don't you see?" Paul whispered. "You can't believe in everything, in all of it, all the time. You fly away..."

"Oh, Ms. Tanner – you have to take it away." Brend begged. "That's all that matters – you have to take it away!"

Ann looked at them a second time that night and, once more, she almost did not recognize who it was looking back at her. This time, what powered the transfiguration was not their outlandish garments – it was the look behind their eyes of genuine fear. Ann took a moment before cautiously asking, "Take *what* away?"

The gun had fired.

He'd pulled the trigger – that much was indisputable. Why there was a 9mm hole in his kitchen ceiling and not in his head was the real mystery. He must have turned just as Dirk had come smashing through the sliding glass doors. There was a small nick near Jeff's temple where the bullet had grazed him, but that was it – unless you counted the massively painful ringing in his right ear which Jeff was fairly sanguine would not be going away any time soon. Dirk, on the other hand, was a complete mess. At first, there was so much blood that Jeff had supposed – to his horror – that he had fired directly into Dirk. But, with the hole in the ceiling and after clearing away most of the safety glass, after helping Dirk to a chair in the living room, and after inspecting his leg, Jeff was confident that Dirk's injury had occurred sometime prior and looked to be the result of a pretty vicious dog bite. He'd need medical attention, but the wound was far from life-threatening.

"Goddammit, Dirk. You crazy asshole," Jeff chided – at possibly the best friend he'd ever had. Dirk was still woozy and not entirely coherent – mumbling a string of elaborate apologies and responses to conversations lost deep within him. Jeff continued picking at the bits of glass embedded throughout Dirk's strange clothing while outpourings of astonishment at what Dirk must have gone through began striking him. Dirk had entered his property from the back yard, which could only mean that he had somehow successfully climbed up through a gauntlet of gated properties all with incredibly sophisticated security measures. It was a miracle that only his left leg had been torn to shreds.

"Dirk, you crazy asshole," Jeff repeated, now more to himself. He sent another nervous look to the security monitor – why there wasn't an entire squad of cop cars coming up his private drive was the real question. The gun shot had to have been heard for half a mile around. But, maybe that was one of the perks, so to speak, of living in L.A. People tended to ignore such things. It was only then that Jeff finally noticed Dirk holding something tight in his fist. At Jeff's first touch, Dirk released his grip and a crumpled piece of paper fell to the floor.

"Jeff," Dirk whispered, now looking directly at him for the first time, "the truth shall prevail...remember that...the truth shall prevail!"

Reaching down, Jeff picked up the scrap of paper and unfolded it. It was the cover to a playbill which read: "*I, Puck: A Musical Fantasia* by Paul Sherman. Performing nightly. The Daft House Theater Company, Los Angeles, CA."

That was when Ann called.

ele

The theater had the aura of a church.

While there had been no effort on the outside to disguise the structure's original function as an automotive garage – in fact, there was little anywhere to suggest that the surrounding industrial park was rapidly becoming a bohemian enclave – the interior had been transformed. Thick velvet curtains masked the exposed girders and the side panels of corrugated metal. Punched-tin star lamps had been suspended throughout and sent their dappled glow over a small stage set at the far end and over the Persian rugs carpeting the center aisle. Ranged on either side were multiple rows of folding chairs, strips of wooden theater seats bolted to plywood bases, and several old church pews painted a variety of colors. The place had the feel of being abandoned – although, except for the front door being unlocked and slightly ajar, there was nothing else Jeff could have specifically pointed to that was responsible for giving him that impression. But it was the emptiness and silence, above all else, that gave the make-shift theater its inescapable spiritual character. The most devout worshiper would have felt eminently at home communing with the universe within those walls. And Jeff did.

He walked slowly down the aisle and took a seat next to Ann.

She had been crying. And, somehow, he felt she knew everything – that she had been crying not only for herself, but for him as well. And he, too, felt there were things now that he understood about his sister that had previously been dark to him. There was nothing to say except to take her hand, to feel the warmth and realness of it – and to stare up at the small, exquisite painting which stood, braced to its easel, at the center of the stage.

CHAPTER 31

T he fire pit had been one of the many things Ann had had restored to their uncle's property over the last several months. In fact, the whole place had been revitalized in preparation for potential buyers. With the gazebo behind them, its fresh coat of paint luminous against the dark night, Jeff and Ann stared out over the garden. Lightning bugs, a particularly rare sight, flickered among the newly trimmed grass and hedges and replanted flowers. Mr. Lee would have been proud.

Jeff added another log to the bonfire. That there had ever been within that tiny inferno a small wooden frame with a canvas stretched across it would have been impossible to ascertain. But were those colors Jeff saw, rising up from the flames like sunlight through a prism? And in those flames and colors, did he see a beloved uncle released from his torments? Did he see a man that he cherished above all others finally free? Jeff looked over at his sister, her coat wrapped about her, and decided to leave Ann to herself – and to leave unspoken what her speculations might be to those particular questions. The last night in their uncle's home had a sacredness he had no wish to disturb.

"Well," he said, looking over at her again and smiling, "here we are in Spain."

"Yep," she said without looking up from the blaze, and with a wryly playful edge to her voice. "Here we are."

Spain indeed. In the weeks following the still inexplicable night that Dirk had crashed into his kitchen, it seemed as though the entire world had changed. First, Ann had finally come to a decision regarding the estate and had opted to donate the entirety of it to the Children's Convalescent Center rather than to accept any of the various offers that had been submitted. The move had infuriated the realtor – and Jacob Pressman had sternly advised against it – but it had not surprised Jeff at all.

In fact, looking back, he was surprised she had not considered it from the very beginning. Then there were her new friends, Brenda and Paul: they seemed to have something of a cult hit on their hands and had extended the run of their show indefinitely – albeit with a new lead singer – because Dirk, that crazy sonofabitch, had just been named head of animation for Family Films, Ltd. Go figure.

Ann, for her part, was not yet ready to start a real conversation, was still recollecting a summer long ago with her brother and Uncle Aaron – a dinner, with french doors open to the cool air, and a question that had been posed to them. Had they, in the end, been trapped by their answers?

"Would you rather be rich and famous but know that your endeavors were worthless – or brilliant and unloved?"

They'd each chosen, and held steadfastly – valiantly even – to their opposing positions. And now, that night, Ann could very well have argued that Uncle Aaron had spent the rest of his life showing them how wrong they'd both been. For the first time, Ann felt herself closer than ever before to understanding.

The night sky, with the crackling fire, whispered to her its answer, and she sighed.

"So...how are things with you and Michael?" Jeff finally asked after a while – sensing that his sister had returned from wherever it was she had been.

"What?" Ann asked, looking up from her reverie.

"How's he doing?"

"Ha – I didn't realize you even knew I was seeing somebody."

"Of course I do. You've mentioned him before."

"Have I? I didn't realize that." She looked back down into the glare of the flames before adding, "Well, that's all over with. Thank god."

Jeff could see there was more to the story, but, again, tonight was a night to let things be.

"And what about you?" Ann asked in return. "Are you seeing anyone?"

He had already told her about Steph and about their break – and that he and Murch were taking a stab at patching things up – seeing that they had a common enemy: it had recently been announced in the trades that Stephanie Strane had been cast in Ronald Lewis' next big costume drama – and the industry scuttlebutt was that she had the lead in his bedroom as well. And neither Murch nor Jeff were anywhere near mature enough to let *that* go.

What Jeff had not mentioned was the note that he continued to carry with him. It was something he had found in his office the morning after the wrap party, on the floor near his sofa, and which had gone originally unnoticed. In that handwriting he knew so well, had been printed: "I hope you don't mind,

I tucked you in for the night. And just so you know, I never stopped believing in it. Or you. –D."

"Yeah," Jeff said after reflecting, "there's someone. I don't know if she knows it yet – or where she may land on the issue – but it's someone I should have reached out to long ago. I'll let you know what happens."

Ann could see there was more to the story. But just as he had generously backed away from inquiries into a wound still attempting to heal, she let his answer stand – and refrained from asking him about the slight deafness in his right ear. She had guesses – but knew that the story would keep until he was ready to talk about it. Even conjoined twins needed their privacy from time to time.

"Hey," she said, now turning fully towards him and with a sudden look of concern, "I thought you had to be somewhere at eight?"

Jeff shook his head. He'd committed to attending the test screening tonight, but there really was no need. What people were going to think of the movie did not require his presence or any analysis of audience response cards – nor was it going to be any great mystery. No, tonight was for Ann and Uncle Aaron. Tonight was for experiencing the answers to questions long in the asking and long in coming – and much too intimate to be said aloud.

"I'm where I need to be," Jeff answered.

"In Spain?" she asked.

"In Spain," he said.

ele

As the film mercifully wound down to its conclusion, a sense of relief permeated the theater. The voice of Carol Beth called out against sounds of a thunderstorm lashing the tiny farmhouse.

"While she slept, I drew a rainbow for mama – and put it in the window next to her bed. I would have drawn a hundred rainbows – and filled every window in the house with their happy colors – if only I'd had the chance. But even rainbows must leave when their time has come. And mothers must too."

The angry thunderclouds slowly lifted and golden shafts of sun burst out across the farm. With rain dripping from the weathered eaves and birds beginning their first, tentative chirps, Carol Beth entered the bedroom of her dying mother. Her eyes moved from the sleeping woman to the dirty rug, the faded wallpaper, the wrought-iron bedstead, the hobnail coverlet, and the curios on the nightstand – all of which seemed to reflect the ebbing spirit of the matriarch who had sustained the family for so long.

It was far too much for the daughter who knew she must soon carry on alone – must take on the responsibilities that she had watched destroy her mother. Kneeling down at the side of the bed, she laid her face near the old woman's withered hand and let gentle sobs pour from her breaking heart.

"*Carol Beth! Carol Beth!*" *her mother's voice suddenly clamored, piercing the gloom.*

"*Yes, mama? I'm here,*" *she said, raising herself up to look into her mother's eyes, now wild with passion.*

"*Carol Beth! Look! It's a rainbow!*"

Following her mother's stare towards Carol Beth's poor attempt at mimicking what only God could achieve, the sad crayon drawing mocked them in the dim light – and Carol Beth was filled with bitterness.

"*No, mama, it ain't!*" *she cried, suddenly turning on her mother with a heart too broken, a mind too angry at Heaven to continue the deception.* "*It's just a picture of a rainbow! Just a damn picture!*"

"*You're wrong, Carol Beth,*" *her mother softly replied, caressing the cheek of her youngest child, the only one who had refused to abandon her.* "*That ain't the rainbow I'm talkin' about.*"

"*Which one then, mama, which one?*"

"*Why Carol Beth, it's like I said, I'm talkin' about the only one that ever really matters...the one in your heart!*"

To a final burst of thunder, the old woman closed her eyes forever – and the drawing that Carol Beth had dismissed, the one she had judged useless, fell from the window pane. And then, in that quiet way of miracles, from outside the window, through a sky now clearing of its recent storm, a beam of radiant, multi-hued light came flooding into the room – and a surging angelic choir lifted their voices in song.

Stepping to the window and into the chromatic brilliance, Carol Beth smiled. She smiled long and hard and deep, for the first time in a long time – because as far as her eye could see, there was before her a glorious new day and a glorious new tomorrow. The rainbows had returned.

The crowd, long since abandoning any sense of decorum, laughed uproariously. As Jeff Tanner had surmised, they experienced a collective sense of seeing something unique to the world of notoriously bad cinema. Already, multiple plans were underway to continue mining the hilarity of their experience at a local pub – and to celebrate their superhuman endurance.

But unnoticed by the crowd that evening – and what would have astonished the much maligned director of the picture to discover – there were, scattered among them, two or three people – maybe more – deep within a spell of perceiving all that was best in the world, of recognizing artistic passion and intent in all its many forms – some because they always had, others because, as fate sometimes ordained, they were still resonating from a recent encounter with something strange or wonderful or extraordinary – an encounter with something magical just off to the side, a moment with an intensity like sunlight off burnished chrome. But, whatever the reason, these lone watchers scattered throughout the audience would go on to say that what they saw that night was the greatest film ever made.

And, perhaps it was.

www.ingramcontent.com/pod-product-compliance
Lightning Source LLC
Chambersburg PA
CBHW031437240626
47154CB00001B/300

* 9 7 9 8 9 9 3 1 7 6 3 0 7 *